Chambers

Chambers

STEVEN W. WISE

Thomas Nelson Publishers
Nashville • Atlanta • London • Vancouver

Published in Nashville, Tennessee, by Thomas Nelson, Inc., Publishers, and distributed in Canada by Word Communications, Ltd., Richmond, British Columbia, and in the United Kingdom by Word (UK), Ltd., Milton Keynes, England.

Library of Congress Cataloging-in-Publication Data

Wise, Steven W.
    Chambers / Steven W. Wise
        p.   cm.
    ISBN 0-7852-8295-5 (pb)
    1. Missing children—United States—Fiction.   2. Kidnapping—United States—Fiction.   3. Satanism—United States—Fiction.   4. Family—United States—Fiction.   I. Title.
PS3573.I798C48   1994
813'.54—dc20   93–45803
                                                            CIP

Printed in the United States of America
1 2 3 4 5 6 7 — 00 99 98 97 96 95 94

For the little armies of Christ, mocked by the world,
yet powerful beyond human understanding.

Within some human hearts, chambers of sorrow hide, so dark and mysterious that they are known only to the spirit world. In these places, both God and Satan seek to dwell, but in the end, only one may remain.

PROLOGUE

Young Arvil Kassley rested uneasily on filthy sheets, staring at the bare light bulb of the ceiling fixture. It was the night of his ninth birthday, and his grimy fingers caressed the edges of the new baseball cards that were his only gift. But he was thinking of the hairy man in the next room. He could hear him; his voice was unlike that of any of the other men his mother entertained in her bedroom. This man's words came from his body, not his throat and mouth like the other men's. The boy could hear the hairy man's words now, mingled with the throaty laughter of his mother, and he wondered why she allowed the man to leave her and come to his room to hurt him.

The harsh glare from the light bulb blurred as tears welled up in his eyes and spilled onto his nose and cheeks. He blinked them away with angry snaps of his eyelids; tears would not protect him from what was about to happen. He could only bury his face in his pillow and clench his teeth and fix his mind on a faraway thought. Sometimes, if the thought was strong enough, Arvil could leave his body, will it to be a thing detached from his being. Maybe he would be able to do this tonight. Maybe he could lose himself in Mickey Mantle's baseball card, be out there in the beautiful green expanse of Yankee Stadium's center field and run down a line drive in the gap with the great man. He held the card in front of his face for a moment, burning the details in his brain, and then he carefully hid the other cards under the mattress. He leaned up on one elbow and placed the special card squarely under his pillow. He would need it when the light flicked off.

When the bulb flickered, Arvil's heart skipped wildly and he steeled himself against what was to come. But the light danced in the bulb for a moment and then glowed again evenly. The room grew suddenly cold and he shivered. It was then that the voice came to him.

"Ar . . . vil." It was raspy, like an old man's voice, yet distinct, as it etched both syllables in the air.

The boy's body tensed in fear, his head straining to turn toward the door, but he could only move his eyes.

"No, Arvil, you cannot see me, but I am here nonetheless. Speak to me, and you will know."

"I . . . I . . ." the words came out in tiny squeaks.

"Yes, I understand. It is a strange thing to you, but you should not fear me. I have a name. Would you like to call me by my name?"

"Where . . . where are you . . . you're scarin' me bad . . . how do you know my name?"

"It is my business to know the names of those I seek to help." He paused. "My name is Razzom. I have come to help you kill him."

"K . . . Kill . . . him?"

"Yes. Do not pretend that you misunderstand me. I know of the man in the next room. Do you want him to be with you this night?"

"No, but . . . but I just want him to go away and not come back."

"But he will always come back, Arvil. We must do it my way."

"But . . . I . . . can't hurt him . . . he's so big and . . ."

"Be silent and listen to me. There is something else under your pillow, beside the little card. Look and see."

Arvil trembled as he rolled over and raised the pillow. The tip of his mother's long scissors lay two inches from the card. The boy had never before seen the scissors in his room.

"How . . . where . . . ?"

"It does not matter how. It only matters that they are here. You may place your little picture with the others. You will not need it tonight."

Arvil retrieved the card and stuffed it under his mattress with the others.

"Listen closely, we have but a few moments. Turn over now and take the scissors in your right hand, under the pillow. Do not place your fingers in the holes, it will weaken your grip. When he comes to you in the darkness, pretend to cry. He enjoys it when you cry and it will distract him all the more. The instant you feel both of his hands on your body, *both* of them, you will twist your body and thrust the scissors with all your might at the sound of his breathing. You will find your mark, do not fear. I will be here with you."

Arvil's fear was waning, even though the sound of the demon's voice still chilled him. The scissors felt cold and powerful in his hand. A strength that he had never known pounded in his veins.

"Ar . . . vil?"

"What?"

"Say my name."

"Raz . . ."

"Yes . . . Razzom. Say it."

"Razzom."

"Say it when the hairy man's blood spills on your hand. Will you do this for both of us?"

"Yes." There was no hesitation. "I'll say it."

"Good. This is very good. For as you say it, we will be bound forever, you and I. I will help you do many things."

The boy did not reply. His fear had left him. When he heard the flick of the light switch, he smiled as blackness took the room.

CHAPTER ONE

The hooded man watched intently as the evening breeze nudged the folds of his black robe against the blood-stained edge of the great flat stone. The man wore no undergarments and the touch of the heavy cloth on his skin was sensual. Except for the rhythmic rise and fall of his wide chest, he had remained motionless for the last twenty minutes, savoring the moments when the moonbeams devoured the last frail offerings of day. White light soon washed clean the flat face of the rock outcropping, save for the old gore, but this was as it should be. The man smiled to himself. Reverently, he lowered his long frame to a kneeling position at the foot of the altar and folded his hands under his chin.

"Oh, Razzom, master of the darkness, hear me now in your place of honor. Come to your altar and give strength to all who will soon attend."

He bent his head forward until the coolness of the stone touched his forehead and the tip of his nose. The coarse texture of the crude altar caused his tongue to tingle and he moved it slowly, allowing the saliva to mingle with the stains. He knew that he would be unable to taste the dried blood, but the wetness was comforting, and the man trembled with anticipation as he thought of the service which would begin in less than a half hour. There would be fresh blood then. He could wait.

The man stood and arched his back against the stiffness as he surveyed the small clearing surrounding the ruins of the old homeplace. Thirty steps away, only parts of two walls stood—worn sentinels that would soon succumb to the callous touch of wind and rain and sun. A few sturdy cedars hovered in the old yard like humble friends, and beyond, the tall grass brushed the trunks of hickory and oak at the edge of the dusky woods that sloped to the creek bottom. The great woods formed a protective oval around the ruins, breeched only by the remnants of an old road, now barely defined, as it stretched a quarter of a mile to a gravel road.

As a boy, he had trudged up and down the lonely road five thousand times, always relieved with the house behind him, and always filled with dread as it loomed before him. He turned to face the remains of the house of his youth and the two walls which had formed the corner of his bedroom, and as he did, the sounds came back—scratchy laughter and guttural cries, men's voices coated with smoke and whiskey, animal-like grunts of passion fused forever in his memory with the slamming of his mother's bedroom door. And then, behind the walls that sealed him in darkness, the man was with him again, and he could hear the coarse entreaties and he could smell the sour breath that clung to the side of his face like a filthy dew.

A shudder jolted the long frame of Arvil Kassley as he withdrew from the past and formed a twisted smile across his thin lips. The child who had reason to dread the ascent up the old road was now the man who delighted in the journey. He had once been Evil's victim, and now he was his conspirator, and the knowledge of this union strengthened him. The smile grew wide as he allowed himself one last remembrance—the wail of agony and the fountain of blood that escaped the hairy man on the last night he entered the bedroom.

Twenty-five years had passed since that fateful night, and Razzom had remained the faithful companion he had promised to be. And more. So much more. Arvil Kassley had learned of the force that drove Razzom—the very reason for the demon's being. He had learned of the one that even Razzom spoke of with deference. He had learned Satan's ways.

The rustle of footsteps in the dry grass of the old road came to him, but he did not turn his head. He slipped his right hand into the deep pocket of the robe and closed his fingers around the smooth leather and the stem of the silver chalice. With practiced ease he unfastened the strap from the sheath and withdrew the dagger, the blade making a soft clink against the small cup. With great care, he placed the knife and the cup at the foot of the altar and then turned to watch as the two robed figures shuffled toward him. The taller of the two carried a burlap sack, and as he grew near, Arvil stared intently at the wriggling bundle suspended from the man's hand. The smaller man also carried a sack of equal bulk, but it was dead weight, and of little interest to Arvil. The men walked within two steps of him before setting the sacks on the ground.

"Good evening, brethren. And a fine night it is to worship him, is it not?"

"That it is," wheezed the larger man, "that it is, Arvil."

Arvil slowly shook his head before he spoke. "Wesley, it is indeed beyond me why you continue to smoke in this enlightened age. Imagine walking up that hill without sounding like a bellows. You would surely enjoy the services a great deal more. A little discipline, my friend. A little discipline is all that is required."

Wesley nodded earnestly in agreement and clamped his mouth shut against the irritating sound, but this only changed the pitch of the wheezing, and he quickly abandoned the tactic. Arvil turned his gaze to the other man who bowed his head slightly in deference to the leader.

"Good evening, Jessie. A pleasure to see a worshiper prepared in body, silent and reverent before the altar of sacrifice." Arvil shot a final glance at Wesley. "And the mind, Jessie? Is the mind prepared this evening?"

"Yes. Yes, sir. It is. I promise."

"Very good then. We shall begin. You may prepare the altar." He turned toward the other man. "Wesley, I should like to examine the animal."

The younger man quickly walked to the side of the stone and emptied the contents of his sack on the ground. There were four wooden stakes, four lengths of sturdy twine, a hammer, and a towel. The stakes were two feet long, with one end sharpened and a deep notch cut in the driving end. Jesse positioned one of the stakes at a corner of the altar and covered the top with several folds of the thick towel. With twelve muffled thumps of the hammer, the stake became part of the hard earth. One end of a length of twine was fastened in the notch and tested for strength.

As he reached for another stake, Jessie stole a glance at Arvil. For the last year, the strangely handsome face had at once haunted and captivated the boy. The forehead was expansive, framed by a thick shock of black hair and unruly eyebrows that joined at the bridge of a strong nose. Eyes, deeply set, were well spaced, foreboding only when he desired them to be. Thin lips on a mouth perhaps too small were the only deficiencies of the long face, and they were seldom noticed. The moustache line guarded the upper lip closely and then curved elegantly as it fused with the evenly cut bristles of chin beard. To Jessie, it was the face of a handsome Lincoln, misplaced in time; yet none of the great statesman's sorrow was ever in this face. Only the power.

The big man held the small dog easily in his powerful hands and smoothed the dark fur with long soothing strokes, and with each stroke, the creature lost a bit of its fear in spite of the masking tape that held its jaws together.

"A fine specimen, Wesley. Purebred beagle male. Five or six months old, I would guess. The collar and owner's tag—did they look expensive?"

"Yes, Arvil, top notch. Look at his coat and feel the meat on him. There's no doubt he was well thought of."

"Yes . . . yes," the voice hissed in the darkness, "he is loved, and that is of great importance to our master. A sacrifice is no sacrifice if the offering is not coveted."

The other man nodded silently.

"Is all in readiness, Jessie?" Arvil asked calmly.

"Yes sir, it is."

Arvil carried the dog to the slab and six strong hands worked in unison as a length of twine claimed each leg. The beagle's fear returned full force. Arvil took his position at the foot of the altar with the other two men kneeling at each side. They joined hands and bowed their heads before offering their chant to the Prince of Darkness.

"Oh, master Satan, you represent the only true and vital existence in this life and the next . . . your wisdom is undefiled . . . please accept the blood of this humble sacrifice as a token of our allegiance to you and your way, now and forever . . . amen."

Arvil picked up the dagger and offered it to Jessie, careful to notice the delicate tremor in the hand of the younger man.

"The honor of first blood is yours tonight, brother. You have made great progress. Only forward now, be strong, only forward."

The tip of the blade inched forward toward the dog, and then, after he exhaled a long breath, Jessie Pacely thrust the blade and quickly withdrew it. The knife passed quickly now from hand to hand, and soon the animal lay silent on the slab. With three fist-sized stones, Arvil secured the chalice under the lowest corner of the slab and soon the crevice that led to the corner became a tiny brook of crimson which emptied into the silver cup.

Arvil leaned over the carcass and made a deep incision into the chest cavity, probed with his fingers for the heart, and cut it free. He laid it on the slab and carved it into three portions, setting one at each position of worship. He paused as his hand found the stem of the chalice, and waited a full minute as the last drops filled the cup. Satisfied, he picked it up and set it between the hind legs of the still creature. As he picked up the portion of flesh, his companions did likewise, and he spoke a single sentence.

"This, the flesh of the innocent, is eaten in homage to thee, our master."

The three men quickly devoured the warm morsels. Arvil took the chalice and extended it over the body of the dog.

"This, the blood of the innocent, is drunk in homage to thee, our master."

The cup was passed about until it was empty, and then the hooded heads bent forward again, the three figures becoming somber statues carved from the great stone before them. For the next half hour, the only sound on the hilltop was the low chant of prayers at the altar and the muted chatter of the night creatures. After the whispering stopped, the men stood and arched their backs to relieve the stiffness.

"Very well done," Arvil intoned. "I'll meet you at the creek." He retrieved the dagger and chalice, then disappeared into the gloom.

Jessie opened his pocketknife and cut the twine from three of the dog's legs before kicking the stakes loose from the ground. He tossed the three stakes into the sack that Wesley held open, and then groped about the ground for a moment before locating the hammer and dropping it into the sack.

"That everything?" the older man asked.

"Yeah, let's go."

Jessie bent over and picked up the stake still tied to its

burden and soon the small carcass bounced along behind the men. They walked fifty yards into the woods before either spoke.

"This is good," Wesley said. Jessie severed the twine near the leg and tossed the last stake into the sack. "Coyotes'll clean him up before morning."

The men changed direction and began the descent that would take them to the meeting place at the creek. Arvil was slinging water from the knife and chalice as he turned toward the approaching men. They walked to the edge of the shallow water and splashed the sticky gore from their hands and faces.

"Do we *believe* what we are about?" the fervency of the question froze the men at the creekbank, and they turned their eyes toward each other but not their heads. Neither offered a reply.

"True enough, we have offered worthy animals—beautiful, healthy creatures, loved by their owners—and I know this must please the master, but . . ." his voice trailed off as he shook his head at the two squatting figures. "I fear that before long, possibly even now, the depth of our conviction might come into question. Is it reasonable to assume that our master will forever be satisfied with our present level of sacrifice? I think not."

Cautiously, Wesley stood and Jessie followed his lead. The older man fought to overcome the pounding in his chest before he spoke.

"What—er—what do you mean, Arvil?"

"I mean that, in time, true followers must upgrade the quality of their sacrifices. I mean that the covens that please him most are those that offer—human sacrifice."

The words dangled in the night air as the tall man drew out the last syllable. Wesley could not stifle the wheeze that leaked from his lungs as he opened his mouth to speak.

"That's a whole other thing, Arvil—people. Pets are one thing, but—people . . ."

"I realize that we would have to take great care, Wesley,

but it is being accomplished all over the world now and you know it. There are humans in this town who would be missed far less than tonight's dog—nameless creatures who roam the alleys or hitchhike I-70—and not all filthy bums that would be unworthy. I have kept close watch for the last month or so, and I have spotted at least four who would do nicely."

"Oh, man . . . oh man . . ." Jessie said through barely-parted lips. Arvil walked to his side and placed a hand on each shoulder.

"You did very well tonight, brother, but it is only the beginning. You should take strength in that. Together we will attain heights of glory that we cannot yet imagine. Be strong now, be strong. I have seen what you are made of, and you are a worthy warlock. Trust me."

The younger man nodded but did not speak.

The three men walked single file, parallel with the gravel road, but never drawing within thirty yards of it. They had walked for ten minutes before the sound of a car engine came to them, and without a word being spoken they stopped in unison and became one with the shadows; the crunch of gravel faded, and the shadows moved again.

Wesley flipped the beads of sweat from his brow with the forefinger of his right hand and looked eagerly beyond the tall man in front of him. He could see it now—the dot of white to his left at the edge of the road; fifty steps more and it became the neat rectangle of Arvil Kassley's mailbox. Wesley's Ford pickup and Jessie's battered Chevrolet Camaro were parked behind the barn, and as their owners approached them, both men wondered what would be said to them in parting. They stood by the driver-side doors and waited as Arvil drew a long breath and exhaled luxuriously.

"I'll call. Week after next, most likely."

Wesley started to speak but could only scratch the question in the loose soil of the barnyard with the toe of his boot.

"No, not next time—but soon. Keep the faith and rise above your fears. Go now. I am going for a drive."

The eyes of the two angels took their radiance from the brilliant, white light that shone around them and reached into infinity. The head of the lesser angel was slightly bowed in deference to the archangel, whose magnificent countenance slowly rotated toward earth. The lesser angel took notice of the sadness in the great face, but he remained silent; he would know soon enough of what was to come. After a moment, the resonant voice claimed the air.

"There is an evil one who has roamed the earth for many generations. He lives now in the heart and mind of a frail soul who knows not our Lord. His power grows in the man like a pestilence. Even as we speak . . . his thoughts are from the pit of hell."

"Are there not many such as this, archangel?"

"Sadly, this is true, but our Lord has directed my thoughts toward the one called Razzom."

The lesser angel knew at once the nature of his charge.

"When shalt thou send me, archangel?"

"Very soon."

Save for the whisper of a breeze, silence again reigned.

The Reverend Arvil Kassley, pastor of Oak Tree Missionary Church, drove at fifty miles per hour on the band of interstate highway as it led past the city limit sign of Wrightville, Missouri. There were four sets of ramps which serviced the highway, and as he neared the first, the man peered into the dirty light beside the narrow strip of concrete, his gaze intent, like that of a great night owl in search of prey. It was on the third, the Leland Boulevard exit ramp, that he saw one. He steered the van off the highway at the next exit, then crossed the overpass above the four lanes and reentered the highway from the opposite side. It took four minutes to reach the hitchhiker; there were no headlights in the rearview mirror of the Suburban as it stopped twenty feet from the bedraggled figure. Reverend Kassley's left foot pressed the brake pedal firmly, while his right rested on the accelerator.

The hitchhiker registered only mild surprise as the Suburban roared down the ramp before his hand could reach the door handle. He had seen many strange people on the highways. He muttered a curse at his bad luck into the night.

CHAPTER TWO

The boy stood thirty steps away, his short legs rooted firmly in the sandy beach, and although she could not see them, his mother knew he was wiggling his toes down where the grains were cool. His head was down, looking at feet that were not there, and from time to time he looked up at the woman but his expression did not change. He soon grew tired of this tiny activity and turned and trundled to the edge of the water, but only close enough for the incoming waves to die at his feet.

His hair was the color of the sand, and when the sunlight came full force from behind a cotton cloud, it caressed the blowing strands and made them more beautiful. Even at nine, he had the look of his father—his head cocked to the right, always the right, and his back ramrod straight—and he appeared to his mother as a tiny figurine of a man, standing in contrast to the infinite green backdrop of the sea.

The roar of the ocean came to Joanie Starmann like a great hymn without words, barely changing in its pitch, yet melodious and carefree. She closed her eyes and for long moments no thoughts cluttered her brain. She allowed only the sounds of water and wind to fill her, only the yellow heat of the afternoon sun to touch her. For these precious moments she was free of the memory—as free as a thirty-year-old widow could hope to be. But they passed swiftly and the nothingness in her closed eyes gave way to his image. The clean smell of the wind in her nostrils became his sweat mingled with cologne—manly and strong—like he was on the last morning of his life three months before. She shuddered slightly in the baking warmth of the sand, not wanting his memory now, but powerless to shut it out. And so he came.

He burst through the kitchen door with his tennis racket in one hand and an empty container of Gatorade in the other, and his presence filled the room as he crowed good-naturedly of victory over a neighborhood rival. It was when he peeled off his wet shirt and handed the ball of clothing to her that the look of utter surprise distorted his features. She had seen the look a hundred times, frozen forever in her mind, and all she could see was surprise. Then he was at her feet, a giant tangled knot of arms and legs, and she was on the floor with him, her face touching his, and she screamed his name but the only sound that escaped him was like the hiss of a mad teakettle. He died before the ambulance came, his tousled head cradled in her lap, and the attendants talked gently and touched her hands, and she let them have her husband.

She wondered now, listening to the aria of the ocean, how many more times she would have to let them take him from her. The boy turned now and came toward her, scuffing the sand thoughtfully as he walked. He plopped down beside her on the beach towel and she tried to smooth his hair in spite of the wind.

"You were thinking about Daddy, weren't you, Mom? I peeked at you from over there. Your eyes were shut tight."

"Yes, baby, I was. Is that all right?" she whispered against his shoulder.

"Does it help?"

"Sometimes yes, sometimes no. But most of the time I can't help it."

Neither spoke for a full minute, and the woman knew he wanted to speak again, and she waited for him.

"It doesn't help me," he said, "but you can if it does you."

"Thanks, Rooster. You're an all right guy, you know?" She hugged him and they rocked gently for a moment, but the child still did not smile.

"Will the others try to call me that?" he asked in reference to the nickname his father had given him. "I don't want them to. Only you and Grandpa and Grandma now."

"Okay. They'll understand. I think they like Darren better anyway. It won't be long before you'll want me to call you Darren too. You'll get tall and handsome and the girls will fight over you, and Rooster won't sound right at all."

He fell silent again and traced the outline of a whale in the sand with a stubby finger. Satisfied with the likeness, he finished it off with a finger poke for an eye before turning his head to his mother.

"I'll always want you to call me Rooster. That's what helps me. Okay?"

Joanie swallowed hard against the thickness in her throat and smiled down at him. "Always. I promise."

She tossed her head backward so that the wind could take her long hair, knowing that some sand would come in exchange for the feel of it, but not caring. The boy stretched out beside her on the towel and folded his hands over the band of his trunks, his eyes closed against the brightness. She turned her head so that she could see his face. Save for the blond heads of hair, mother and son shared few features. His eyes were wide-set and thoughtful and even now the look of his nose was strong and the lips full, almost pouty, like photos she had seen of Donald Trump. You could have taken something of mine, she smiled to him. Her own features were attractive, though not striking. Makeup had never been a crutch; the clean lines of her face were womanly, the skin tone robust and colorful. Maybe she would need to cheat later when her love for the outdoors had robbed her of good skin and the wrinkles came creeping in the night. But not now, not at thirty. Her body was hard, but the lines were feminine, and she knew that if she chose to, she could get up and jog steadily in the heavy sand of the beach for three miles and only be winded in a pleasant, athletic sort of way. Charles Starmann had been like that, too, churning away on a bike or gliding after a tough corner shot on the tennis court—forever moving with the grace of an upright cat. They had joked, years before, about who would outlive the other, and had settled on ninety for him and ninety-two for Joanie.

"Just missed you by a mere sixty years, buddy boy," she whispered too loudly.

"What'd you say, Mom?"

"Oh, nothing, son. Just daydreaming."

"I was thinking now with my eyes closed . . . about what he's doing up there. They don't have stocks and bonds in heaven, do they?"

"No, I'm sure they don't, Rooster."

"Then why did God need him?"

"I—He didn't need him for that, son. We'll all have different things to do in heaven."

"Is he just laying around like us now?"

"No, I don't think so. I think heaven is a busy place. A wonderful, busy place."

The boy studied the incoming waves as they slapped the beach. "If God was strong enough to make the whole earth and stars and all, I don't see why He thinks He needs Daddy too." There was an edge to the words, nearly sharp, and his mother detected it.

"Oh, Rooster, I want him here, too, but we can't change it. We can't be mad at God. It would almost be like being mad at Daddy."

The child's chin quivered and he fought bravely against the tears for a moment, but they won the small battle. She held him, but shed no tears of her own. At least she was beyond that now—the weeping. It had been a cleansing thing, somehow right and good, but it was behind her now. Another day at the beach, and they would go home and live and love and do the best they could for all their tomorrows.

Rooster wordlessly extended his left hand, palm up, and Joanie filled it with a tissue fished from her beach bag.

"I'm tired of doing that," came the tiny voice.

"Don't worry about it, son. It'll stop when it's supposed to. It's not a bad thing."

"I want it to stop now," he said defiantly. He drew a jagged breath. "That's enough. That's gonna be the last time."

She looked at his red eyes as they flashed at her, and she loved the boy with a depth that almost frightened her. She playfully balled her fist and nudged his chin.

"You're a tough Rooster aren't you, buddy boy?"

It came now, the hint of a smile, and Joanie Starmann knew that together they had breached a wide chasm. He sniffed one last time and looked back at the ocean before speaking.

"Can't do that forever."

The Reverend Arvil Kassley stood in the doorway of the small but stately brick church building on Tower Lane and spoke in deep, measured tones to the departing members of his congregation. He smiled easily with his flock, accepting their words of praise for the sermon just delivered, bowing his tall frame deferentially to the older parishioners, sturdily shaking hands with the younger people as he exchanged pleasantries. They ate from his hand, these fawning worshipers with their stupid smiles and clinging fingers. They were as malleable as wet clay, and he smiled inwardly even as the lie of a smile on his face warmed their hearts; it was so incredibly easy with them.

It was only with the children that Arvil Kassley had to be on guard. He longed to touch them, caress their roseate cheeks and feel the silkiness of their fine hair, but he seldom allowed himself this pleasure. Many times, parents would fairly shove their offspring to him, and Arvil would discreetly fend off the diminutive offerings, barely allowing himself the passion of a fingertip. He had touched them a year before when he first came, but quickly learned that he must deny himself.

Some of the children knew his heart, just how, he could not be sure—perhaps something in his touch or the way his eyes probed theirs—but they knew, and he soon stopped touching them, and now they lived only in his imagination in ways that would gag their parents. But there was great solace in that; it would have to suffice for now. So he only looked.

The stream of people thinned gradually until finally only the face of Gladys Fairchild remained, peering up through squinting slits resting tiredly on clown-red cheeks. The old woman was always last to leave the sanctuary—by design, Arvil felt sure, and he despised her for it. There was no reason for her to hurry her comments, no easy way for Arvil to dismiss her. He drew a deep, steady breath and calmed himself as she shuffled one step too close and the stale old-woman odor drifted to his nostrils.

"Morning, preacher," she said.

"Good morning to you, Miss Fairchild," he answered evenly.

"Another fine sermon, preacher . . . scholarly," she drew out the syllables, "I believe would be the right word."

"Well . . . thank you, Miss Fairchild . . . I try to . . ."

"No law against letting the Spirit creep in now and then though, preacher. Don't take me wrong now," she quickly added, "few indeed can explore the Old Testament like you. Few indeed. Thing is though, the Spirit is in the New Testament and, well, even old has-beens like me want to hear about that part of the Good Book once in a while. I've known some mighty good preachers in my time, I have for a fact." For a fleeting moment her cloudy eyes sharpened and a strange light came to them, but it passed before Arvil took notice. "Some of them go way back, I'll declare, preacher. Way back."

Arvil's smile was thin over clenched teeth. Calm now, stay calm. The scratchy old record of a voice was winding down.

"Well, anyhow, don't take no offense, preacher. Just a thought from an old woman's brain. Lucky to find you, we were. Young, and with your career ahead of you. Wonder some crowd in St. Louis or Kansas City didn't snatch you up. Who am I to offer advice to the likes of you?"

"That's quite all right, Miss Fairchild, you may . . ."

"Just something to think about, preacher, that's all. Maybe you could see fit to humor an old woman one of these soon Sundays. Probably ain't got a lot more," she wheezed a short laugh.

One can only hope, Arvil struggled against lips that wanted to release the juicy thought poised on his tongue.

"You take care, preacher. See you next week, God willing."

"Good day to you, Miss Fairchild."

He swung the heavy door toward him and enjoyed the metallic sound of the latch as he shut out the bright light of noon. The paneled study awaited at the rear of the building, and he walked to it with purposeful strides. He flipped the light switch off and settled into the comfort of the desk chair. That there was no window in the small study had been a point of minor embarrassment to his welcoming committee at the outset of his pastorate. He had feigned mild disappointment—perfectly he thought—while delighting in his good fortune.

Now, in the near darkness, he closed his fingers around the smooth silver object in his suit coat pocket. He would remain in his study for an hour, fondling the raised edges of the pentagram and talking with Razzom.

CHAPTER THREE

Wesley Livingston's hand banged against the edge of the nightstand as it groped like a flesh-colored tarantula in search of prey. Thick fingers closed around the crush-proof pack of Marlboros and drew it to the bed. With the third swipe, the bookmatch hissed its sulfur into the heavy air of the bedroom. Wesley drew the welcome heat deep into his lungs and shot a neat trail of smoke toward the ceiling. He glanced at the sheet-covered lump beside him and waited for it to stir; it always stirred before his second drag. First, tangled brown hair emerged from under the sheet, and then the fleshy profile of Twila Livingston's face contorted in protest at the morning light. She did not speak until the smoke from her husband's third drag hung over her, but her eyes remained clamped shut.

"Looks like you could wait till you get your rear out of bed before you stink up the room."

"Don't do it every morning, woman."

"You do it often enough, seems to me."

"Can't help it. Love 'em too much."

"I ain't gonna argue that, Wesley," the woman said tiredly as she swung her legs over her side of the bed and sat up. "Don't suppose you and your loved one could manage to turn on the coffee for a working woman."

A groan befitting two hundred out-of-shape pounds on a

five-foot-ten-inch frame filled the room. "Sure. Be glad to help with your habit. Don't rag me about mine."

"I don't poison nobody around me with black coffee as far as I know, mister."

Wesley waved his hand in a final gesture as he padded heavily from the bedroom. He reached the kitchen and flipped the red button of the coffee maker which Twila had readied the night before. He remembered two cream-filled rolls in a crumpled sack on the counter and grabbed a half-gallon carton of milk from the refrigerator as he passed on his way to the kitchen table. The doughy sweetness was pleasing in his mouth, and he chewed slowly as he thought of the day ahead. Twenty-seven acres of alfalfa hay to bale for cranky old Ed Higbee, if the baler didn't act up again. Bounce along on the tractor in the sunshine with a little cooler of iced tea tucked beside him. Yes, he could manage that, and beyond that, who cared?

The woman worked steady at the plant; loved it, too—her and her bunch of loose-jawed women cronies, carrying on about their worthless men and unappreciated lives. Just flat loved it. Couldn't fool him though; no silly woman could. He half-smiled through the wad of pastry as he heard her approaching. Wordlessly, she filled a tall plastic container with the steaming black liquid, then finished her preparations to leave. She paused for a moment at the door and spoke over her shoulder.

"You got work today?"

"Yeah. Balin' some hay for old Higbee."

The back door banged shut and welcome silence closed in around him. Since Arvil had found him, he had come to covet the silence. Sweet silence that allowed his thoughts to wander and contemplate things unimaginable only a few months before.

He had at first been hesitant to take a job from the new preacher in town, although working for members of the church had proven suitable. They paid without whining and didn't come up with too many distasteful jobs. But when the voice of Arvil Kassley filled his telephone receiver, a vague apprehension tugged at him, and he determined instantly that he would turn down the job offer. A churchgoer was one thing, but a preacher, that was something else—too close to great God Almighty for comfort. But he did not turn it down; he *could not* turn it down. Such was the force of the man. A voice on the telephone, and stubborn Wesley Livingston, who took great pleasure in declining work, had eagerly accepted.

He smiled ruefully as he remembered the first meeting with the Reverend Kassley. They had worked all day side by side, reroofing the storage shed behind Arvil's house. And yet, the dreaded sermon that Wesley knew would come sooner or later never spilled from his lips. Many words did come from the man though—words strange for a preacher, words that confused at first. And Wesley listened raptly, even without understanding; he could do no less. After the seventh job for Arvil Kassley, Wesley was confused no longer. The soul of the reverend was finally revealed, and the details were forever etched in Wesley's memory.

They had worked on a section of fence until late in the evening, and the light came to the barnyard meekly, filtered through clouds pouty and gray with rain. The two men had not spoken in several minutes and suddenly Wesley felt the stare of eyes on him as surely as he had ever felt the rays of the sun. Arvil held a sledgehammer in his right hand as Wesley looked up from his task into a face now stern yet somehow fatherly. The nine pounds of iron and wood slid from his fingers and thudded ominously to the ground.

"Haven't you ever wondered, Wesley, why I've never spoken to you about religion?"

So now, he had thought, now it would finally come— the Bible thumping, loud-voiced, spit-slinging pitch for God Himself. His eyes dropped as he steeled himself for the onslaught. Wesley Livingston had never made a more erroneous assumption in his life.

"No, Wesley, not that. Do not worry." The words were soothing, reassuring. "Have you ever heard of a double agent?"

"I, uh, I think it's about spyin', ain't it?"

"Yes, but more than simple espionage. Much more indeed. It is a situation wherein an agent who appears to work for one master, in reality, works for the 'enemy'."

He paused to let the word hang in the air as he found Wesley's eyes again and would not let them go.

"Who do you think I work for, Wesley? Who is the enemy?"

"Arvil, . . . I—uh . . . I'm not sure."

"Don't be frightened of the truth. There is great power in it. Think of the power in this world. Who is stronger, God or Satan? Who was stronger at My Lai, Wesley, when the soldiers chopped up the women and children with bullets? Remember the photos? Who was stronger at Auschwitz when the gas spewed from the shower heads? Who was stronger in Kansas last week when the tornadoes killed twenty-eight?"

The questions came end-to-end, pounding at his brain and he said nothing.

"We must all choose sides in the world, Wesley. I have just chosen the strongest side. The side that gives me some of the power."

"But how can you—"

"Preach the 'word'?" His laughter filled the barnyard. "For now, it gives me great pleasure to toy with them, their expectant hearts all atune to me up in the pulpit—me! an agent of the master to be sure, but not their master. Give me a few short years, only a few I promise you, and I will seek out those worthy, those teachable, and deliver them from their ignorance."

The tall man closed the six feet that separated them, and clamped a great hand on each of Wesley's shoulders, and his face drew near as he spoke. "Trust me, Wesley. Just trust me, and I will take you to heights unknown. You will feel the power course through your veins like the blood that gives you life. Just follow me."

The blurry outline of the cluttered countertop sharpened into focus as Wesley left the memory. "I have," he said aloud in the empty kitchen. "I have so far."

Jessie Pacely studied the metallic green sheen on the back of the blowfly as he carefully raised the swatter for the kill. On any other object it would have been a beautiful color, but here, creeping over the bone of a chicken leg beside the plate, the green was one with the fly—something to be destroyed. Before he could unleash the swat, the ugly little thought flitted through his brain. "Green like you, Jessie boy. Green like you." He lowered the swatter to the table and the insect buzzed into the air with an irritating drone.

With the sound, Allene Pacely turned from the kitchen sink and looked at her son's empty face. "Jessie, for pity sake, will you swat that thing?"

"Won't land right," he lied, pushing away from the table and tossing down the fly swatter. The screen door clapped behind him as he stepped onto the wood floor of the back porch and plopped into a metal chair. The woman shook her head at the soapy water that sloshed over her hands.

The old chair protested with rhythmic creaks as Jessie toed the rough wood of the floor. The lazy breeze that puffed through the backyard had little effect on the hovering warmth that would remain even in the coming darkness. His eyes picked over familiar objects in the yard: the faded bulk of his car, the tin-covered shed, the neat garden plot, the scattered yellow of dandelions reflecting the last offerings of sunlight— they all came to him unhurriedly but there was no pleasure in the sight of them. He heard the screen door open but did not turn his head.

"Whew! Still swelterin' out here, huh?" Allene asked. Jessie nodded but said nothing. She sat down in the other chair and her weight barely compressed the metal frame.

"Son, I know you've been worryin' over your job, but it'll work out in time."

He had been moved to the eleven-to-seven shift at the garment factory five months ago and for the last two of those months, he had been cut to three days a week.

"You ever work a graveyard shift?" he asked, his lips moving only enough to let the words escape.

"No . . . I don't reckon I have. Not in a factory or on a job as such. I do remember bein' up a time or two with you when you were little, when most folks were sleepin'."

"Ain't the same. I got to worry with it all day while I try to sleep in the daylight, and then supper's breakfast, and then breakfast is bedtime . . ." His voice trailed away. "And to top it all off, I ain't even workin' steady now."

"It's better than bein' laid off altogether like some down there," Allene said softly. "And besides, Reverend Kassley's got some work for you on off days, and that's been a real blessing."

His head half-turned toward her at the mention of the man's name and she thought for a moment that a smile would come to him, but it did not.

"Yeah . . . yeah, that has been a help," he said evenly. His chair creaked louder.

His mother sensed an opening and began very carefully. "What a solid man. I'm glad you got the chance to be around him some . . . even if it's just around his farm." No reply. "We were lucky to find him before some bigger church snatched him up. At least that's what all the deacons are sayin'. I don't know much about such matters, Lord knows."

She laughed easily at herself as she glanced sidelong at Jessie's profile. A bit too thin maybe, but it was a handsome face, a young man's face without the creases and heaviness that would come soon enough. His sandy hair was too long to suit her, but that was a small thing, a meaningless thing really, and she thought little of it anymore. It was his heart that worried her and was the object of her prayers. She had done as well as she could through the fatherless years of his boyhood. She could not remember the last time he had asked about Frank Pacely, but she knew that it had been years. She hoped he would not ask again.

"Anyway," she continued after a few moments, "it might be a nice thing for you to do, just for the reverend mind you, if you'd come to services some Sunday . . ."

"You think all we talk about is barnyards out there?"

She could not suppress a smile at the thought of her son receiving private counseling on the higher matters of life from no less than the pastor of her church, but she determined not to bubble over and risk showing too much approval. "Course not, son, I expect you do talk about other things now and then."

"Yes we do, Mom. We do for sure. Fact is, there ain't much need for me to come to church when I got him private-like." He did smile now, she was sure, but in her gladness she did not recognize the emptiness of it, and it passed quickly.

"Well . . . I just know it'll help your thinkin' and worryin'—bein' with him and all. There is higher powers to rely on, son."

"Yeah, I know."

Neither spoke for several moments and only the soft sounds of the evening came to them. Jessie stood and stretched his long arms toward the ceiling. The thought of going inside and dressing for work did not trouble him now.

"You ever kill it?" The strange question nearly startled the woman.

"Kill—what?" she asked.

"The fly. You ever get him?"

"No," she laughed, "he got away when I opened the door."

CHAPTER FOUR

Joanie Starmann expertly wove the silver Dodge Caravan in and out of the steady Sunday afternoon traffic on Highway 74 as it stretched toward the dull orange sunset and Charlotte, North Carolina. She flicked a sidelong glance at Rooster, and as he returned the look, he hooked his thumbs under the shoulder strap of the seatbelt and purchased a bit of freedom.

"I know, bub, they do seem to get a little tight after a long ride, but . . ."

"Yeah, I know. Don't say it," he said as she felt his tiny stare. He singsonged the words, "Better safe than sorrrrry."

"Twenty minutes to the front door, Rooster. Hang on."

They rode in silence for five more minutes before the boy spoke again. "Bet Grandma'll be outside waiting for us."

"Bet you're right."

Highway 74 became Independence Boulevard, and the familiar sights zipped past Joanie's gaze as the red dot of a traffic light hung over Idlewild Road. Left for a block, then a quick right onto Knickerbocker Drive, and then she finally gave in to the road weariness that prickled against her hips and back.

"Whew! I'm ready to climb off this horse, Rooster, how about you?"

"I'm ready to get out from under this thing, that's what

25

I'm ready for," and he eyed his mother as his left hand edged toward the seatbelt release.

"Don't you dare. One more block, you wiggly worm."

"Told you so," the stubby finger poked over the dashboard. "Out there messing in the flowers."

The face under the sunbonnet beamed at the sight of the van as it turned into the driveway, and the woman stabbed the trowel into the black soil at the edge of the railroad tie border. She half trotted toward them and extended a wagging dirty hand to both Joanie and Rooster.

"Hey there, you two beach bums," she said, gathering her grandson to her bosom.

"Hey to you, Grandma," the boy said.

"Great day, will you just look at the sun on that handsome face?" She petted Rooster's cheeks and forehead. "Heaven's sake, daughter, you didn't scorch this child did you?"

"No, mother, I did *not* let him get sunburned. Give me a break, will you?" She chuckled at the crinkled eyes that danced at her from the shade of the floppy hat brim.

"You got cookies in there, Grandma?"

"Do chiggers itch?"

The boy yelped in delight at the sassy answer and bounded for the door.

"Mother, I'll swear. I can't get a straight answer out of him half the time. Guess why?"

"Nothing wrong in that. Person gets tired of plain old yesses and nos all the time."

They embraced, and the old skin of Norma Hunt's cheek felt good against Joanie's face, and the women took comfort in each other.

"He seems better, honey. How'd he do down there?"

"Not very good at first, Mom, but the last day . . . the last day something good happened, I just know it. He left some bitterness down there. We crossed some kind of bridge . . . I don't know exactly."

"That's good news, honey, real good news. I been wearin'

out God's ears on this thing. It'll be all right, just you wait and see."

She caressed her daughter's cheek with the back of her hand and loved her with a love that was almost pain.

"Where's Daddy?"

"I sent him to Harris-Teeter. We're gonna do up some chicken on the grill tonight. Sound okay?" Joanie nodded. "Let's go rescue the Rooster before he founders on the best chocolate chip cookies in the south."

Joanie watched her father and her son through the sliding screen door that led to the patio. They were stacking charcoal briquets in a black pyramid, the man directing gently and the child exercising tongue-biting care with the delightful task. Floyd Hunt wore his sixty-three years well. A few more pounds than necessary had accumulated around his middle, and his five-foot-nine-inch frame could not hide them well, but it was of no real consequence—something for Norma to tease him about. His hair, once coiled in inky waves, had thinned to long strands, barely reminders of his youth, but he continued to comb it as if the years had not robbed him. His face was square and strong with well-formed features, the best of which was a mouth that smiled easily and without pretense. He reminded Joanie of a handsome Karl Malden. His hands were large for a man his size, and Joanie loved them as the thick fingers caressed the back of Rooster's head.

He had been a rock for Joanie during the turbulent weeks just past, masking the grief that she knew had eaten at him like a living thing while he attended to funeral arrangements, appointments with lawyers and insurance agents, and a hundred tiresome details that meant little to her then, but a great deal now. She remembered little about the meetings and the papers she signed, but in the netherworld of her sorrow, even then, Joanie knew she had become his little girl again, for however long it was necessary. He had become her rock again;

both knew it but neither spoke of it. It was his way. It had always been so.

Joanie turned to her mother and watched her for a moment as she cut up the second of two fryers for the grill with practiced strokes of the heavy knife. The short, graying hair was permed in a clean fashion that fit well with an active lifestyle. She had battled the crinkles at the corners of her eyes for the last twenty of her sixty years, and for the most part had held nature at bay. She smiled as easily as her husband, but it was spritely, even childlike, the corners of her mouth turning up quickly at the slightest provocation. Her eyes were the color of the green Atlantic ocean that she cherished. It had been her idea for Joanie and Rooster to retreat to the ocean for healing.

"As close to the sound of God's voice as we'll ever know, this side of the Jordan," she had assured her daughter. And she had been right. The seemingly eternal call of the sea had been a balm for mother and son alike. Joanie knew that she would not need their near-daily support much longer. The knowledge of her growing independence was a good thing. She could feel her spirit returning to her in tiny increments like sand oozing through an hourglass.

The dancing eyes caught Joanie's gaze, and Norma made a silly face as she spoke. "Still can't chop up one of these little birds like old Mom, can you?"

"No way, Mom. You're a butcher deluxe, and when you're not here, my other butcher deluxe is five minutes away at Harris-Teeter."

"Rats' tails! Those guys couldn't cut up a fryer proper if their life depended on it. When's the last time you bought a breast piece with a pully bone in it?" She held up the prize piece like the crown jewel. "Hah! Harris-Teeter my foot. If it wasn't for me, poor little Rooster wouldn't have broken a pully bone yet."

Joanie chuckled at the good-natured lecture and waved her hand at Norma as a wet forefinger jutted toward the two figures hovered over the grill. "Would you please ask those two if they're gonna build a replica of the pyramids or just start me a little cook fire?"

"I heard that in there," came the deep voice from the other side of the screen.

"I hope so. I'd like to eat before we get past your indigestion threshold. Like sleeping with a hundred-and-seventy-pound grasshopper, when you eat too late."

Rooster laughed at the exchange, his eyes darting from tormenter to tormented. "Grandma's gettin' cranked up, ain't she, Grandpa?"

"That's a safe thing to say, boy. You better run and get me the matches before she says something downright ugly about your poor old grandpa."

Joanie opened the screen door and the boy shot through it on his way to the kitchen, his laughter trailing behind him.

The chicken cutter looked at the pyramid builder, and they winked at each other; the boy's delight was their joy, and each knew that the other was silently thanking God for it.

On any night other than a sacrificial night, Jessie Pacely would have been amused at the sight of Wesley Livingston ambling across the asphalt pavement in front of the convenience store. Like a life-sized cartoon caricature with a cigarette clamped in his teeth, the big man ignored the water puddles and splashed forward, the paper sack a brown pendulum at the end of his right arm. But Jessie did not smile at the spectacle of his friend, the man with whom only an hour before he had drunk the blood of a calf. The night had not gone well for the three worshipers. A rain shower had crept in from the southwest, and with the first drops on the stone slab, Arvil's irritation had mounted. The ceremony was rushed, and the blood washed away far too quickly.

With a huff and a small cloud of smoke, Wesley plopped into the car seat and slammed the door. Jessie pulled the gear selector down into drive and eased the vehicle onto Sinclair

Drive. Wesley placed the sack on the floorboard between his feet and fished for a can of beer. The metallic pop released the heavy odor in the close air of the car, and it mingled with the smoke but bothered neither man. Wesley extended his left hand to the driver while his right was already groping for another can.

"Whew! I don't like bein' around him when he's like that," Wesley said after savoring the first taste of the beer.

Jessie paused before he spoke. "In a way, I guess I know what you mean—but—"

"But what?"

"It's just that—I don't know exactly. Don't get me wrong, I'm scared of him, too, when he starts ragin' like that, but to see it—to be a part of it. It's just awful strong. You know what I mean?"

"I reckon I follow your drift, but I tune in better when he's in control—like some black-robed god of some kind, all the words comin' out just perfect and all."

Wesley crumpled the can and tossed it into the sack, replacing it with a fresh one.

"He'd wring our necks if he knew we split a six-pack after the services, wouldn't he?" Jessie said.

"Wouldn't like it, that's for sure," Wesley replied.

They rode in silence through two traffic lights before Jessie spoke again. "I can feel a little of it now."

"Feel what, Jessie? Would you talk straight out? Dangnation. I ain't no mind-reader."

"What you said before—about him bein' in control. I can feel some of it for myself now, and I like it."

"Power's the word, Jessie. Power. Where else me and you got any power in this stinkin' world? Foreman's on your butt every time you go to the restroom or sneak a ten second break. My old lady or some dumb-head farmer's raggin' me about some piddlin' thing four or five times a day. And then the time comes up there on the hill, and it's just us and him and something livin' that's about to die . . ." his voice trailed off.

The word came from behind the steering wheel, and it was but a whisper, "Yeah."

"First time, I couldn't believe it was me up there," Wesley continued, "gougin' with that dagger of his and chantin' to the devil, him a preacher and all, but now—now it's the strongest thing in this world for me, and I don't aim to quit. It's the power of it."

"They're real, ain't they?"

"Who?"

"The voices." Even now, the word spilled from his lips haltingly, uncomfortably.

"Yes. Real as anything I know of. How could you ever look in Arvil's eyes and doubt that?"

"No, I didn't mean it like that. I know they're real too—I just meant, well, before, I could only feel them close up there on the hill, but now, sometimes I feel them close at the house or at the factory . . . I hear them inside me."

Wesley lowered his head and turned the can slowly in his hands, and he nodded, but did not speak.

"He didn't say nothin' about . . . doin' a human tonight," Jessie said.

"Surprised me, too, but I guarantee he ain't forgot."

"Does it still scare you like it did the first time he said it?"

"No. Not as much. You?"

Jessie ran the fingers of his left hand thoughtfully through his long hair before he replied. "Not as much for me either."

Arvil Kassley stood next to a flat-topped fence post twenty paces from his back door, facing the breeze as it whipped the cold rain against his face. He had not removed his robe of worship and the heavy cloth clung wetly to his skin, but he did not shiver when the night breeze nudged its folds. The discomfort of it would merely add to his penance. The sacrificial service had been a disaster and the feeling of rage he took from the altar had slowly mutated into a spirit of contrition. He had offered his words of repentance to Satan with all the fervor he could muster, but he knew that it was not enough. Razzom had confirmed his feeling. Something more would be required tonight to make amends for his slovenly leadership, his tardiness in taking the necessary step to truly meaningful sacrifice.

The rain fell throughout the night and into the dingy grayness of dawn, and Reverend Kassley remained a part of it, thinking his thoughts.

There would be no more animal sacrifices on Arvil Kassley's altar of worship.

CHAPTER FIVE

Hazel Dobson sat with her back stretched comfortably against the wood of the bench as she squinted through the noontime glare at the front door of the church building. Her fingernails tapped like falling dominos on the worn leather cover of her Bible. She spoke to the lady sitting beside her without turning her head.

"There she goes again, Bessie, jawin' at the pastor. She's gonna wear out his ears one of these Sunday mornings."

"Only time she says anything to anybody. Reckon she's got to make the most of it."

"Suppose so . . ." Hazel's voice trailed off with a touch of irritation. "I can't figure out how she's been around for months without us coming to know her—at least a little."

Bessie adjusted the rose-colored hat on her head and gently smoothed the feathers over her right ear. "She's a strange one all right. Got to be an old widow like us, for sure . . . that is, if she ever had a man."

"If she tried catchin' one with her looks or her mouth, she ain't no widow."

Bessie chuckled at the remark, and peeked at Hazel's face as the corners of her mouth twitched upwardly.

"Aw, I know I shouldn't be so ugly toward her, but dang it all, who we old cronies got if we ain't got each other?

Seems like she'd want our company sooner or later. I got about a hundred questions I'm dyin' to ask her . . . why she moved here so late in life? . . . kinfolk close by? . . . what she used to be? . . . how'd she find that nice little house so close to the church? . . . you know. Looks like she'd want to know something about us too. We're all in the same boat."

"She's pleasant enough and all," Bessie said. "It's just that she's—a loner, I reckon, Hazel. Some folks are just loners."

"Well it ain't natural, I tell you. Old lady churchgoers ain't loners. Least I never knew of one before her."

"Looks like she's turnin' the preacher loose for today," Bessie said.

"Here she comes." Bessie squirted the words out of the side of her mouth.

Gladys sauntered toward the bench and smiled, nodding pleasantly at the two women. "Good day to you, ladies. My but you make a fine picture here in the Lord's own sunshine."

"Thank you, Gladys," Bessie answered. "I don't think anybody's told me I looked good in forty years."

Gladys laughed easily with her.

"Don't suppose you'd care to join us down to the cafeteria for a bite?" Hazel asked.

"So kind of you to ask me, but I must decline. Some things I need to attend to. Thanks so much for the offer. Good day to you, ladies." She nodded and smiled again before shuffling away from the bench.

"Now what in the world's she got to *attend* to?" Hazel huffed. "She's got to eat something—somewhere. Plenty of meat on those old bones."

"Oh, Hazel, leave the poor thing be. I kinda like her somehow . . . hard to put your finger on. You know? You don't really *dis*like her, do you?"

Hazel pinched her chin between her thumb and forefinger and looked over her glasses at her friend.

"No. Dang it."

Gladys Fairchild's strides slowly changed from shuffling to purposeful as she neared the squat white house at the end of Turner Avenue. The asbestos shingle siding was worn but not unsightly, and the roof shingles, although old, were serviceable. The tiny lawn was neatly trimmed and two yellow barberries stood on each side of the concrete porch. The shades were drawn over every window in the house.

The small form of the woman quickly stepped onto the porch, opened the unlocked door, and disappeared into the house.

Across the street, the girl stood silently beside her bicycle and watched the door of the white house swing shut. The midday sunlight filtered its way through the maple leaves and found her face and bare arms and made her think of the pitcher of grape Kool-Ade at home on the middle shelf of the refrigerator; she turned her head and began to ride away from her vantage point.

If she had watched the white house for a moment longer, she would have noticed that a bright light, greater than the sunlight of noonday, illuminated the window shades for two seconds and then was gone.

Nearly four weeks had passed since Arvil's night of penance in the rainstorm. It had been a time of contemplation and planning, and his resolve had strengthened with the passing of each day. His fawning congregation continued to lavish him with everything from praise to food, and he played the part of the stalwart servant masterfully. He had met with Wesley and Jessie several times at the altar, mainly for quiet communion and prayer, and he was sure that they were prepared for the next level. The plans had been meticulously made; all was in readiness.

The phone jangled from the countertop just as Wesley forked in a mouthful of pinto beans, and his wife glanced to see if he would make a move to answer it, knowing full well that he would not. She took a hurried sip of coffee and pushed away from the table.

"Hello. Yeah, he's right here." The receiver dangled from her fingers for a moment and as Wesley swiped a thumb over his mouth and stood, she covered the phone with the palm of her hand. "Sounds like your preacher buddy. Hopefully, he's got work for you. Remember that ugly four letter word?"

Wesley snatched the phone from her hand and offered a quick scowl. "This is Wesley."

"Good evening, Wesley. Do you feel like a cup of black coffee tonight?"

Those were the code words. Wesley felt the prickle of gooseflesh between his shoulder blades, and he knew that his wife was watching. He took an even breath and with all the nonchalance he could manage, he answered the deep voice on the other end of the line.

"Sounds—good to me, Arvil."

"Excellent. Be here in an hour."

Wesley placed the receiver back in the cradle.

"Well?"

"You were right. He wants to talk about a job. A big one."

"Hallelujah!"

"I might have a brew or two after we're done talkin'. Don't look for me back early."

"When have I ever, Wesley?"

Allene Pacely wiped the soapy water from her hands with a faded dishtowel as she crossed the kitchen floor to answer the insistent ringing.

"Hello. Why, good evening to you, Reverend," she tried mightily not to gush. "Yes—yes, doin' fine, thank you, Reverend. Hope you are. Yes, he's out back, I'll go get him for you."

She spoke through the screen door into the semi-lit backyard. "Son, it's Reverend Kassley on the phone for you." Jessie walked directly to the kitchen and took the receiver from his mother's hand. The woman returned to her task at the sink and busied herself, but Jessie was sure that she would strain for every word from his mouth.

"Hello."

"Good evening, Jessie. Wesley and I have decided to share some black coffee tonight. Would you care to join us?"

There was no hesitation. "Yes, sir. I would like to."

"My farm in an hour. Till then."

Jessie hung up the phone and answered his mother's unspoken question. "Long stretch of fence he wants to work over this week."

Allene turned her head and nodded a smile. "Sounds good, son. Weather's supposed to hold nice like this for the next few days."

"Yeah, figured that. He watches the weather real close." He smiled into the backyard, but Allene could not see his face. "Think I'm gonna cruise town for a while. Go on to bed, I may be late."

Willard Honeycutt sat on the end stool at the restaurant counter, his forearms resting on the cool formica as he carefully studied the neat rows of pie slices in the metal cooler. Despite the fact that he did not have enough money to buy one, he allowed his eyes to caress each piece, and he decided that if he could buy one, it would be the banana creme with the beautiful meringue piled two inches high.

He closed his eyes and tasted the smooth, sugary yellow of the filling and the light touch of the beaten egg whites, and he swallowed against the saliva that pooled under his tongue. Willard Honeycutt had tasted such pie before at a hundred restaurants like this one, and he was confident that he would savor it again somewhere down the great highway— a hundred miles, perhaps a thousand—it did not matter. He could wait.

The highway stretched forever, and he had roamed it for the ten years since his wife had cast him aside like a soiled cloth. There would be a sympathetic ride who would shove a ten dollar bill at him as he climbed from the vehicle. There always was—somewhere down the long highway.

The man studied his face in the mirrored backdrop behind the counter and passed a rough hand over smooth cheeks and jawbone. He took great care to keep it clean and shaven, and he knew that it had garnered him many rides that would have passed him by had he been unkempt. Oh, it had weathered some, to be sure, but Willard did not think that the square face appeared more than two or three years older than the forty-three that he had owned it.

The drone of the interstate called to him now from a hundred yards, and he was eager to return to it. He slipped the green ticket from beside the porcelain cup and hoped that the waitress would not notice the absence of a tip, but she appeared as if by magic and drug a wet cloth around the cup and saucer, popping her gum with practiced ease as she shot him a tiny glance.

"Next time, hun."

"Right, pardner," the gum snapped louder, "next time."

Willard Honeycutt stood, and as the waitress watched, he reached for his backpack and sucked down the last drop of coffee he would ever drink.

Three pairs of eyes peered through the clean glass windshield of the long black vehicle as it slid along the westbound lane of the interstate, but one pair saw far more than the other two, even though they belonged to the driver.

"There." The deep voice filled the darkness of the vehicle. "Just at the top of the ramp." Arvil jerked a forefinger toward the right corner of the windshield.

"Yeah, you're right. It's a hiker all right," said Wesley.

The pitch of the engine changed as the Suburban sped forward toward the next exit and crossed over the highway.

"We will take a closer look," Arvil said as he maneuvered

back onto the interstate. "It looks promising. I have spotted some worthy specimens at that exit."

Arvil braked smoothly as the vehicle reached the top of the ramp, the left turn signal ticking like a slow clock. Arvil glanced to his left across the overpass. The man was halfway down the opposite ramp, walking steadily backward, his right arm held nearly straight out from his body. They would reach him in less than forty seconds.

"Prepare yourselves."

Wesley squeezed his bulk over the console and between the high-backed seats, taking his position directly behind the passenger seat. Jessie was already crouched behind Arvil's seat, a short crowbar clutched in his right hand. Two thick-nesses of a small towel, tightly secured with thick string, covered the last twelve inches of its length. Wesley's palms were slick with sweat and he cradled the cold steel of the .38 revolver in both hands, thankful that it was empty. There was no need to risk accidental discharge, Arvil had instructed. Their guest would never suspect.

Arvil had worked the plan through in his mind a dozen times, and the only possible flaw was the hitchhiker's line of sight as he entered the front seat. It was possible that he would notice Jessie through the narrow space between the seats. This problem was easily solved with the application of three sturdy strips of duct tape over the light switch inside the doorframe. Darkness would prevail in Arvil Kassley's Sub-urban.

"Calm now, brethren. Remember your duties. I will do all the talking. Jessie, should we need your assistance earlier than expected, I will simply call your name. Remember. No blows to the sides or top of the head. Straight from the back, and do not be afraid to wield some force; the skull of an adult male human is extremely strong." He paused for a moment. "Questions?"

Only the sound of faint wheezing from behind the passenger seat.

"Very well. Let's have a closer look at our friend."

Willard Honeycutt blinked at the headlights of the big vehicle as it approached, and the familiar anticipation came to him as the vehicle slowed twenty feet away. He liked the monied look of it, shiny even in the dim light, and he slowly lowered his outstretched hand.

Inside, a single word was hissed. "Yes."

Arvil leaned over the passenger seat, unlatched the door, and pushed it with his fingers. Willard swung the door open, and a flicker of apprehension registered in his brain as he noticed that the dome light did not illuminate the interior, but the friendly voice of the driver overcame it.

"Evening, friend. Hey, I'm only going as far as Kansas City, but I'd enjoy the company."

"I'm much obliged, mister. Thanks."

"I'll toss this in the back for you," Arvil said as he reached for the backpack.

Willard slid into the seat and drew the heavy door closed with a solid thud. The engine churned into the night. "Rides pretty smooth if I do say so myself, friend. Bet you've been in worse, huh?"

"You got that right, mister."

Arvil laughed easily with the man as his peripheral vision caught the dark form rising slowly. With the malignant snick of the .38 revolver hammer, Reverend Kassley's folksy tone vanished.

"Remain calm, and no harm will come to you. My friend back there is very jumpy with firearms. Do you understand?"

Willard jerked a nod and tried to speak, but could not. The deep voice was speaking again, but the words were far away and he could not tune them in. His mind spun with the horror of the moment, and he struggled against the nausea that climbed up his throat like a small animal.

The tales he had heard from other hikers tumbled through his mind, and he searched through them for some small thing with which to arm himself. *It couldn't be money, that much was certain. Hatred of bums? Maybe. A beating at worst, surely . . . surely they wouldn't kill him. Sex? . . . could be that. It had happened to the young guy in Oklahoma City he had spoken with last year. Yes . . . that was likely it. The long back compartment of the vehicle . . . it was there that he would become the object of their attention.* Whatever, he could live through that if he had to. And he did have to. The muzzle of the gun against the back of his neck assured him that he would have to. He could speak now. He needed to. The driver had stopped talking.

"Mister—please—whatever you want with me—I'll—I'll go along with it. No trouble, I swear. Tell him to put the gun down. Please."

"Take it from his neck, but keep it trained on him through the seat."

"Thanks, mister—I swear—no trouble."

"What do you think we want with you?" The voice was resonant, yet without a trace of emotion.

"I—I reckon . . . you want to have your . . . way with . . . me."

Reverend Kassley's mind sprang at the opportunity. It was absolutely perfect. The wretched drifter thought they desired sex. With only a little care, he could be led to the altar with a minimum of commotion. How perfect indeed.

"I trust you do not object to the . . . gay lifestyle?"

"No—no—no problem," he lied, and swallowed the revulsion.

"Very good, mister hitchhiker. If you can manage to relax a bit, the night should not prove to be totally unenjoyable for you. My apologies for the gun, but I'm sure you understand. We never know in the beginning whether we have met friend or foe." Arvil reached through the darkness and gently stroked the man's thigh, and although he flinched involuntarily, he did not resist.

"I know of a wonderful spot only ten minutes from here where we can find some privacy. A favorite of ours, I might add. I think you will like it. Then, money for a hot meal, and back to your highway. Fair enough?"

Willard nodded as he spoke, "Yeah . . . no problem."

Within minutes, the beam of the headlights found the familiar gravel road, and soon three of the men knew that they had passed Reverend Kassley's house, but none turned their heads. When the Suburban turned off the gravel road, Arvil turned the headlights off and steered the blocky vehicle up the slope with only the moonlight to guide him.

With each foot of elevation gained, the thud of Jessie's heart magnified and he could swallow only with great concentration. He needed the whisper from within, and he prayed for it, and thought of the power that would soon be his. But the whisper did not come.

Wesley Livingston would have given anything he owned for a cigarette. Seven gratifying drags of rich smoke pulled deep into his lungs; the mere thought of the act was incredibly strong, and he willed it away from himself even as he fidgeted for the pack that was not there. Higher thoughts now, he chastised himself. The greatest adventure of his life was minutes away, and all trivial matters must be laid aside. He could see the long profile of Reverend Kassley's face in the moon glow, and he took strength from it as he always did when they climbed the hill together.

Willard fought against the trembling of his hands as his fingers dug into denim trouser legs. For a fleeting moment he comtemplated a quick lunge out the door, but he dismissed the thought immediately. He had not seen the other two men who now sat behind him in the rear seat, but he had seen the driver, and the thought of angering him nearly gagged Willard. No, he would somehow make it through the next hour—he hoped it was only an hour—maybe less if he was lucky. Calm. Just stay as calm as possible. He could not anger the big man. There was a strange solace in the certainty of this fact; it was the one thing that Willard did have some control over, and no matter what harsh treatment awaited him, he would not anger the owner of the great voice.

The vehicle stopped. The trembling man drew one ragged breath before the padded crowbar whooshed forward in a level arc, and then nothingness.

He came back from the void with dull fragments of consciousness, and then the throb at the back of his head was his total being. But he struggled against it with all his will because now an eerie sensation enveloped him, and as his mind cleared, the horror of it was made known. He lay naked on a huge stone of some sort, each limb of his body stretched to a corner, his wrists and ankles tightly bound with coarse rope. He attempted to speak but the rolled cloth drawn through his mouth only allowed him to utter animal-like grunts. His mind grew clearer, and he blinked wildly and turned his head toward the sound of footsteps in the grass—closer, ever closer. Now a shadow moved beside the stone, and another, and yet another, taller than the other two. He could see the loose robes over their bodies and the faces were lost under peaked hoods, and then the voice came from the tallest.

"He has regained conciousness; all is in readiness."

The three figures moved in unison as they knelt and crowded to the edge of the stone, one on each side; the great voice directly over his head.

"Until this night, your life held little, if any, value, but this is soon to change. You will be made one with us, one with the master of darkness, and even in your agony, you will be made one with the truth of the world."

The doomed man arched his back and rolled his eyes rearward and sought the eyes of the voice, and when he found them, he knew beyond the slightest doubt that he was going to die. He could see the long dagger now, its blade pale in the weak light, and he watched in disbelief as his tormentor laid it gently on his stomach. They joined hands now, these insane beings from hell, and the words from their lips sounded like prayers.

Willard Honeycutt screamed into the wet cloth for death to take him quickly.

CHAPTER SIX

Sunday morning dawned splendidly through the stately oaks and hickories behind Arvil Kassley's barn. The sumptuous aroma of the freshly brewed coffee wafted up to his nostrils, and they flared slightly with the delicate pleasure. The sacrifice of the previous night had gone wonderfully well, and the reverend was still aglow from it all as he relived the climactic moments; it had far exceeded his greatest hopes. Wesley had performed very well, and Jessie, acceptably, he thought—oh, a slip of resolve here and there—but nothing of consequence. Jessie would only grow in strength now under his tutelage, and he had his eye on another potential worshiper, and a young woman at that. What lovely spice that would bring to the ceremonies; the fairer sex with the long dagger in her dainty white hand. Yes, he would pursue that project soon enough.

He glanced at his watch; plenty of time to concoct a silly sermon for his flock. He might even tease them, especially the old woman, with a few words about the great Jesus of Nazareth, the lamb for the Roman slaughter.

He smiled into the morning light and hummed an airy tune with the early morning songbirds as he retreated to his house so that he could select a virtuous Bible passage for the service.

He first noticed the change in Gladys Fairchild from the pulpit, and he was sure that it had been with the mention of Jesus' name. He had made a point to seek her eyes out, to enjoy the mockery of it all as she smiled her tired smile back at him. But no smile came to him then, only a strange coldness as she patted the worn Bible in her lap. Perhaps she had passed the point of senility; could not the old fool comprehend the words she had fairly begged to hear?

And now, as she drew near with her shambling gait, there was no dance to her eyes, no hint of familiar anticipation of the motherly admonishments she would mouth. There was only resolve, and a grim resolve at that. She stood before him now and did not wait for his greeting.

"So . . . you finally crossed the line, preeecher," the word scratched from her throat.

"I—uh—yes, Miss Fairchild, I decided to draw a sermon from the New—" her eyes probed his like tiny blue torches and his discomfort mounted by the second, "Testa—"

"More than that line, preeecher, you have crossed far more than that line."

"I—uh—I don't under—"

"Yes. Yes you do."

The eyes, the cursed eyes would not unlock his, and he could feel the hair at the nape of his neck move like tiny feathers. The voice came again now, but it was more than the sound of an old lady, and he at once hated her and yet was in awe of her presence.

"Very soon, you must seek the Christ that you mock." She turned to leave the doorway, but Reverend Kassley did not see her move away. He was walking toward his study as steadily as his legs would allow, and his right hand groped for the pentagram in his coat pocket.

Twila Livingston scanned the Sunday paper with her fifth cup of coffee as she lay curled like a lazy cat in the corner of the faded couch. Between sips, she took notice of Wesley, who stood at the front door peering through the glass panes into the late morning light. She had been asleep the night before when he returned to the house, well past midnight, and had only awakened with the hiss of the shower head from the cramped bathroom, less than ten feet from the bed. She feigned sleep as he joined her in bed, and she thought her thoughts, as she did now, looking at his profile at the door. Ten, maybe closer to fifteen, pounds had melted away in the past month, and this despite the fact that his smoking had decreased dramatically. His appearance had also improved; he sought clean clothes and combed his hair, and even now on a Sunday morning stood clean-shaven in his own living room. Strange goings-on for sure for Mister Wesley Livingston.

Twila took a thoughtful sip of coffee and pretended to read the paper. Another woman? Couldn't be, not even with his new look. It was simply too much trouble for a man who didn't really like women that much. No, not likely that, she decided, even though the idea of her old man having an affair would have been a source of amusement rather than jealousy. Maybe the great Reverend Kassley, in all his pomp and splendor, had rubbed off on him. They had surely spent enough time together in the last few weeks. Wesley with a big dose of religion? The idea at once intrigued her and yet sent a spark of resentment through her brain. Anything but that, please. She could cope with clouds of cigarette smoke, other women, wanderings for half the night, six-packs—anything but the dreaded "R" word. She would pick at him and find out; she needed to know.

"Just look at you, Wesley Livingston. If I didn't know better, I'd swear you were runnin' with some young thing in town."

Wesley huffed a little laugh and cocked his head at her for an instant before resuming his watch over the front yard.

"Maybe you're fixin' to start attendin' church services with your buddy the reverend? Ha! That'd be a major deal, now wouldn't it?"

She dropped her eyes to the top line of the paper but she was looking at him and he knew it.

"Since when does whatever I do mean spit to you?"

She was surprised at the venom in his voice; a tender spot had definitely been roughed up.

"Hey, don't get excited, Wesley. Sorry if I wasn't respectful enough for the reverend. Maybe you should just squeeze into your Sunday-go-to-meetin' duds and prance on down to the church house for a hymn or two."

She glanced up from the paper ready to smirk with the sting of her needling, but she did not. There was something in his face that would not allow it, and she wanted to avert her eyes, but he would not let them go.

"Maybe I just will someday soon, woman. I've learned a lot from him already, and I've never set foot in his church house. Maybe I just will." And with that he jerked the door open and stepped onto the porch. He would not speak to his wife again until the next morning, but he would look at her and dare her to speak, and she would not.

Allene Pacely could not keep the spring from her step as she approached the back door to her house. Scarcely fifteen minutes before, she had exchanged pleasantries with the Reverend Kassley at the front door of the sanctuary, and what a perfectly wonderful conversation it had been. She had mentioned Jessie to the leader of the flock, and he had virtually assured her that he would soon prevail on her lost son to begin attending services. She had tried not to gush, but it did not matter; Reverend Kassley understood her joy and clasped her hand warmly as he gave her a quick hug about the shoulders. His presence remained with her even now—the smell of his rich cologne, the strength in his great hands as they drew her to him, the timbre of his voice—oh, such men were few and far between indeed, and such a man guided her only son.

Jessie was sitting at the kitchen table when she entered and turned his head as she greeted him. "Hungry, son? I got a nice pot of beans and hamhock simmerin' here. Smells mighty good to me."

"Not very—I mean—hungry, Mom. Yeah, they smell good. You go ahead. Maybe later."

"I can wait a while. Think I'll change out of this dress anyhow. We don't get much chance to talk it seems. I'll make a pone of cornbread after a bit. Never known you to pass on a chance to pinch the edges of my cornbread."

She smiled at him and paused for an instant to give him a chance to reply, but he remained distant and said nothing.

"Well, I'm gonna get out of this dress." Allene stepped away quietly to her bedroom and closed the door.

She had awakened the night before when Jessie had returned, but did not look at the lighted face of the alarm clock. It was late, very late, but it did not matter really. The boy was young, wasn't he? It was only natural for a young man to run some late at night. After all, it was a Saturday night in the summertime. The beer would soon be less of an attraction, she was sure. The more time he spent at the reverend's farm the sooner he would move on to important things, things of the heart. It was hard for a young man to cross over the line, especially one who had endured adolescence without a father.

"In good time," she smiled to herself as she fastened the buttons of the worn blue jeans. Allene toyed with ideas about how she would work the dinner conversation around to her little talk with the reverend. It should not prove to be difficult, what with the number of odd jobs Jessie had worked for him lately. She was eager to see some hint of the progress Reverend Kassley had mentioned. It would be a fine Sunday dinner. She had just turned the doorknob when she heard the low rumble of Jessie's car and the crunch of tires on the gravel driveway.

It was two hours after the Sunday evening services before Arvil began to collect himself. Gladys Fairchild had been thankfully absent, and the sparse gathering of worshipers had demanded little of their pastor; indeed, he had little to offer from either the pulpit or the front door of the church building. Arvil vaguely remembered the sermon topic that he had stumbled through during the service. He sat now in the darkness of his kitchen. His clenched fists finally began to loosen and his breathing deepened into a normal rhythm. Thin light touched the table top and the man accepted the offering of the moon and wondered if any of his brothers-in-arms were looking at the same light, or if perhaps they were about their master's business. He needed them now, oh, how he needed them now, and one in particular.

He pushed away from the table and flicked the light switch, blinking the glare away as he sought the small Rolodex at the corner of the countertop. His fingers made quick work of the task and he punched the eleven digits into the telephone.

"Hello," the male voice was deep and forceful.

"Devon, this is Arvil Kassley. I am glad that you are home. Do you have a few minutes?"

"Certainly, Arvil, it's good to hear from you, although I must admit that I detect a hint of distress in your tone. Nothing of consequence, I trust?"

"Oh, I—no, nothing of consequence, I'm sure, Devon . . ."

"We are brothers in service to the same master, Arvil. You know me very well; there is no need to mince words. Unburden yourself."

"Yes, you're right—as always. Forgive me the false start. It is a member of my flock, an old woman—unfortunately not old enough to be an invalid—but old enough that she should be harmless. She has pestered me about my lack of attention to the New Testament . . . things like that . . . from time to time . . . until . . ."

"Until what, Arvil?"

"Oh, Devon, this should be a call of great victory. Only yesterday I and two of my pupils reached the second level of worship—a thing beyond my wildest dreams—and then this—this confrontation . . ."

"My congratulations, brother, on your great victory. This is marvelous news, although I am hardly surprised. I have long known of your strength and level of commitment. But this—confrontation—as you say?"

"The old hag wandered up to me as usual after the service— always the last one, always and forever, the last one. All the better to hound me with no one in line behind her to speed the cursed process, you see. Anyway, I had decided to toy with the flock and toss the great Christ's name about for a bit, and had done so rather well I thought, and she says to me, 'You have crossed over the line, preacher.' I naturally assumed that she referred to the New Testament passage, but she interrupted me in mid-sentence and said, 'More than that line, preacher,' . . . and the look of intensity in her eyes, Devon, it was as if she knew about . . . it . . ." the words tumbled from Arvil's mouth.

"Arvil, Arvil, calm yourself, please. I'm sure that you have read something more into this than there really is. Members of my flock have been an agitation from time to time also . . . some great agitations, but that is all there is to it, trust me. Especially with the aged. Who knows what will spill from them next. Silly rantings, that's all."

"But the look of her, Devon, and the way she said 'More than that line' . . . it was dreadful . . . what if somehow she found out . . ."

"Not a chance, brother. Your pupils—they are trustworthy, I'm sure, knowing you as I do. There is just no chance of a security breach, especially involving someone like an old woman. It was nothing more than verbal drool from her rotting flesh."

Arvil drew a deep breath and released it over the receiver. "Oh, I suppose you're correct, Devon. You usually are." Arvil managed a small huff that could have been a laugh.

"That's the spirit, brother. I can't imagine the Reverend Arvil Kassley being slowed down by a senile old bag spouting nonsense."

It was a laugh now that Arvil shared with his friend, and he felt the tension begin to drain from his hunched shoulders. Devon continued. "Remember that haughty professor of Hebrew in seminary? The one with that idiotic gold tooth gleaming like a penlight?"

"Yes, who could forget?"

"You worried about him for a time also, didn't you—thought he was onto us, remember?"

"Yes, Devon, I remember. Must you rub it in?"

"It's not my intention to rub anything in, brother, I just want to remind you of your own strength against such trivial creatures. Brush aside the trivial in your quest. Ignore the old hag. She will fade away soon enough, but you will not." He paused to allow his words to echo in Arvil's mind. "Two pupils you say? Marvelous. In a few months' time too. I have only one that I completely trust, along with two underlings . . . but they do show promise. Not second level promise just yet, mind you, but soon enough. My trustworthy one is something special. Devoted family man, beautiful wife—choir soloist from time to time—two children . . . too good to be true. It is an incredible story how we found each other. I want to tell you in person. We must get together soon, Arvil."

"Yes we must, Devon, we must indeed."

"You are all right now? You seem yourself again."

"Yes—yes, I am all right. Thank you, brother. I needed you. It does seem a bit silly now, I must admit . . . ."

"Not at all, don't think that. I may be the one calling you

next time. We must support one another. We must remain bound to the cause."

"Yes . . . the cause, Devon. I will drink to you at my next service. Thank you again."

"Until next time."

"Until then."

He sat in silence for five minutes before Razzom's voice filled the room.

"I heard the last of your conversation. If you needed reassurance, why did you not call on me? Do you think that another human could better serve you?" There was a touch of anger in the demon's voice, and Arvil shuddered at the sound of it.

"Cer—certainly not, I—just . . ."

"Needed to speak with another human. Yes. Yes, I suppose that is forgivable—this time. You must remember that I have others that I am helping. I cannot be at all places at once. *But,*" the word stung Arvil's ears, "I am able—*always*—to hear your cry for help. Do not ever forget this."

"No—I, uh—I will not, I promise."

The chill air of the room warmed instantly with the departure of the evil spirit. It took a quarter of an hour for Arvil to calm down and again organize his thoughts. He dialed the seven digits of the next number from memory. "Wesley, good evening, this is Arvil. May we speak freely?"

"Yeah, she's gone with her cronies somewhere."

"Good. Listen, you remember our discussion about the need for a solid pornography contact?"

"Yes, Arvil, I remember."

"Have you had any success at either store?"

"Yeah, I think, but you'll have to decide for yourself. I bought four of 'em. You got any idea what these dang things cost? I couldn't believe . . ."

"I'll reimburse you, Wesley. Do any of them deal with . . . younger subjects?"

"Yeah, some of 'em do, but like I was sayin' . . . you'll

have to see for yourself—these ads—some of 'em don't make much sense to me. The words and all—like some kind of code or something, I don't know . . ."

"Yes, well, just see that you get them to me soon. Tuesday at the latest. I am eager to make some useful contacts for future . . . levels."

"I'll get 'em over to you tomorrow evenin', if that's okay. Right after supper maybe?"

"That would be excellent, Wesley. I'll be expecting you. Good night."

CHAPTER SEVEN

Reverend Kassley's thumb gently fanned the tops of the gold-edged pages of his Bible as it searched for the last of the square cut-outs from the magazines. They were tucked safely in the pages of Lamentations—rather appropriately, Reverend Kassley thought to himself—since the delectable lamentations of the innocent would soon fill his ears.

Wesley had procured four pornographic magazines which specialized in children. Arvil had pored over the pages with great intensity, searching for advertisements which might lead him to a suitable contact. He spent little time with the photographs. They were interesting enough, to be sure, but they lacked purity or purpose, and Arvil dismissed them as gratuitous. Evil without purpose was, after all, merely an exercise, unfit for an offering to the master. But evil with proper direction was an incredibly powerful thing, and this was what Arvil sought.

He felt the scrap of paper with the tip of his thumb and pulled it into his hand, rubbing it slowly between his fingers. There had been seventeen telephone calls within the last two weeks from several phone booths scattered about town, and all had ended in frustration. The advertisement in his hand had been cut from a magazine named *Sweet Lad,* which had seemed the most promising, and which had been saved until last. The phone number was for a location in St. Louis; Arvil had checked with directory assistance. The ad had instructed that calls should be made between ten forty-five and eleven o'clock. The digital clock in the dashboard read ten-fifty. It did not matter that the light coming from the edge of the grocery store parking lot was poor; Reverend Kassley had memorized the number. A small box of quarters lay on the console near his right hand and he picked up several as his left hand reached through the open car window for the phone.

"Hello." The voice was ordinary, like that of a shop owner answering his telephone in the midst of a routine business day.

"Yes, I'm calling to inquire about the ad in *Sweet Lad* magazine."

Silence. "So?" asked the voice.

"Yes, well I'm calling to—uh—learn of the possibility of making—contact with . . ."

"With?" The voice was unchanged.

"Well, the ad mentioned specifically that—this could possibly be arranged . . ."

There was another pause, ten seconds long, as Arvil's words dangled in the one hundred twenty-five mile space which separated the two men. Ten seconds was all Joey Fazor needed to be sure that the inquirer was the genuine article. In his own way, Joey was as perceptive as a practicing psychologist, probing into the minds of his callers, listening for the telltale word or phrase that did not fit, ever listening for voice inflections that sounded alarm bells in his own mind. There were no alarm bells now.

"Listen to me. You are in a phone booth, right?"

"Yes."

"That's good. I like dealin' with a thinkin' man. Maybe I can help you, maybe not. You ever done this before?"

"No."

"I didn't think so, but that's okay. First-timers don't make many mistakes. They tend to be real particular about doin' exactly what I ask. And I don't make *any* mistakes. And I don't like doin' business over the phone. What number you at?"

Arvil stuck his head out the window and carefully read the digits from the receiver.

"Good. How far apart are we?"

"About two hours."

"That's very good. You be at that phone at exactly eleven tomorrow night, and I'll set up a face-to-face, okay?"

"Yes, I'll be here."

"One more thing. I'm sure you know we're not talkin' about small change here, huh? Professionals get professional fees."

"I understand."

"Later."

The sharp click on the line separated Reverend Kassley from the man who had traded in the lives and bodies of children for the last eleven years.

The thick tread of the tires on Reverend Kassley's sleek Suburban hummed pleasantly as they peeled away the miles of I-70. The voice on the phone had instructed Arvil to enter the St. Louis metropolitan area on U.S. Highway 40, and at the east edge of Wentzville the black vehicle swung southeast from the interstate and merged with the highway. Eleven o'clock was the appointed time. The green digits of the dashboard clock read 10:10; Arvil tapped the coast button and brought his cruising speed down to fifty-five. He was comfortably on schedule.

It seemed only moments, but twenty-five minutes passed before Arvil's eyes began to scan the overhead signs for his exit. The voice had warned that Eleventh Street exited on the left side of the highway. Arvil skillfully manuevered the Suburban into the left lane a mile before the exit. The ramp curved downward to a stoplight, and a quick right turn led down one block, and then another right placed him on the street of the meeting place. It was an area of old masonry warehouses, some abandoned, and the street lighting was poor. Arvil squinted into the gloom along the left side of the street, seeking the three-story building with the loading dock that jutted nearly to the street.

Arvil's pulse quickened slightly as his eyes fell on the old concrete dock. He turned off the street just beyond it, nosed his vehicle against the dirty brick wall of the warehouse, and switched off the headlights. There were no other cars in sight. He had been instructed to remain inside his vehicle.

A slow minute passed, and then another, but no headlights were visible from either direction along the street. With a start, Arvil jerked his head toward the rearview mirror; the beam of the flashlight was a tiny strobe as it probed the interior of the Suburban, and then it disappeared. Two dark forms, one on each side of the front doors, blocked out the thin yellow light. Two taps on the left window glass and three on the right. Arvil breathed a sigh and watched as the two men walked quickly to the building door.

Arvil slid from the seat and followed them into the building, picking his way over shattered bottles and chunks of broken concrete. He paused at the doorway before it swung open with the groan of old metal, and he recognized the voice as the one from the telephone.

"Come on in."

Arvil stepped over the threshold and blinked at the two men in the shadows. The door was left partially open, and as Arvil's eyes adjusted, he could see faint outlines of the two faces, but that was all. They would forever be things of the shadows, and Reverend Kassley knew that he would never see them clearly. One of the men moved two steps closer to Arvil before the other man spoke.

"First things first. My friend here ain't very big as bodyguards go, but some people think he moves kinda like a cat, and he has this nasty habit of carryin' very sharp things in his pockets. I can't do much with him when he gets excited—

you know what I mean—hey, I hate to even mention this stuff, but I meet some real weirdos every now and then and, well, you just never know . . ."

"I understand."

"Good. I knew you would. You sound like a businessman to me." He nodded his head toward his companion.

The beam of the flashlight cut into the room as the men took two more steps to Arvil's side. "Easy now," the man said softly as he removed Arvil's wallet. Arvil silently cursed himself as the man with the flashlight handed the wallet to his partner.

"I like to know who I'm dealin' with, Mr. Kass—ley. Am I sayin' that right?"

"Close enough."

"Good. Good." He replaced the driver's license and handed the wallet back to Arvil. "I never forget a name or address, Mr. Kassley. Habit of mine, you might say."

He huffed a little laugh, but Arvil did not acknowledge it.

"Well, time to get down to business, huh? I need to know just what type companion you have a hankerin' for, Mr. Kassley. Boy or girl?"

"Boy."

"White, black . . . other?"

"White."

"How old?"

"Eight . . . nine."

"Keepsake or date?"

"I don't under—"

"One to keep for your very own for as long as you want—your disposal problem, or a date for a night and back to me—my disposal problem."

"Keepsake."

"Let me guess the rest, huh? Nice handsome face, blond, blue eyes—green would do—clean, not big for his age . . . that about got it?"

"Yes. That would do nicely."

The man paused for a moment, and although Arvil could not see his face, he knew he smiled as he spoke. "Man, I love you chickenhawks. Know just what you want, not bashful, smart, money, the whole package. I love it."

Arvil remained silent, and the man continued. "Mr. Kassley, what you want can be arranged, but it is a fairly big deal. That's no surprise, huh?"

"No."

"For what you want, we're talkin' a ton of cash in small bills."

"How much is a—ton?"

"A ton, Mr. Kassley, is twelve thousand dollars."

"That will be fine."

"Good. We're done here then. I'll go to work. You check in with me every three or four days. I don't think it'll be long. I know most of the pros out there, and before I hit the sack tonight, some of the best will be helpin' us."

"I'll stay in touch," said Arvil as he turned to leave. As he neared the door, the voice came to him just above a whisper, and he could not tell which man spoke.

"Sweet dreams."

Six days after the meeting between Reverend Kassley and Joey Fazor, a man and a woman casually pushed open the big metal doors that led to the Cafe Court area of Southland Mall in Charlotte, North Carolina. As was their custom, they began to stroll leisurely along the major wings of the big shopping center. They paused at a shopfront display now and then, and to anyone who threw a casual glance at them, the couple appeared to be perusing the items for sale. But they were not.

The man wore a thin nylon jacket despite the warmth of the evening. However minor, this was a noticeable thing, something that made him stand out from the milling shoppers, and, as such, was a bad thing for the couple. But it was simply the lesser of two evils, and it had been an easy decision to make in the beginning. A thin jacket on a warm evening was much less memorable that even a cursory glance at the jagged slabs of muscle that formed the man's arms. He stood an inch over six feet and had the easy walk of an athlete, his lithe frame gliding over the floor of the mall with smooth, even strides. His brown hair was neatly trimmed around his forehead and ears and did not protrude beyond his collar. His features were ordinary—brown eyes, straight nose neither too large nor too small, lips perhaps a bit narrow, square jaw line—a face that fit in nicely with fifty others on any given night at Southland Mall.

Like the woman, he wore expensive athletic shoes, although they had been purposely soiled and scuffed to conceal their newness. The footwear of the couple was the single most important item of dress. There were many times when swiftness and silence of movement was paramount, not to mention the miles they regularly covered on hard surfaces.

The man felt a twinge of pain in his right index finger and he glanced down at the flesh colored Band-Aid that concealed the two-week-old wound. It was healing well and the pain would soon be gone. He knew that it should have been attended by a doctor—human bite wounds can be nasty things—but this was not possible, and the woman tended it as best she could. She had told him more than once that the pain would serve as a proper reminder of the consequences of sloppy work.

The false moustache matched his hair perfectly and was well-fitted except for the right tip, where the adhesive had not bonded well, causing an irritating little itch. He twitched the corner of his mouth every few steps, imperceptibly he thought, but the woman at his side noticed. His sister noticed everything.

"Do you want to be known as the twitching mouth of Southland Mall, Percy?" she asked, turning her head toward him, and there was not a hint of levity in her voice.

"No, Sis, I didn't think anybody could see . . ."

"I did. And if I did, somebody else might. Stop it right now."

Leva Arstead's eyes were cold and foreboding when she desired them to be and Percy looked straight ahead. They were a deep sea-green and should have been beautiful, but they were not. Her features were not striking, although, with modest effort, she could have made herself very attractive, even memorable, but this was something above all else that she avoided. She allowed herself some flexibility with her shoulder-length hair, albeit merely a functional exercise that allowed for drastic changes in her look. Tonight it was drawn into a loose ponytail with wispy bangs in the front, matching her age of thirty-six years. But five minutes with a brush and hairpins, coupled with the application of rouge high on her cheeks and an ugly shade of lipstick, could add twenty years to her appearance.

They sauntered along with the shoppers and the mall-walkers, their eyes ever sweeping about the space around them. None of the shoppers could have ever imagined that they walked with the most dangerous couple that had ever entered the giant shopping center.

The traffic was beginning to thin out in the main shopping wings. In fifteen minutes, the movie theater would empty near the Cafe Court area and some of the movie goers would depart for the parking lot while others made for the food and drink concessions and the video arcade room at the opposite end of the court. It was this group, the one that unfailingly made its way to the arcade room, that interested Leva and Percy Arstead. This was the group with all the lovely children.

It took them only ten minutes in the noisy room to sort out the possibilities. They sipped soft drinks at a cafe table thirty feet from the arcade as they discussed the children.

"I see four that might work out sometime, but only two that might work for Joey," Percy said.

"You're right about the four, but only one might work for

Joey," Leva said. "The smaller one in the red shorts is a no-go. Mom and Dad both hoverin' over him like he was the only kid on earth. Never take their eyes off him. No way he'd ever get near the rest room alone."

Percy nodded thoughtfully, like a student listening to a learned professor.

"The bigger blond," she continued, "things are lookin' better and better with him. Second Friday night in a row he's been here. A really pretty kid."

"Yeah," said Percy, "I remember. Nobody but his mother with him last week too."

"There isn't anybody else, Percy. Didn't you see Mom's naked ring finger?"

"You think he goes to the rest room by himself?"

"Got to. Oh, she'd stay around the door somewhere all right, but he's way past goin' in the ladies' room with her." She paused. "I feel really good about him. We'll see what Joey thinks."

Leva brought her purse to her lap and fished for a tissue, which she brought to her nose with her left hand. Her right hand appeared to be arranging the things in the purse as it skillfully cocked and positioned the small camera.

"I'll be right back" she said.

The woman and the child did not notice Leva as she meandered her way toward them. The boy was perched atop a step which elevated the smaller patrons to the proper playing level for the video game. Great splashes of orange and red washed over the screen as the child gleefully zapped one space invader after another. His mother clapped dutifully in response to each delighted glance he cast her after a victory.

Leva was two machines away, then one. The light from the flashing game board reflected into the boy's face. Leva waited until he laughed at another victory over his electronic foes before she raised her purse slightly and probed for a tissue. Neither the woman nor the child was ever aware of her presence.

Leva returned to the table and tossed a nod and a half smile toward Percy. They sipped their drinks in silence as they watched the mother and child slap high-fives and hug each other before moving to another game machine. Ten minutes before closing time, the woman and the boy departed the arcade, but they did not walk toward the front doors. They walked toward the corridor that led to the rest rooms.

Leva and Percy exchanged looks of satisfaction as they pushed away from the table. Neither spoke until they reached the parking lot.

"We'll express mail this roll on Monday, and I guarantee we'll hear from Joey within a day. He's gotta love the face, not to mention that we've got 'em patterned."

Percy nodded. "Got to be at least a five-thousand dollar kid, don't you think, Leva?"

"At least. I'll try for six when we set up the deal. I think I can get it."

Percy started the engine of the big conversion van and slipped the gear selector into drive.

"Rooster." She nearly spat the word from her mouth, and then laughed a tight little laugh.

"What'd you say?"

"Rooster," she repeated, louder this time. "That's what momma called her little boy."

They both laughed.

CHAPTER EIGHT

Joanie Starmann stood beside her mother at the kitchen sink, watching her as she formed perfect hamburger patties with practiced ease. She peeked at Norma with a sidelong glance; the older woman was already looking at her, shaking her head and smiling.

"How many burgers you reckon you've watched me pat out, Joanie?"

They both laughed easily. "Mom, it may have been a thousand, but we both know I'll never do it like that. That's why I've got this little plastic beauty that squishes them out just right every time."

"And packs them down so they don't cook right. Pshaw!"

Joanie shook her head. "I'm going to see if the firestarters have done their thing."

"Just as well I do them all. Hadn't been for me, poor little Rooster would be all grown up without ever tasting a juicy burger. Great day! Just think about that."

Joanie threw her hand up in surrender as she began to walk toward the patio door. Floyd Hunt stood beside the barbeque grill, bent forward with his hands on his knees looking for all the world like a sixty-year-old umpire without a uniform. He watched intently as Rooster painstakingly stacked the last few charcoal briquets near the peak of the black pyramid.

"Good, son, very good," he coached. "About three more, don't you think?"

The boy nodded, the tip of his tongue jutting from the side of his mouth.

Joanie looked at the two of them through the screen door and loved them intensely, frighteningly even, she admitted to herself. Maybe it was because the link of one generation between them was gone. The grandfather had become more of a father figure to the boy in the last few weeks; she had watched it happen—smoothly, gently, firmly—her father's way, without Rooster ever suspecting that a subtle but important change had taken place in their relationship. It was sacrificial on Floyd's part; like all doting grandparents, he had welcomed the freedom of being a granddad. But now he had added a necessary dimension to their kinship, and he would maintain it as long as it was necessary.

"Good heavens," came Norma's voice over her shoulder. She had come from the kitchen to check on the fire. "You two making another one of your ancient pyramids or what?"

"Take it easy, Grandma," Floyd said quietly. "If you build a charcoal fire, you should build one that lasts a while."

"Well, that one should do real well. Time it burns down and we fire up these burgers and eat 'em, it'll be eight-thirty, and you know what that means, Floyd Hunt."

"It means you'll turn into a big grasshopper, right Grandpa?" Rooster chirped.

Floyd shook his head and gathered Rooster with one arm. "Squirt some starter fluid on it and torch it, ladies. We men are going to retire to the ballgame for a while."

Norma picked up the can of fluid and began to soak the briquets with brisk strokes, prancing around the cooker like a woman half her years. The fire caught slowly at first, and then, with the evening breeze fanning it, grew orange and tall, and the women backed away from it a few steps before they settled, arm in arm, to watch it.

"I'm beginning to feel better about him all the time, honey. He's going to weather this all right."

"Me too, Mom. He's a strong kid and he's got us. I feel good about him too."

They were silent for a few moments and both knew what the other was thinking. Joanie answered the question that her mother did not have to ask.

"Yes, Mom, I'm beginning to feel good about me too."

They stood quietly with the fire dancing in their eyes until the roar of the crowd at Fulton County Stadium in Atlanta came to them from the television set. A young slugger named Dave Justice had just launched a towering home run, and above the noise of the crowd, the women could hear the howl of delight from Rooster Starmann.

It was nearly one o'clock in the morning, but the bedroom light from unit number 2-B of The Cascades Apartments in southwest St. Louis glowed into the row of evergreens that lined the rear boundary of the complex. Joey Fazor was working late. He was propped comfortably on two pillows that rested against the headboard of his bed. He had just showered to clear his head before he made his final selection. The sensual feel of the silk bathrobe was delightful, and he allowed himself a few more moments to concentrate on its caresses.

Three eight-by-ten photographs of excellent quality lay on the sheet to his right. He picked up the first and studied it carefully, as if for the first time, although he nearly had the boy's beautiful features memorized. He ticked off the pros and cons. Kansas City—great logistics regarding both pick-up from the snatch and delivery to the customer; solid two-man team with a good track record; very strong plusses, he nodded to himself. On the down side, his contact had stretched the truth about patterning the child's movements. Joey always knew when someone was lying to him—even a tiny lie. Tiny lies could prove very costly in his business. Beyond this, the boy had not been seen without both parents with him. He tossed the photograph back on the bed.

He picked up another photograph. Memphis—very suitable logistics; a man and woman team with no history of screw-ups; again, excellent quality as far as facial features and body. But the boy appeared to Joey to be an old nine, maybe ten, and he was big for his size, athletic looking, maybe a soccer type. A tough snatch even for pros. The photograph fell lightly on the first.

Joey picked up the last one. Charlotte—the least desirable pick up and delivery of the three; but this was the only negative. There was no doubt that the boy would make Mr. Kassley very happy. He looked at the smiling face in the photo. Somehow, Leva always managed to take the best shots. Leva and her gorilla brother were simply the best out there, no question. And they had him patterned. Joey had known this was the boy even before the shower, but he had enjoyed the final selection process nonetheless; it had become a ritual with him.

He glanced at the radio clock. It was 2:10 Eastern Standard time, but he would call anyway. Leva would want to know of his decision at once. Besides, he smiled to himself, maybe she would be easier to deal with when she was a little sleep-fuzzy. He grabbed a pair of jeans from the back of a chair and quickly dressed for the short ride to the phone booth.

The telephone on Leva Arstead's nightstand jangled three times before she answered thickly. "Hello."

"Evenin', babe. I know it's late, but this car you're tryin' to sell me is really on my mind."

"Where you at?" the voice had lost its thickness.

"Three," came the reply, referring to the coded location number of the phone booth Joey was in.

"Give me ten," Leva barked.

Click.

Eight minutes later, Joey plucked the phone from its cradle. "Hello again, babe."

"You want to talk first, Joey, or should I?" Her voice was crisp, businesslike.

She did not hear his sigh of resignation. "It's a go with your kid. I'm not gonna waste our time tryin' to hassle over money with you. Top dollar. He's worth five thousand, and I know it, and I know you know it too . . ."

"Wait—wait a minute, Joey. Where is it written down that five is top dollar?"

"Come on, babe—"

"Don't 'babe' me, Joey. I've heard through the grapevine that there's deals goin' down close to seventy-five hundred in Atlanta and Miami."

"Hey, Leva, this is the cornbelt here where I am, and you ain't exactly in Miami yourself . . ."

"I'm not sayin' he's worth that, Joey, but he's worth every penny of six, and you know it. Look, I'm not tryin' to keep you from makin' a decent living. But I know you got some high-roller chickenhawk slobberin' on your hand up there, and I know that there's a lot of room for your cut. Me and Percy are down here lookin' at a mall snatch—rest room maybe, parking lot maybe—both tough snatches. Whose neck's on the block here, huh?"

"Hey, I hear you, hun, okay? Let me think on it till morn . . ."

"Here's the deal, Joey. I'm wide awake now and I'm not goin' back to bed before I make some other phone calls. You're not the only good mover out there. So, before you're sniffin' your mornin' coffee, this kid might be promised somewhere else. It doesn't much matter to me who I—"

"Easy—easy. I give up. We deal at six."

Leva drew a long breath that Joey could not hear. "Good. We're set to try this Friday night. Have your guy on call. If we pull it off, we'll pass him to you in Nashville. Stay close to your phone between nine and ten, your time."

"Gotcha. Good luck."

"It's not bingo, Joey. Luck's not got much to do with it."

Click.

Joanie Starmann stood in the doorway to Rooster's bedroom, watching her son as he slept. It was nearly four-thirty in the afternoon and she knew that she should have awakened him from his nap before now. But it was a special day, and there were only four more weeks of summer vacation left.

Rooster stirred slightly, and Joanie smiled at the tiny man-to-be. He looked for all the world like a miniature track star, left leg drawn up in mid-stride, head back, chest thrust forward as it strained for the finish line. The smile faded. In truth, the child had been in a race, and she with him. A race away from sadness and hurt, away from loss; a race toward some semblance of peace and, if not yet true happiness, at least a zone of comfort in a world that both gave and took.

There was no pressure on the boy now, that was the most important thing. Even when school started, Joanie doubted that this would become a problem. Grade school was after all, grade school, a time of exploration and unpressured development, a time of small friendships and teachers that dabbed at tears with tissues. He would do well, of this Joanie was certain. Her smile came back as she thought of the night to come. There would be no pressure on this special night of the week, a night that had become a happy routine for mother and son.

Joanie walked to the bedside and began the gentle process of waking him. After he had rubbed both fists into his eyes and blinked himself awake, she reminded him that tonight was Friday night at Southland Mall.

Percy Arstead peered intently at his sister's deft hands as they wielded the needle and thread. A long-sleeved gray workshirt was spread over her lap as she sewed the bright red logo of Southland Mall over the left breast pocket. Percy moved his eyes to look at the lightweight nylon jacket hanging from the corner of a chair. He would wear it into the mall building and then, at the proper time, fold it and put it into his right rear trouser pocket. Percy could remove and fold the thin jacket into a neat square within seven seconds. His left rear trouser pocket already bulged slightly with the two black plastic trash bags. Percy had just finished lining one bag with the other and carefully refolding them into a precise square. At double strength, they could be trusted to contain up to eighty pounds without tearing. Percy Arstead could hold a double trash bag filled with eighty pounds of weights in either hand and run in place for five minutes without pausing. By Leva's estimate, there would be a safety margin of eighteen pounds. Leva Arstead was incredibly accurate at estimating the weight of small children.

Percy reached up and adjusted the black-framed glasses with the clear plastic lenses. He had worn them since early morning, allowing himself ample time to become accustomed to their feel. The elastic headband that secured them in place was comfortably snug. The dirty looking athletic shoes were light and perfect on his feet, with the strings double-knotted and well above floor level.

Percy returned his focus to his sister, whose eyes had not moved from her lap for the last five minutes. He stole a glimpse at her face and wondered, as he had a hundred times before, if she looked like their mother or father. Whichever, Percy knew that he looked like the other parent. He had always believed that Leva looked like her father; it was difficult to imagine a woman with eyes of cold steel. Surely, in his life, Percy had never encountered their equal.

He looked quickly to her hands; it was never a good idea to look at Leva's face for very long. It was as if she could see into his brain and sort out the electrical impulses that gave life to his thoughts. And if she saw him peeking at her now, she would know that he was thinking soft thoughts, thoughts of long-dead parents, thoughts that could interfere with the life Leva had ordered for him now. She had ordered things for him as long as he could remember. They had been united as one forever. His memory had shut out many things long past, things of dread and nightmares. But he could still remember some of the night sounds that came from the old orphanage tucked away in the tall pines of southern Georgia, and he could still remember his sister's face as the pale light of morning unmasked her sad features. And he could remember the night that they had walked away from the place, never to look back.

He had asked her once, when he was eleven and she was thirteen, about their parents. The look of her eyes in that instant was seared for all time in his brain, and he saw a malignancy that sucked the breath from him. He had not mentioned their parents again in all the years that had passed. He never would.

She was finished now, and she held up the shirt to inspect her handiwork. Once satisfied, she turned to Percy and handed it to him.

"It's time to go get momma's little Rooster," she said quietly. There was no emotion in her voice.

CHAPTER NINE

The woman seated beside the younger man at a table in Cafe Court sipped her Pepsi-Cola through a long straw, filling her mouth with the sweet liquid and holding it there for a delicious moment before swallowing. Her hair, drawn atop her head in a tight bun, held a faintly grayish tint that matched the wan features of a face totally devoid of makeup. Her blouse was plain, tan, nearly colorless, and tucked into faded blue jeans. Leva Arstead looked exactly as she wanted to look—like a harmless nondescript woman of fifty-five.

Percy sipped ice water directly from his tall paper cup; he preferred to work without a trace of caffeine in his bloodstream. His actions over the next thirty minutes would determine success or failure; it was as simple as that. His performance, if precise and machine-like, would make Leva very happy, and it would cause Joey Fazor to be very happy. And when Joey became very happy, a brown grocery sack stuffed with small bills would be theirs. The consequence of slightly sloppy work would be Leva's displeasure at the loss of so golden an opportunity. The consequence of very sloppy work might well be a prison term.

But Percy did not dwell on such possibilities. His body was a wonderous mechanism that amazed even him from time to time. More often than not, he could will the perfect amount of adrenaline into his system, allowing his body to accomplish nearly any humanly possible feat, and yet, not enough to push him over the edge and cause foolish things to happen.

Leva's short fingernail tapped insistently on the table, drawing his attention to the exiting moviegoers. He trained his gaze on hers, and soon he could pick out mother and son, hand in hand, as they walked excitedly toward the arcade.

"Hope he had plenty of soda in the movie," Percy said.

He could see Leva's head nodding before she spoke. "Did last Friday."

Percy moved his head a quarter turn to face the wall and picked out a light fixture as a focal point. He stared at it until it became a fuzzy, faraway thing, and only then did he mentally rehearse what he was about to do.

It would not matter if the boy chose the child-level urinal or a stall. The boy would pay no attention to the janitor with the plastic trash bag until he had zipped up his trousers and turned around. The janitor would be on his right knee, and his eyes would be on the same level as the boy's, and when the child froze in that instant of inquiry—in that perfect half second—it would happen. The jab would be thrown with the speed of a snake's tongue from no more than fifteen inches, directly onto the point of the chin. It would be forceful enough to crush a large orange without exposing the pulp. The small body would never touch the floor of the rest room; it would be gathered quickly into the double trash bag, and then the janitor would be free to leave.

The tap of Leva's finger came to his arm, not the table. "What are you doing?"

"Just thinking, Sis, just sort of practicing in my mind."

She paused and cocked her head. "You okay, Percy?"

"Sure, Sis. Never better. No problem."

"Your finger still sore?" It was more than a question.

"It's okay now. Good as new."

"See that you keep it that way."

He nodded without speaking and they both turned their attention back to the arcade entry. Twenty minutes ticked by. The crowd was thinning out nicely now; it was only ten minutes before the main section of the mall closed, and then only a small area of Cafe Court would remain open for business in order to catch the patrons leaving the late movie.

Rooster jammed a small fist into the air as the last of the space invaders fell to the might of his ray gun. "Did you see that, Mom? Never had a chance, did he?" came the delighted squeal.

"No Rooster, you're the baddest invader zapper in Charlotte, no doubt." She tousled his hair.

"Mom, I gotta go to the bathroom, and then—"

"No *and then,* mister. Poor old Mom wants to curl up at home with a book before bedtime for a little while."

"Oh, Mooom . . ."

"Let's save some invaders for next week, what do you say, Rooster? Let's call it a night."

"Oh, all right, I guess. But I really do gotta go to the bathroom."

"I think I can wait for that. Let's go."

Fifty feet away, the aproned attendant cleared the two tall paper cups from the empty table. She took notice of the contents. Anything to divert her mind away from the monotony of her job. They had both looked like Pepsi drinkers to her, but one of them was not. One cup had a small amount of dark soft drink remaining; the other had only ice, but it was not discolored. Probably Seven-Up or Sprite, maybe water, she guessed.

Joanie watched carefully as Rooster entered the men's rest room before taking her place across the narrow corridor; the door to the rest room was clearly visible. She paid little attention to the woman who stood facing away from her, twenty feet distant, near the door to the women's room.

Rooster knew the rules very well. They had been implemented within the first few weeks after his father died. Never enter a public rest room without his mother standing outside the door. Always check to see who was in the rest room and then come out and tell her. Then back in to do his business. It all seemed a bit much to the boy, but he had always complied. She had gently explained the necessity of it, although he saw no reason to be afraid; most important, it made her happy.

He looked around the room, and, except for the janitor who was preparing to empty the trash can, it was empty. He hesitated for a moment, about to leave and report to his mother, before he picked out a stall and pushed open the door. Surely the janitor didn't count. A guy had to draw the line somewhere. He latched the door. The man in the gray work shirt listened to the toilet sounds, and when they stopped, he moved silently to the stall door. Fifteen seconds. That was all the time he needed.

The belly of the fat man spilled over his plaid trousers, leading the way down the corridor like the rounded prow of a small ship bobbing through choppy water. Leva had locked her peripheral vision on the man from the time he turned off of the main mall corridor and headed toward the rest rooms. He was wearing a watch. Her plan came to her automatically; variations of it had worked quite nicely in other times of crisis. Ten more huffing steps, and then she would step in front of him, humbly begging his pardon, and inquire of the time. Leva never wore a watch when she was working. She would then ask him if he was sure of his timepiece, quietly incredulous as to the lateness of the hour and the where-abouts of her elderly mother. Was there a security officer close by? Would he assist her in locating him? The delay would last as long as Leva desired.

He was three steps away now and as Leva took a steadying breath and gathered herself, she heard the faint squeak of the men's room door. The fat man barrelled past her and nearly collided with the janitor as he emerged from the rest room, a full trash bag in his right hand.

"Hey, sorry, bub," he laughed, "I'm about to bust."

The janitor did not reply.

At first, Joanie was more irritated than startled at seeing a man come through the door, but then she saw the bright logo on his shirt and the full trash bag, and knew that she would say nothing to her son. Janitors would not count. The man moved steadily away and she directed her gaze to the fat man, who was as harmless looking as any man could be. She did not notice that the woman in the corridor was gone.

The first sixty seconds passed easily enough, but with the passing of sixty more, the seed of apprehension took root. Joanie chased the silly little thought away and shook her head at a mother's capacity for paranoia. Thirty more, and she could not chase it away. *Surely,* the fat man was nothing to worry . . . . The door was opening. The big man's face contorted into a polite smile.

"Excuse me, sir, I hate to bother you, but my son seems to be taking a rather long time—and—"

It was when the man's eyes registered wonderment at her statement that Joanie Starmann felt the horror close about her throat like a pair of strong hands. She shoved him aside and lurched into the empty rest room. The first sound that came from the rest room seemed to the fat man like that of someone strangling, but it was the second sound that sent him careening down the corridor toward Cafe Court. It was the sound of a woman dying in agony.

The rear door of the van opened as Percy approached. He gently swung the plastic bag into the rear compartment as Leva guided it in. He moved quickly to the driver's seat and started the engine, and within seconds, the big vehicle lumbered out of the parking lot. Leva tore away the plastic bags, found the boy's left arm, and plunged the needle deep into the deltoid muscle. He groaned and attempted to move his head toward her, but his eyes did not open, and soon he passed into a dreamless sleep. Leva stripped the child of his clothing and made a careful inspection, using the beam of a flashlight like a surgical tool as it swept from head to toe. The bruise on his chin was angry looking, but the jawbone and lower teeth were normal. She positioned the ice bag over his chin, propping it with a folded blanket.

His skin was flawless. Well-proportioned body, clean, extremely well-kept. A chickenhawk's delight. Now that she had time to look closely, Leva was sorry she had not fought for another thousand from Joey. She wadded his clothing into a ball and tucked it into the remnants of the plastic bags. She would keep the items until she could watch them burn with her own eyes. She dressed the sleeping child in new clothing— white underwear, dark sweat suit, cotton socks, and black tennis shoes. She repositioned the ice bag and arranged two more blankets around him before crawling to the front seat.

"Very nice work, Percy."

"Thanks, Sis. What was with the fat guy at the door?"

"I was one second away from jumping him when I heard the door. I thought it worked out real well."

"Couldn't a' been better."

"First c-store out of town, we'll stop and find a phone. I got a happy call to make to Mr. Fazor."

They drove for three more blocks before the black and white police cruiser pulled alongside the van at a red light. Neither Percy nor Leva registered the slightest alarm. It had been a perfect snatch. The cop might as well have been on the other side of the moon. Leva thought of the valuable cargo behind her; only two thin pieces of sheet metal and three feet of air separated it from the cop.

She turned to Percy as the light changed and the cruiser pulled away from them. "So near and yet so far away, huh?"

They both laughed softly.

Police captain Marlon Stoner stood with one hand jammed deeply into a trouser pocket and the other wrapped around a Styrofoam coffee cup as he peered through the glass office door at the three people who had just been smitten by tragedy. His bushy eyebrows moved imperceptibly in tandem with the thoughts being sifted through his head. The features of his well-formed face were incongruous with the untamed eyebrows—soft eyes wide-set and thoughtful, almost vulnerable for a man of his profession, short straight nose, full lips, round jawline. His neatly trimmed hair was flecked with the salt and pepper of fifty-three years, twenty-eight of which had been spent as a cop. His suit, though well made and properly fitted, made him appear smaller than he was, and, at five-ten and one hundred seventy hard pounds, he was not a large man.

Joanie Starmann and her parents sat pressed together in a huddle of anguish, shoulders touching, six hands meshed in a strained knot of flesh and bone. Words that Stoner could not hear—words that he did not wish to hear—tumbled from the mother of the child alternately with spasms of grief. The woman's mother was doing most of the consoling and encouraging; her face held a strength that was meant for her daughter, and the captain knew what she was doing and admired her for it. The woman's father seemed at first somehow detached in spirit from the women, and Stoner was puzzled until he noticed the almost imperceptible movement of the man's lips, and although he was not a religious man, Stoner was certain that the man was praying. Other than possibly allowing the old man to better cope with the situation, the captain doubted that it would do any good.

As a professional policeman, Marlon Stoner knew he was good, and he was confident that he could re-enter the office and say things to these people that would give them some hope. He had no trouble with the fact that the things he said would be half-lies. At this point, it would serve no purpose to lay it all out for them—to tell them that the person, or persons, who took their precious child were as cunning and heartless as an eagle that streaked from the sky to sink its talons into the flesh of a young lamb.

He would not tell them that the boy was probably drugged and unconscious in the back of a van that sped to destinations unknown, and that the best hope was that he would be abused and abandoned alive in a place where he could be found by human beings with hearts of humans and not of animals. No, he would not tell them these things. He would tell them that an all-points bulletin blanketed the area, complete with a detailed description of the boy and a surprisingly good description of the janitor who was not a janitor.

He shook his head and smiled ruefully as he remembered his first impression upon seeing the excited fat man inhaling cigarette smoke to the bottom of his lungs and rubbing his sweaty palms on the legs of his trousers. He would have wagered a hundred dollar bill against a stale doughnut that the witness would prove useless. But for a very long time Captain Stoner had been a master at calming excited witnesses, and the calmer the fat man became, the more he remembered. Even so, it was probably of little consequence. The one piece of the puzzle that was most needed—the one thing that could possibly lead to the return of the boy unharmed—was missing. There was no vehicle description. The cold fact was that when the snatchers had cleared the building with their precious trash bag, they had probably won the victory.

Captain Stoner allowed himself the tiny luxury of the last gulp from the coffee cup before he tapped lightly on the office door and joined the small circle of misery.

The first sensations that returned to Rooster were the vibrations that flowed like harmless electricity from the tires of the van up through the floorboard. His eyelids seemed as if they were glued shut; no matter how hard he tried to lift them, they would not budge. There was no sensation of light, but this did not trouble the boy. He was comfortably a part of a strange, heavy world, almost silly, and he wanted to giggle, but he knew that he could not. So, the child lay on his tingly bed in the middle of his silly world and drifted closer to consciousness.

The change in the vibrations caused him to redouble his efforts at opening his eyes. He was aware of motion now and he could feel his body shift slightly as his world slowed down and forced his weight to the right side of his body. His eyelids moved a fraction, and he could feel the seal of sleep break. There was light now, uneven and ever changing in its look and intensity. His weight shifted suddenly toward his head and shoulders.

Rooster Starmann knew that he was in a vehicle of some kind and that it had stopped. His comfortable, silly world was gone. Fragments of thoughts darted through his brain— bright red flames of a dying space invader, his mother's smile, the metallic sound of the latch on the rest room stall door, the look of the dark-framed glasses on the janitor's face— they were all mixed up in the great whirl of his mind. But the last image returned and overcame all the others, and with it came the urge to cry for his mother.

He could open and close his hands now, and soon he would be able to open his eyes fully and see who the people were who spoke over him in low, calm tones. His chin throbbed with each beat of his heart and he lifted his right hand to caress it, but strong fingers wrapped around his forearm and pinned it to his side. There were two forms hovering over him; the voice from one was a woman, and he turned his head toward her just before he felt the sharp prick in his left arm. More hands closed about him and then under him, and he was lifted from his hard bed. Cool air brushed his face for a moment before the hands laid him on another bed, much like the first one. Bulky, soft things were stuffed against his body. He was afraid now, and he wanted to be with his mother. He would ask them where she was. His tongue felt thick and stupid as he tried to say the words, but before his voice came to him, his eyelids slid down like tiny iron gates, and he gave up.

CHAPTER TEN

The night breeze came to Floyd Hunt from the west and the direction of the city. Somewhere in the east edge of Charlotte, four miles away as the crow flew, a church bell chimed the hour of the morning to any who could hear it. The bell tolled only twice. The man stood on the sidewalk that separated his own church building from the asphalt parking lot behind it. Great teardrops slid from the corners of his eyes, touching his lips, and when enough had gathered he wiped away the salty wetness with a sweep of his tongue. He had been strong and brave for his daughter at the police station. Captain Stoner had tried valiantly to extend some hope, but Floyd Hunt was not deceived as he aided the captain in shielding his daughter. And he had been brave here, inside the sanctuary, where friends had gathered to pray for the lost one. But now he needed to weep, and he did it alone. It was a good thing, as badly as he hated to admit it to himself. For if he did not weep, he would hate with a ferocity that could consume him, and he would soon be of no use to anyone, even himself.

He heard the door behind him open quietly and he was not surprised by the familiar touch of soft arms around his waist and the head that rested on his back. He removed his hands from his pockets and covered Norma's.

"Just look at this parking lot, hun," Norma said. "Middle of the night, and there's two dozen cars in it."

"God bless 'em all," he sniffed. "I need my handkerchief."

"Save it." She handed him two clean tissues as they untwined and faced each other.

"Had to have a little air, Norma. Had to let it out."

She nodded silently.

"Some old church, this Cedar Valley Baptist Church, huh?" Norma said as much to herself as to her husband.

"It is that, woman . . ." His voice trailed off.

They had been members for over forty years now; there were only a handful who had been members longer. Back then, in the beginning, the church grounds lay fifteen miles from the city limits; now only five by road, and seemingly growing closer by the month. The membership had been steady at around one hundred fifty—small even by long-ago standards, but no one ever worried about it. Few but strong, the old-timers liked to say—let The Almighty worry about numbers. They would just come, tithe, work, pray, and not whine. Just tend to His business as best they could. Good people moved away from Charlotte and good people came and replaced them. It had worked very well that way for a long time.

The door opened behind them, and they turned toward the sound. Without a word being spoken, the small, bent woman walked to them and joined hands with both. Her voice was thick with emotion, the words tumbling out in spurts.

"I've known you two for thirty-seven years—good times, bad times, weddings, funerals—we've been there. And I'm telling you now, there's never been anything stronger happen in that building than what's happening in there now. The Spirit's in there—so strong I want to look around and try to *touch* Him, even though I know I can't. *Keep* your hope . . . in the precious name of Jesus . . . keep your hope."

"Thank you, Lucy," Norma said. "Thank you so much."

The old woman tiptoed and kissed the cheek of both Floyd and Norma and turned to leave.

"Lucy," Norma stopped her. "Do you know who put the candle on the communion table?"

"Pastor's wife—Kathy—put it there. Says it'll stay burning till the child's home safe."

"Thanks, I might have known."

"I want to go back inside now," Floyd said. He handed the wad of tissues to Norma. "I won't need these anymore tonight."

They walked hand-in-hand to the rear of the sanctuary and stopped beside the last pew at the center aisle. Seventy feet away, their only child lay on the carpet in front of the communion table, her comforters kneeling about her in a circle of prayer. Every few moments, a hand, sometimes several hands, reached out gently and caressed her head or her hands, like mothers or fathers touching a feverish infant in her misery. Only two overhead lights burned at the rear of the sanctuary, allowing for the flame of the tall white candle to bathe the area around the communion table.

Norma first saw the old woman seated on a pew, well to the right of the communion table, where the soft light turned to shadows. She peered for a long moment, certain that she would recognize the woman, but there was no doubt that she had never seen her before.

"Floyd, who's that woman down there on the right? I've never seen her before."

He looked intently for five seconds before shaking his head. "Me neither. Must be kin to one of the members, or maybe a friend of somebody's who heard from them."

"I suppose. Whatever, I'll slip down there in a minute and thank her. Somebody that's not even a member out here this time of night, dressed nice like that and all . . ." She shook her head in amazement.

The couple walked slowly down the aisle and melded into the edge of the prayer group. A woman of fifty, clad in the housecoat that she had hastily thrown about her when the call came, leaned over to Norma and whispered. "She just went to sleep a few minutes ago, bless her heart," the woman said in reference to Joanie. "Strangest thing—no, it was a beautiful thing, that's what it was," she continued. "That old lady back there . . ." She tossed her head toward the shadows behind them without looking. "Sang the prettiest verse of *Jesus Loves Me* that you ever heard in your life. Nobody even breathed. And then Joanie—she just curled up like that and went to sleep . . ."

"Who is she?" Norma whispered.

"Never saw her before. Nobody else seems to know either."

"I'll be right back," Norma said.

When she turned around and looked to her right, only empty pews met her gaze. She must have left in the last few moments, Norma thought to herself. She walked hurriedly to the rear door and opened it to the parking lot, but the old woman was not there. Norma walked around the perimeter of the building and then, back inside, checked the ladies' rest room. It was empty. She peeked into the sanctuary before making another circle around the building. Once more in the parking lot, she looked inside of each of the twenty-three vehicles. When Norma Hunt confirmed that the last car was empty, she began to feel the tingle at the base of her neck, and for an instant she was sure someone was near. She whirled around on the asphalt and scanned the parking lot. She stood alone.

The only sound that came to her was the night song from the trees as the west wind filtered through the leaves.

The girl stood astraddle her light blue bicycle, a tennis shoe-covered foot firmly planted on each side. Except for the slight movement of her ponytail as she swished it idly over her neck, she had not moved for five minutes, and five minutes was a very long time for a child of eleven to stand still. The little house looked whiter than it really was with the late afternoon sun painting its worn siding. The girl wondered if the old woman would come out so that she could wave at her. She doubted it. Saturday afternoons were not the best times to see her. Probably tomorrow noon, just before Sunday dinner, she would slip from her house while her mother was busy frying chicken and her father's face was lost in the sports page. The old woman would probably be arriving home from church, a silly bright hat perched atop her head, the big Bible tucked against her right side. But still, there was a chance this afternoon; the girl had seen her a couple of times on Saturdays. She rolled the chocolate Tootsie Roll Pop lovingly with her tongue, judging that it was over half melted, and she decided that she would watch until the last chewy morsels were nibbled away from the stem.

In some way that the child could not identify, it was satisfying to exchange waves with the old woman to whom she had never spoken. The smile seemed genuine enough, even from across the street, but it served as an unspoken pact between them; there would never be more than smiles and waves. The girl wondered if the woman knew the real reason that she watched the house from across the street; maybe that was why she never stopped to talk.

The white light had burned from inside the house on two separate occasions as the girl had watched. The first time, the girl was frightened and thought that a fire had flashed up, but before she could lift a foot to find the peddle of her bicycle, it was gone. She had told no one, not even her parents. She had no truly close friends, surely none that she would share this find with. It was far too great a thing to divvy up with the little secret-tellers, whiners, and motormouths. As for her parents, maybe she would tell them one day, but she was not certain.

The sweet chunk of candy in her mouth was very small now, and she was about to chop it up with her teeth when the tingle came to her spine. The light was far brighter than the afternoon sun and for an instant it looked as if the inside of the house would burst from the brilliance of it, and then it disappeared as quickly as it had come. The girl's eyes had involuntarily closed and when she opened them the black spots danced before her. It was like looking at the flash of a camera, only the spots that came now did not fade so quickly. She realized that her hands were clenching the handlebar grips almost painfully, and she loosened her fingers. Her tongue touched the outside of her lips, and she was surprised to learn that the stem of the sucker was no longer there. Blinking eyes swept the sidewalk, finding the white paper stick beside a dirty tennis shoe.

It was just a squatty white house now, not unlike a hundred more she could see if she rode her bike for a half hour. But the girl knew that what she had seen was so far beyond her world that she could not begin to describe it—even to her parents. She loved them, trusted them, but—something—the way the old woman's soft eyes fell on her from across the street. Something—something—bound them, and the child was certain that the secret would remain theirs alone. Maybe forever.

Wesley Livingston gently hung up the telephone as his wife watched from the doorway. He did not wish to look at her now, much less speak to her, and he did his best to avoid her eyes without being obvious, but his efforts were ineffectual.

"The great reverend, no doubt."

Wesley nodded as he passed her in the doorway. Her words chased after him. "He invite you to church services this Sunday?" Wesley stopped and paused for a moment before turning to face her.

"No. If you got to know every little thing about my life, woman, he asked me and Jessie to go to a ballgame in St. Louis with him."

"When?"

"Tonight."

"Kinda short notice, isn't it? I mean, looks like he'd be

up all hours and such on Saturday nights sweating over his preaching notes for Sunday morning." She huffed a little laugh.

"I don't reckon he needs to sweat too hard to think of something to say, as long as he's been at it." He locked on her eyes, wanting them now, waiting for her to say something else.

"How you plan to get by without drinking half a case of beer? I mean—I doubt if his holiness would approve, huh?"

Wesley savored the next five seconds, for within the brief interval, mere dislike had evolved into hatred. He had wanted to hate the woman for years, never quite able to manufacture the necessary bile, but now, in this delicious moment, it was a thing alive. His smile was thin and crooked as he spoke, and his eyes were as cold as he could make them, almost like Reverend Kassley's he thought.

"Oh . . . Twila, you wouldn't understand I reckon, but there are other satisfying things to drink in this world."

He could see the unease leaking through her hard features like cheap makeup melting in the summer sun, and the rush he felt from it was a marvelous thing, a powerful thing. Just as Arvil Kassley had promised it would be. He spoke once more before turning casually and leaving the room.

"Maybe someday I'll show you what I mean."

Allene Pacely carefully turned the big pages of the photograph album that rested in her apron-covered lap. The handsome face of Frank Pacely smiled easily at her as he cradled the baby boy in the crook of his arm. It was like looking at a ghost now, even though the woman knew that her husband was probably still alive somewhere, far away no doubt. Part of her wanted to hate him again, as she had for the first several years after he left. But hatred was a hungry thing, and it required nourishment and attention. One day Allene Pacely realized with an awful clarity that in the end the hatred would demand all of her—body and soul—to satisfy it. Then, slowly, painfully, she starved the evil thing to death. There had been only two women at the church with whom she could bare her soul, but, along with the Spirit, they had been enough. The boy, they had reminded her, the precious boy could not grow properly in spirit with a mother full of hatred.

So there was no hate in her as she looked at the man's image and clung to the few good times which they had shared. She only wondered now, less frequently as the years went by, how she could have made it turn out better, but the conclusion was always the same—she had done her best—and in that, there was a fragment of peace.

The album was filled mostly with photos of Jessie, and as she turned the pages, she smiled with the memories of another time, a time when her worst fears were falls from bicycles and chicken pox and feet that outgrew shoes seemingly overnight. The smile faded as she thought of him now, sullen and withdrawn in his room. Something had changed inside of him within the last few weeks, but she could not identify it. The strangest part was that the change coincided with his association with Reverend Kassley. At first, she had reasoned that Jessie was struggling with his religion—beliefs long dormant—that the reverend was no doubt arousing. But lately . . . oh, how could she doubt him, a man of God of his stature. She felt ashamed. Had not Reverend Kassley himself assured her of revival stirring in her son? Time, he had reminded her, time was the precious commodity that was necessary.

And yet—the foreboding lingered. Allene folded her hands on the album page and bowed her head.

Dear Lord God . . . what is it in me that weighs so heavy now? Why now, Lord? Why do I doubt my own preacher trying to help Jessie? I—I just can't make sense of it. Help me . . . help me know what to do. I just can't lose Jessie too, Lord. Let me live to see him stand tall with a family pointed to you . . . please . . . let me live to see that.

She heard no voice in her head, but Allene knew precisely

what she was to do, and she was to do it now. She had seen the photo only moments before, a couple of pages back. She flipped the pages. There, in the lower left-hand corner. She kept it there because it was one of her favorite portraits of Jessie, and more often than not, she slipped it from the plastic cover as she did now and held it in the palm of her hand. He was nine then, his hair sandy, like wheat in the sunshine. Dear God, he was a beautiful child, wide-set green eyes over a perfect nub of a nose, full lips, almost pouty. Allene could not remember who had snapped the photo, but whoever had taken it had done a marvelous, or extremely lucky, job. The boy had just turned toward the camera as laughter lit up his face, and his expression was one of pure childhood joy.

She climbed the stairs quickly and knocked softly on the closed door. "Jessie? Jessie, can I come in for a minute?"

"It ain't locked."

Allene opened the door and stepped into the room. Jessie was lying on his bed, fully clothed, staring at the ceiling. He did not turn his head toward Allene as she approached.

"It's nothing really," she began, "I was just looking through the old album—and—well, I found this picture of you—when you were little."

Jessie's head turned toward her and their eyes met for an instant before he dropped his gaze.

"It's billfold size—and—silly enough, I reckon, I thought you might like to have it now. 'Course, they'll all be yours in due time, I know. Most of 'em are pretty big, but this one's been cut down, looks like, I don't remember why exactly, but anyway, like as not, it'll slip out one day and get lost. So—I just thought—I'd give it to you now."

She extended her hand, but Jessie had returned his gaze to the ceiling, and if he saw her gesture, he ignored it. As she laid the photo on the nightstand, the telephone rang downstairs.

"I'll go get—"

"No, I'll get it," Jessie said, springing to his feet in one motion.

Allene listened as she descended the stairs. With the first "yessir," she knew that Reverend Kassley was on the other end of the line, and the feeling of dread returned to her. The conversation was brief, and after Jessie hung up, he spoke to Allene as he climbed the stairs.

"Gonna go to a ballgame in St. Louis with the reverend and Wesley. Don't wait up, I'll be real late."

He was in his room for only a few moments. He did not speak to Allene as he brushed through the back door. The low rumble of the car engine filled Allene's ears, and then he was gone. She walked back to the living room and looked down at the album on the coffee table. The tiny square in the lower left hand corner of the page was white, and it mocked her as tears welled up in her eyes. Where had the silly thought come from? It had felt so right—the answer to a prayer.

The door to Jessie's room was open. Allene's eyes sought the photo on the nightstand, but it was not there. She walked closer and looked at the spot where she had placed it, and then to the floor, all around the nightstand, and under the bed. She searched the top of the dresser drawers and the jumble of things that he kept in a loose pile beside the mirror, but it was not to be found. She emptied the contents of the wastebasket on the floor and picked through each item before refilling it. Finally, she sat down on the edge of the bed and allowed the realization to sink in. It had not been a silly self-delusion, it had been exactly what the Spirit told her— somehow, an answer to a prayer.

The photograph of the laughing boy was gone.

The long black hands of the wall clock held Reverend Kassley's attention. He had stared at them for only a few seconds, but they were no longer six-inch slivers of molded plastic; they were sleek daggers, their needle-nose points nudging ever closer to the hour of glory. The irritating sweep of the second hand finally broke the spell, and he realized that he had only ninety minutes before Wesley and Jessie would arrive. It was time enough; all was in readiness. There would be ample time for a quick walk to the altar and precious moments of meditation.

Arvil covered the familiar ground with long purposeful strides, clinging to the shaded edge of the woods that paralleled the gravel road, and then up the old road to the clearing. The summer haze hovered oppressively over the altar grounds, and as he touched the stone slab, the heat radiated through his fingers. The stone had been barely large enough to accommodate the last offering, but it would be more than adequate for the one to come. He closed his eyes and waited for the voice that would surely come. It always came when he needed it.

Sometimes the voice came as if from someone standing beside him, other times it came from within his head, malevolent yet enticing, so much a part of him that Arvil almost wondered if it was really a separate being. But in his heart, he knew that it was a power distinct from his own. Razzom was someone else, some*thing* else. Arvil was as sure of that fact as he was of his own life.

The demon came in the man's head as an unearthly coldness crept over his body. Even the mighty force of the summer sun was made trivial in its presence. Arvil Kassley trembled and waited for the voice.

"It is good that you seek me today. I know that you come to prepare for the slaying of the young lamb, and this is good, very good. But—beyond that—" Arvil sensed immediately that something was different today. The demon had never before paused in speech. The words were always perfectly spaced, the rhythm unchanged. But now the voice had paused, almost unsure of itself, Arvil was certain. "Yes . . . today I must tell you of . . . someone else who is attempting to interfere with our plans."

"I don't understand . . ."

"Silence! You fool. Of course you do not understand. That is why I have come to help you with . . ." The voice was no longer in his head. At first it was very close, but Arvil could not understand the unintelligible rantings that spewed forth. The demon's voice rose now and the wild screechings careened through the edge of the woods as a foul smelling wind jerked the branches to and fro. The final cry was like the horrible groan of a great beast in its death throes, and then the smell was gone. And with it, the wind. Silence now, an incredible silence; the only sound Arvil could hear was the beating of his heart in his ears.

Then another voice came to Arvil Kassley from the shadows in the woods, but it was an ordinary voice, and there was no malice in it, only pleading. It was the voice of an old woman, and even as the man ran wildly from the clearing, he could not escape the words.

"Take back your soul . . . take back your soul . . ."

CHAPTER ELEVEN

The house that Charles and Joanie Starmann built five years ago stood proudly, its brick veneer front and dark green window shutters facing Wisteria Lane. The lot sloped upwardly from the street and the curved sidewalk leading to the front door made an elegant gray "S" between the low shrubs and flowers meticulously planted along its edges. Captain Stoner had entered a hundred such homes, and as he studied the Starmann residence from his unmarked police car a half block away, he tried to remember how many times his visits had marked happy occasions. He could recall three. He shook his head and nibbled thoughtfully at the inside of his lower lip. Three . . . in twenty-eight years. In fifteen minutes he would enter the Starmann house again and it would represent yet another entry on the sorrowful side of life's ledger.

There had been no breaks since the kidnapping. He glanced at his watch. Twelve forty-five P.M. Nearly fifteen hours had passed. That no ransom call had been made was hardly a surprise to Stoner; he would have been surprised if a call *had* come. The Starmanns, even when the man was alive, had never represented the kind of wealth that attracted kidnappers for ransom. The kidnappers who had taken Darren Starmann desired the child for reasons of the flesh. They desired his youth, his purity, his beauty; or if not the kidnappers themselves, the person or persons at the end of the trail—like the end-users of a product.

He had long ago ceased the futile effort required in attempting to understand such people. They were simply enemies now, antagonists to be met on a battlefield of concrete and steel—a battlefield that afforded them a thousand crevices in which to hide. The sad fact was that the most dangerous enemies were seldom seen. They were cunning, ruthless creatures, like great timber wolves of the North that moved swiftly with the shadows of the forest—their eyes all-seeing, muscles rippling, senses alive—driven by a hunger for the flesh. Stoner doubted that he would ever see the wolves that had pulled down young Darren Starmann.

Still, he had to play it by the book. Against her wishes, Joanie Starmann had agreed to spend what remained of last night and this morning with her parents in her own house—the house with her son's empty room, the house permeated with the memory of her husband. The call *could* come. Stranger things had happened. The phone was bugged, and a technician was stationed in the house. Stoner had patiently instructed Joanie concerning the proper method of handling a ransom call, but given her state of mind, he harbored little hope that she would be able to remain calm and stretch out the call. Whatever. He shook his head again in frustration. It was a moot point; there would be no call. The hands of his watch read twelve-fifty; he would wait until one o'clock, no longer. He would end a bit of her misery and allow her to leave with her parents.

Norma Hunt knelt on the carpet in front of the sofa, cradling the hot bowl of soup in a dishtowel. Carefully, as if spooning a tiny portion for a child, she raised it to Joanie's lips.

"Please, baby, you've got to keep your strength up. I know you don't want it, but you need it. Open now, just one spoonful at a time."

Joanie raised her head and opened her mouth, accepting the spoonful of soup. "Mom, it'll just come up I tell you . . ."

"It may, Joanie, it just may. But if it does, we'll just clean up and try again in a little while. We'll work through it. Take a sip of this Seven-Up now. Little nibble of saltine, that's it, baby . . . good . . . one little bit at a time."

Together, they managed a half bowl of the soup and three cracker squares before Joanie raised her hand in caution. "Okay, Mom, maybe a little later, okay? That's it for now."

"Sure, hun, that was a good start. A good one. You rest some now."

Floyd was in the kitchen, staring out the window over the sink. "She eat anything?"

"Little soup, few bites of cracker, some soda."

He nodded in reply. Norma placed the bowl and glass in the sink and leaned her head against Floyd's shoulder. "Lord knows, I can't blame her for not wanting to be here now," she said. "I mean—just about the time she's able to cope with Charles . . . and now—this. Dear God . . . "

Floyd swallowed deliberately and shifted his gaze through a different windowpane. "There's no use in Stoner making us stay here. There won't be any ransom call. There's not that kind of money involved here, he knows that. Got to go by the book for a while though, I guess. But I'm not going to make her stay here much longer."

The sentences were clipped and sounded harder than Floyd intended for them to. They were like hammer blows to Norma. In the silence of the next few seconds, he realized what he had done. If not ransom, then what? And in the "what" lurked unspeakable horrors.

"Oh, Norma, listen to me spouting off like I know as much as a veteran police captain . . ."

She cut him off with her eyes as she turned to face him. "It's—all right, Floyd." Her chin trembled, but only for a moment. "I needed to know. I want no silly false hopes. I needed to know."

He gathered her in his arms, wanting for all the world to console her, but he could not.

Her voice was a whisper in his ear. "It's like—like Satan himself has him. Dear God . . . Dear God." She broke the embrace and looked into his face again, snapping the tears away. "It's beyond human help, isn't it, Floyd? No police force in the world could help us, could it?" The questions were statements. "It's almost like the child is a part of the spirit world."

"Yes, you're right, Norma."

"But you know what? We're not exactly strangers to that world are we, Floyd?"

"In Jesus' name, woman, we're not. We can fight in that world . . . tooth and claw."

"I want to go back to the church with the others. Now. You tell that policeman in the study to get ahold of Captain Stoner. We've had enough of this cat and mouse stuff."

Floyd turned and began to walk toward the study, but before he had taken five steps, the front doorbell chimed.

Thirty minutes later, when Floyd Hunt manuevered his blue Ford sedan into the parking lot of Cedar Valley Baptist Church, he saw even more cars than he had the night before, but he recognized nearly all of them. The very heart of the church, he thought to himself. The living, breathing, beautiful heart of the church. Joanie sat between her parents, clasping Norma's hand. It was a different Joanie Starmann from the trembling woman who had left her house a half hour before. Floyd Hunt had laid it all out for her during the car ride. He had taken a chance, but he could shield his daughter from the truth no longer. It was time for Joanie Starmann to take a stand and fight with the body of Christ. And one could only fight armed with the truth.

"Oh, look at the cars . . . just look," Joanie said.

"Yes, girl, I feel better already. Let's hurry and get inside."

When Joanie neared the communion table, her eyes locked

onto the flame of the tall white candle. First one bowed head, then another and another, became aware of her return, and like tall wheat in the breeze, arms rose and bent toward her. She stood for a moment in front of the candle, gathering herself, drawing in the first long, steady breaths she had taken since the ordeal had begun. Slowly, she turned to face her friends.

"The love I feel for you all—I can't put into words. It's like the love I feel for my parents, like the love I still feel for Charles, like the love I feel for . . . my son." Her chin quivered for only a moment. "My father has just laid it on the line for me . . . and I'm glad he has. You must know too. You all must know the truth, so we can face it and know what to pray for." She sighed. "It seems like I've lost a lot of strength in just a few hours, and even my voice is puny now. So Daddy will talk to you . . . but know this. I stand *with* you now; I do not lay at your feet. There is another soldier here in this little army."

She looked at Floyd. He took a few steps forward and stood by her side. He motioned for Norma to join them.

"Well . . . here we are again—the family with all the sorrow." He raised his hands a few inches and let them fall to his sides. "Why? I don't know. Who can say? It will be interesting when we can see the great puzzle from the other side— the side where all the pieces fit together. But for now . . . for now, thank you all for standing against this thing with us. The truth Joanie speaks of is this. There was no ransom call. There will never be a ransom call. The people who took Rooster took him for reasons of darkness, reasons of Satan. I feel this so strongly in my heart that I cannot believe otherwise. The only chance he has—that is a very hard thing—to say—the only chance he has is through the power of our prayers. The police, God bless them, the FBI, if they get in it, whoever, it doesn't much matter. They simply haven't got anything to work with. The description of a man who was probably in disguise; Joanie vaguely remembers a woman across the hall. Then they both vanish. Gone in some vehicle—lost among another hundred thousand."

He paused and drew a long breath, passing a hand over his brow. "No, we can't wait for the police to deliver Rooster back to us, can we? The fight is far beyond them now. The fight is in the air—where spirits and angels dwell." A sound like laughter escaped his lips, but it was not laughter. "Oh my, people. If the world could see us now, all huddled in our little country church—oh, they would laugh at us, they would pity us. They would give us no chance."

Floyd's eyes found those of Clarence Rosecrans, the pastor, who stood at the fringe of his flock. The tall man was nodding his head and smiling at the man who had helped him through many troubles of his own.

"How far from the truth would the world be, preacher?" Floyd asked, now smiling grimly himself.

"As far, Floyd, as far as the east is from the west. Can we get another witness to that, brothers and sisters?"

"Hallelujah, you tell 'em, preacher!" came a woman's voice.

A man's voice arose from the rear of the gathering, "There's power in the blood!"

More voices, then more, and from somewhere near the front, the voice of a boy, "Jesus loves Rooster."

"Yes! Yes! He does, son," the pastor lifted his voice. "Let's sing about it. Let's raise the roof off this place!"

> *Jesus loves me, this I know,*
> *For the Bible tells me so . . .*

They sang it all, the little army of Christ. They sang it from deep within themselves. And then they sang it again.

The Reverend Kassley's black vehicle melded with the gloom near the loading dock of the warehouse nestled below Highway 40 in St. Louis. The three men inside the unlit interior had sat in silence for three minutes following the hush of the engine. Jessie Pacely willed his heart to beat less violently; he was sure that the thudding was audible to Reverend Kassley and Wesley, but he could marshal no control over the thing that had a will of its own. In truth, the only sound that could be heard was the faint wheezing that defied Wesley's will and escaped his lungs despite a tightly clamped mouth.

Calm and dignified, Reverend Kassley sat behind the wheel, his eyes trained on the six-inch opening of the big metal door of the warehouse. There could be nothing wrong; he had followed the voice's instructions to the letter. Slowly the opening widened, and then, like moving shadows, the two men slithered to the Suburban, one stationed on each side. The beam of a powerful flashlight probed the interior, pausing to search meticulously the faces and bodies of Wesley and Jessie. Joey Fazor tapped lightly on the window beside Arvil's head.

"Listen close. Crank it up, but don't forget—don't turn your headlights on. Pull around the side of the building here all the way to the back. There's another dock like this one with a truck door beside it. You're gonna back in through it. We'll guide you with flashlights."

When Arvil finished backing into the warehouse and stepped from the vehicle, he saw the bulk of a conversion van whose rear doors were no more than six feet from the bumper of his Suburban. Joey's silent friend opened the doors of the van.

"Want to step over here and take a look at your little buddy, Mr. Kassley?" Joey said.

Arvil closed the distance and followed the beams of the two flashlights to the rear compartment. When the beams converged on the disarray of sandy hair and then the sleeping face, Arvil drew in his breath audibly in spite of himself, and the tiny sound pleased Joey greatly.

"Yeah," Joey said, stretching the word out luxuriously,

"what a beauty, huh? Special delivery from the land of Dixie, down Charlotte way." He imitated a southern drawl.

A faint odor came to Reverend Kassley's nostrils, but he knew that only he could detect it. Razzom had come to him, filling his being as surely as warm liquid filled a cold belly. Thirty seconds passed silently, and in the half minute, man and demon communed in the unknowable power of the spirit world in a way that would have melted Joey Fazor with fear had he been aware of the communion. Finally, the words came inside the man's head. "Take him quickly from these fools and claim him as your own."

"Can we get on with it?" Arvil asked, breaking the silence.

"You bet your bottom dollar we can, Mr. Kassley. Let's do get on with it. Speaking of dollars . . ."

Arvil spun away from Joey's van and took three steps to his Suburban. He lowered his head to the open window and spoke in muffled tones to Jessie. When he reappeared, Joey's eyes fell greedily on the paper grocery bag. Arvil extended his arm and the little man received it gently with both hands and bowed slightly from the waist.

"Thank you kindly, Mr. Kassley." Without looking behind him, Joey passed the bag to his companion. "Won't take but a couple of minutes, he counts real quick. I don't mean to insult you, Mr. Kassley . . . I'm sure it's all there, but . . . well, you might say it's just a business habit of mine. Sometimes people who don't handle that kind of cash very often . . . well, they get a little careless with their counting . . ."

"I'm very thorough with details; it is all there."

"Yeah, yeah, I'm sure it is, but humor me, okay?"

Reverend Kassley did not acknowledge the words.

"Listen, one thing I should've mentioned early—I can't believe I didn't—I hope you didn't . . ."

"No, I did not draw the money out all at one time. As I said, I'm very thorough . . ."

". . . with details. Yeah, I remember, Mr. Kassley. Hey, I

believe you are for sure. I like detail men. Makes for good business relationships, you know."

The great head in the shadows did not move, and though Joey could not see its eyes, he could feel them, and the feeling was a terrible thing.

"Hey, back there, how about it, huh?" Joey spoke the words much louder than he had intended.

"It's okay," came the voice of his partner, "It's all here."

"Good. Let's pass the kid and hit the highway." There was a new urgency in his voice.

Arvil retreated a step and tapped on the rear glass of the Suburban. The power window whirred down and Arvil opened the door and lowered it forward. Joey and his partner lifted the child from the van and settled him in the nest of blankets that Arvil had prepared. Joey reached in his jacket pocket and retrieved the loaded syringe.

"Here, you might need this. He's been shot up quite a while now, but one more probably won't matter. I'd feed and water him before long, but that's up to you."

Arvil took the syringe, and nodded.

It was finished. Vehicle doors snapped shut until only two remained open. Joey could see the outline of Reverend Kassley looming at the driver's door, and he knew the eyes were on him again. He had never left a customer without a friendly parting word—a token of good will that might lead to another grocery bag full of small bills. But he was speechless now, and he had no will to think of an appropriate remark. The invisible eyes held him a moment longer, and then the long shadow oozed into the vehicle. The two engines came to life simultaneously, and for a moment the warehouse was filled with the sound, and then it was mute and empty.

The driver of the dark conversion van had smoked a cigarette and half of another as he slid the big vehicle through the highway traffic, but no words had been spoken since the transfer of the boy. The driver pilfered a sidelong glance; his partner sat stonefaced, eyes straight ahead. It was unusual behavior for Joey to display after a delivery; he was normally jovial and talkative on such occasions. The driver decided to wait until he finished his cigarette before probing the silence.

Joey Fazor was in the throes of a mental struggle with himself. That the tiny spark of a thought had flickered and then flamed was at once a source of great agitation and bewilderment, but the flame burned. It was an undeniable fact that the man whose stone-cold heart was a posssesion of great value felt a touch of pity for the child he had just sold. The flame would have to be snuffed, and quickly, for Joey could not imagine anything more dangerous in his chosen line of work.

So the thoughts darted back and forth in his brain, and now, after ten minutes of needed silence, he began to get on top of it—this stupid little thought—and he was certain that if he could sustain his train of thought for only a few moments longer, he could kill it. The coarse texture of the heavy paper bag at his side was comforting and Joey stroked it with his fingertips, thinking of the tightly packed bills nestled inside. Yes, it would soon be extinguished.

His partner's voice nearly startled him, "Geez, we seen some spooky ones before . . . but that guy . . ."

"Just shut up and drive, will you? I ain't in a talkin' mood."

"Yeah, sure, Joey, whatever you say."

CHAPTER TWELVE

The Reverend Kassley had prepared a tidy basement room for his temporary little guest. The ten-by-twelve foot room was the only finished area of the basement and was added as an auxiliary study. At least that was what the church finance committee believed. It had no windows, and the door was very sturdy. The floor was not covered with carpet; Reverend Kassley had specified vinyl to the mild surprise of the committee. The committee could not imagine that there would ever be many messes to clean up, but in the end they considered it merely a personal preference and thought no more of it. They would have been somewhat surprised to learn that the furnishings in the basement study consisted only of a roll-away bed and a small chair. They would have been very surprised to learn that four short lengths of rope were draped over the bed.

The finance committee had offered to finish out a much larger room, but Reverend Kassley graciously declined, advising the committee that the church's generosity had been extended quite far enough. After all, he reminded them, the church had already outdone itself in making him feel welcome. Oh yes, he had assured them, the room would do very nicely indeed.

The door was locked now, and not even a sliver of light penetrated the blackness of the room. But it did not matter to Razzom; locked doors and darkness caused him no distress. Like a vapor, he entered the room and waited for the sound of a vehicle engine.

The beam from the headlights swept over Reverend Kassley's neatly trimmed lawn and then the whiteness of his house, and before it was extinguished he knew that the house was not empty. The trip from St. Louis had been uneventful and only during the last ten minutes of the journey had the boy stirred. Wesley had been given the responsibility of the wheel and had driven expertly and according to instruction—between sixty-two and sixty-five miles per hour, low beam headlights, no sudden lane changes, no reaction to an aggressive driver. Jessie was stationed in the rear seat, close enough to Arvil and the boy to lend assistance if necessary. The reverend was very close to the child, and from time to time Jessie noticed the beam of the penlight from the corner of his eye.

"Pull around behind the house, Wesley, and back up to the door," Arvil instructed.

Wesley positioned the vehicle and after lowering the rear power window, switched off the engine. He walked quickly to the rear of the Suburban and lowered the door. Jessie was beside him now, and they stood silently as Arvil crawled out and stood between them. He took the key ring from Wesley and found the house key, pinching it between his thumb and forefinger.

"Here," he said, extending the key to Jessie, "open up and hold the door for us."

Arvil gently tugged the end of the pallet forward and gathered the child into his arms. "Collect the rest of the blankets, Wesley, and follow me."

When he passed by Jessie, Arvil tossed his head toward the Suburban. "Raise the window and lock it before you join us."

Wesley led the way through the kitchen and down the stairs, flipping light switches along the way. He turned the handle of the outside-mounted dead bolt lock and opened the door. The room was very cool, even for a basement room, and Wesley shivered involuntarily as he entered, but Arvil did not.

"Pick up the ropes."

Arvil placed the small body in the center of the bed and draped a blanket over it. He glanced at the doorway as Jessie entered the room, and as he did so, Arvil trembled slightly as Razzom became one with him.

"Come see our little friend, Jessie," Arvil invited.

Jessie took three strides to the side of the bed, looking for the first time at the boy's face, and when he did, it was pain that coursed through his body, as strong as an electrical current. The gasp that slipped from his lips was clearly audible, but Arvil interpreted the sound as one of excitement and was pleased.

"Yes, Jessie, yes," Arvil clasped an arm around Jessie's shoulders. "He is absolutely stunning, isn't he?"

Jessie Pacely could not speak, and even with Arvil's powerful arm wrapped around him like a steel band, it took all the trembling strength he could muster to keep his feet under him. Within the next few seconds, thoughts like tiny arrows stabbed his brain, and he struggled to sort them out—his mother cradling the small photograph in the palm of her hand; his own hand reaching down, against his will, to pick it up and put it into his pocket; the gleam of the moonlight on the dagger that took the hitchhiker's life; the dark blood that flowed on the stone altar—these things whirled in Jessie's mind and he could not sort them out. He only knew that the face of the child before him was a near perfect match with the image on the small square photograph in his pocket, and the certainty of that caused him to swallow hard against the bile that rose in his throat.

Arvil's voice was a faraway thing, hollow and unreal, and Jessie could barely comprehend the words.

"Oh, brethren . . . we are about to embark on a journey

of the soul that defies description. A more perfect sacrifice I cannot imagine."

The hard eyes turned first to Wesley, and they were a question. "Yes, Arvil, he is near about perfect, there's no doubt."

Then slowly to the left moved the eyes and head, toward Jessie. "Tell us what you think, Jessie, I know that you are moved. That is easy enough to see."

"I—I—yeah—he . . ." The whirling in his brain had slowed, but it had not stopped, and he did not trust himself to say more. There was much less chance of Reverend Kassley knowing his thoughts if he just remained silent. Jessie Pacely knew that his own life hung in the balance, for if the Reverend Kassley learned of his weakness, nothing short of Jessie's death could ensure the sacrifice of the beautiful child. So he clamped his mouth shut and waited and trembled.

"Yes, I understand perfectly, Jessie. It is quite all right. I myself was struck nearly mute when I first laid eyes on him. It will pass . . . it will pass."

The great arm released Jessie, and he half-staggered to the doorway. Arvil turned to Wesley, but he spoke to both men. "Leave us now, brethren. He is waking, and I want us to get acquainted with as little confusion as possible. I know you will understand."

"When?" The question came from Wesley.

"We will not wait long. I want to enjoy my Sunday sermons tomorrow with my faithful flock." He paused and threw back his head as the deep laughter spilled from his half-open mouth. It was a sound that neither Wesley nor Jessie had ever before heard, and this was because the laughter was Razzom's. It died away slowly, like a great bellows that was losing its air.

"Ah, yes, Monday most likely. Monday . . . just after twilight."

They were alone now, the Reverend Kassley, his demon, and the child, and the only sound in the close air of the room was the whimper of the boy. Reverend Kassley left the room and returned with a glass of water and a paper towel on which he had laid a slice of whole wheat bread covered thinly with peanut butter. He placed the glass of water and the bread on the floor near the head of the bed and waited patiently for the boy to fully gain consciousness. Razzom waited patiently with Reverend Kassley, making suggestions in a raspy whisper concerning the sacrificial service which was now less than forty-eight hours away.

Once again, Darren Starmann's eyelids strained to lift their own weight. The hum of the road was gone now, and although he was aware that he was lying down, the feeling under his body was soft and soothing; it was a bed now, not a pallet. He was sure. His eyelids cracked open and the incandescent light of the room caused him to pull them down for a moment. But he wanted desperately to come back to life and he raised his eyelids halfway, accepting the discomfort. With this small pain came greater hurts. The point of his chin throbbed and the pain radiated along his jawline all the way to his ears. He tried to lift his right hand to touch his chin but before he could accomplish this, the rawness of his throat burned its way into his new-found life. His lips peeled apart and he attempted to swallow, but the incredible dryness would not allow it. The bare wall of the room became visible, and he could see the line that it formed with the ceiling. Slowly, painfully, his head rotated to the left, and the great body that was Arvil Kassley filled his vision.

It was then that Darren Starmann broke down and cried openly, but the tears were not caused by his pain. The tears came from the fear the boy knew when the coldness of the eyes fell upon him. His first impulse was to throw himself from the bed and run from the room, but he sensed that this would be futile. He glanced at the long hands that hung loosely at the sides of the tall man, and he knew that one of them would snare him and hurt him more. So he turned his head to the wall and cried as softly as he could.

"That will not help." The voice was low, even, and like the eyes, cold and void of emotion. "You should stop the weeping and turn to me. Sooner or later we must talk."

Rooster shook his head twice and turned it farther toward the wall. The room was silent for long moments, save for the muffled sobs.

"You must know that I can make you look at me, don't you? I would prefer to do it the easy way. Think about that for a moment. You may turn your head away from the wall if you agree. I will not wait very long."

Slowly, like the second hand of a clock, the tousled blond head turned to the left, but the eyes were focused downwardly at the knees of the man.

"Much better, young friend, much better indeed. I can see that we will get along very nicely during your visit."

Rooster summoned all of his courage to speak, but the only sound that escaped his lips was a scratchy, throaty thing that made no sense.

"I'm sure that your throat is very dry after your trip. I have a glass of cool water for you. Sip some and then we can talk." He extended the glass and held onto it as Rooster rolled to one shoulder, but the boy still would not look at the face of the man. He gulped greedily against the burning thirst and coughed after several swallows.

"That will do for now. A bit more later perhaps."

Rooster rolled onto his back and stared at the ceiling. The sobs had subsided but his chin quivered despite his efforts to control it.

"You must look at me if we are to talk. Otherwise, I will not speak, and I know you have many questions of me."

The small head moved again and the wide-set eyes snatched a glimpse of Reverend Kassley's face but Rooster could not hold the eyes. He decided to focus on the man's mouth—surely that would satisfy his demand.

"Very well now. It is not such a terrible thing, my face, is it?"

Silence.

"I know you are frightened, but there is no need for that . . ."

The small voice broke in, barely audible, scratching its little sound in the air, and it was a wonderful thing for Reverend Kassley and Razzom to hear.

"I—I—want my mom—I want to see her now."

"I am afraid that this is not possible just yet."

"Where—where is she?"

"Not close by."

The boy's chin quivered again.

"No, do not start that again. It would upset me, and you do not want to upset me." He waited. "That is better. Just be quiet for a moment and listen and I will tell you all you need to know. More water?"

Rooster nodded and the glass was extended to him.

"You are here with me for a very good reason. Do you know what the word 'ransom' means?"

Rooster shook his head but he had a fuzzy idea of the meaning.

"It simply means that I have to hold you here until I get some money for you—from your mother and father . . ."

Reverend Kassley's explanation continued but Rooster had locked onto 'father'—the man did not know that his father was dead and the boy could not decide if this was a good or bad thing. For now, he would not tell him. " . . . so you see, we will be together for a short time, perhaps two or three days."

"We're not . . . rich."

"Oh, I am not greedy. Your parents are wealthy enough to satisfy my small needs, I suspect."

"I—I don't care—we're not rich." A bit of courage welled up within him now. "And . . . anyway . . . this is real bad of you to do this."

The Reverend Kassley tilted his head back and laughed.

"Bad, you say—bad indeed. And what makes you think you know what 'bad' is?"

"I just—I just know this . . ."

"You know *nothing*," and it was Razzom who hissed the word at the child. The man's eyes changed and Rooster shrank back flat on the bed and trembled in fear. "If I were to show you what 'bad' is, you would do more than whimper like a sickly dog." He paused to allow the impact of the words to sink deeply into the boy's brain. "You would do very well, my little friend, not to tell me I am baaaad."

Even though Rooster dared not look at the man, he could sense that he had relaxed; he was now the same as before— before the hissing voice came.

"These are the rules. Do not break them or I will become very angry. I will always have food and water at hand during the day. You will not eat or drink after six o'clock; I do not wish to take you to the bathroom at night. If you must use the bathroom at times other than when I come to see you, just knock on the door quietly. I will hear you. You will make no loud noises; besides, it would not matter if you did. No one can hear you down here in the basement and we are in the country—far away from other houses. Do not attempt to tamper with—bother—the doorknob. You will only hurt yourself; it is very strong. If you bother it, I will know. If you show me that you can do as I ask, I might bring a small television down for you later. Am I clear?"

Rooster nodded.

"Good. One more thing. Are you afraid of the dark?"

"I—I think I might be . . . now."

"Then hear me well. If you anger me I will take the light bulb from the fixture, and it will be dark all the time in your room." Reverend Kassley paused for a moment. "You may finish your water now and eat your bread and peanut butter. I will check back on you in a short while."

CHAPTER THIRTEEN

Joanie Starmann sat on the bed in the room that was hers for the first eighteen years of her life. It was not a large bedroom; she thought that she could remember her father once saying that it was ten-by-eleven, but whatever the size, it was a wonderful room for a girl to grow up in. And now—now it *should* be a wonderful room to pray in. Joanie Starmann had learned of prayer very early in life from a mother and father who knelt with her and never put words in her mouth. "It's between God and you, Joanie," her parents would softly remind her when she had hurts too deep to discuss freely even with them.

But she also remembered something else they had instilled in her very early in this sacred room. Sometimes, they told her, the hurt was so great that a wounded soul could not effectively pray for herself. Sometimes the agony had to be borne by others through their prayers, at least for a while, until the sufferer could stand with them. She had told her church congregation that she stood with them; she had said these words only a few hours before, but now, now she was not so certain. Now, alone in the bedroom of her youth, with darkness descending like a dirty veil over the window glass—now, as the same darkness came to her son—wherever he was.

The tears came softly at first, but they soon fed on each

other and the sufferer fell to her side and refused to fight against them. It was the coming night that was more than she could bear. The darkness that no one could stop, the darkness that would come to cover Rooster, the darkness that would hide the monsters that had taken him away from her, the darkness that would hide the things they might do to him. These thoughts the woman could not bear.

"Dear God! Dear God! This is more than I can bear!" The words pierced the walls of the room. Pounding footsteps came down the short hallway, and the door flew open, both Floyd and Norma rushing to the bed.

"Baby, stop . . ." Norma said, laying down beside Joanie. Floyd hurried to the opposite side of the bed and covered both women with his arms. "It's all right now . . . don't do this to yourself, baby . . . we'll be all right now."

"Oh, Mom . . . Daddy . . . I felt so brave this afternoon at the church—so strong . . ." the words came in spurts, between the sobs, "and now . . . it's getting dark . . . and . . . Rooster . . . I can't stand it now . . . in the dark."

"Oh, baby, he'll be tended in the dark just like he is in the daytime. God's angels don't stop watching just because it's getting dark. You know that. Hold on to that now, Joanie. There's such prayer aimed at little Rooster—you can't imagine it, we can't imagine it. Just cling to that with us. I'm as sure of it as anything I've ever known in my life."

"Oh, Mom, deep down in my heart, I *do* know—I *do* know, but . . . I want to hold him now, to touch him now . . ."

"I know, child, so do we, but we just have to hang on for a little while. Let the angels hold him for us now. Let them for now."

Norma pulled a tissue from the box on the nightstand and offered it to Joanie. She blew her nose and reached for another. The sobs subsided, and she raised herself to one elbow.

"Can we go back to the church now? I want to see the rest of them . . . to touch them . . ."

"Joanie, listen to me. More than anything else right now,

you need to eat and sleep and build your strength back a little. I know how you feel, but just let them do the work for you tonight, okay? Daddy's going back directly. He'll be there most of the night. Daddy and the rest of them will keep the candle burning tonight. You can trust them."

Joanie reached a hand to her father's face and stroked the evening stubble along his jawline. He covered her hand with his. "Let me look after him tonight, child. He won't be alone. Let Mom help get you back on your feet. It was really you talking this afternoon . . . don't worry. You just need some good rest and a little food, then you can join us in the morning. It'll be Sunday, you know. There'll be a service that'll raise the roof off that place for sure. Stay with Mom, okay?"

Joanie rested her head on his shoulder, and he could feel it nod. He kissed the top of her head.

"Okay now, missy," Norma said as she rose from the bed, "I'm gonna warm some more soup and pop a fresh can of Seven-Up. Gonna pour soup down you till you holler for me to drive to Burger King and get you a cheeseburger. Up with you now, girl. Tomorrow's Sunday, and you're gonna walk in that church house on strong legs."

There was no clock in the room that Reverend Kassley had prepared for his young guest, so Rooster did not know that it was close to midnight. The food and water had been taken up by the tall man, and the door had been locked for the night. Rooster's body shook slightly from the stress and fatigue of his ordeal. The food and water had helped a bit, but not enough to provide any semblance of comfort. The light from the overhead fixture raged at him now, but as much as he disliked it, the mere thought of a dark room was an unspeakable horror to him.

He turned to the wall and curled his legs up near his chin. He wondered if the strange man who had locked him in this room was telling the truth about money. He had learned something about ransom from snippits of conversations among adults—shakes of their heads as they spoke of news-paper articles they were reading—and he could remember television newscasters as they had intoned solemnly of the terrible thing called kidnapping. But it made no real sense to him; the tall man did not even know that his father was dead. The whole, crazy thing made no sense, and his mind was cloudy with fear and dread.

He thought of his mother and hoped that she was not mad at him for breaking the rule about rest rooms. Oh, how he hoped she was not angry. A janitor should not count. How could he have allowed someone to take him? He was sup-posed to work for the mall . . . how? It made no sense. He remembered opening the door and then a face with black-rimmed glasses . . . and then nothing. It all whirled around his head now, and he dug his fingers into the hair over his ears and knew that he would soon cry again. But he knew that he must do it softly; the tall man must not hear him crying.

Before the first sob welled up in his throat, Darren Star-mann felt his hands relax, and he did not know why. Then his legs straightened out comfortably, and he rolled easily onto his back and knew that he would not cry. The voice came softly in the room, and it did not frighten him, though part of him knew that a voice with no body should frighten him. It was a sweet voice, the voice of a woman, older than his mother, more like his grandmother's, only it was not hers. He was very sure of that. It was the sweetest voice the boy had ever heard. It was only with him for a moment, and with it, a warm, bright flash of light as it spoke the only words he heard before sleep gently took him.

"Your mother is not angry with you, child. Go to sleep now."

The only light in Jessie Pacely's bedroom was weak and yellow as it slanted down from behind the little lampshade on his nightstand. Jessie lay fully clothed on his bed, and his eyes were fixed on the faraway circle of light that ascended from the lamp to the ceiling, but he did not see it. He could barely remember driving home from Reverend Kassley's farm and dashing into the house and up the stairs to his room.

Allene Pacely stood, silent and motionless, behind the closed bedroom door, one hand pressed over her face, the other poised over the doorknob. Her mind was a whirl of thoughts that could not be stilled—her son had just returned, nearly a madman in appearance and action, from the company of Reverend Kassley; the feeling of evil hung in the air like a stench; and yet, strangely, pervasively, the knowledge of other forces, things of light and good, came to her also. The woman knew that the forces of evil were things with which she could not battle directly, but she also knew that the forces of light were things which she could cling to.

So the woman clung with all her heart and soul, and she slipped from the door without ever having touched the knob. And when she left, she knew that she would never again set foot in a sanctuary where the Reverend Kassley preached.

It would be four hours before a fitful sleep came to Jessie Pacely, and in the sweaty interim, the young man's damp hands would open and close over the small photograph a hundred times.

Sunday morning came to Marlon Stoner in lovely shades of red, filtered through the clouds of dawn, but the beauty of early morning was unappreciated. Sleep had been sporadic and flimsy; he was relieved that the pitiful effort was finished. He backhanded his eyes and sat up in bed, looking through the open door into the small kitchen at the coffee machine that squatted on the countertop. In five minutes, it would click on automatically and brew the four cups that would propel him into the day.

That it was Sunday morning mattered little to Stoner; all of his days were built around case files and the lives outlined inside the manila folders. There were five folders stuffed with papers and photographs littered about the apartment. Two lay on the kitchen counter, another pair on the desk in the other bedroom that served as a home office, and one lay on the floor beside his bed, near where his head had rested. The all-cap letter heading on the tab read: STARMANN, DARREN.

Stoner rolled on his hip and swung his legs over the side of the bed. His eyes fell on the proud family portrait standing on the dresser top. A son three inches taller than himself, handsome and bashful in his young-man smile; a daughter who was no longer a child, her long black hair a sheen of soft curls; and the woman who was no longer his wife. Stoner had studied her image in the photograph for each of the thousand days since the woman had ceased to be his wife. It had been too much to ask, too much to expect, of any woman, even one of her stature, he assured himself. He had never blamed her; he never would. There were finally, ultimately, too many manila folders for her to share him with. He left pieces of himself in them—ragged, bloody pieces of himself—and then one night, in the angry light of their bedroom, at two o'clock on the morning of a double homicide, she looked at him with haunted eyes, and he knew that his family would be gone when he returned.

He leaned forward and picked up the STARMANN folder. There was little substance in it, save for the photograph of the lost boy. Stoner held the photograph gently before him and allowed the red sunrise to touch it. A beautiful kid. A really beautiful kid. In a few hours, even now possibly, his family and church friends would lament to the God hidden somewhere behind the red sunrise. Stoner wondered if the God who made beautiful children would hear them.

More than that, Stoner wondered if the child had lived through the night. The human animals who enjoyed children were very fond of the night. The man sat on the edge of his bed, feeling another piece of his flesh being torn from him, and he could do nothing about it, and he took the pain.

When Stoner buried the boy's face in the folder, he wondered what the wolves of darkness would leave for him to seek.

The Reverend Kassley had been awake for a half hour before the light of dawn crept into his bedroom, and now, at seven o'clock, he stood in front of the window dressed only in his ceremonial black robe. Razzom had instructed Reverend Kassley to put it on. The demon's presence was becoming an indwelling phenomenon, his power ever increasing day by day, his voice nearly a constant in Reverend Kassley's head— at times a whisper deep within his brain, other times a voice raspy and alive in the room. Razzom's voice was a thing alive in the room now.

"Look out the window, beyond the grassy field, at the tops of the trees on the hill," the demon instructed. "It is only a short distance on a straight line to the altar. See it in your mind's eye; see the old blood."

Razzom etched a laugh in the air. "I am growing very excited in anticipation of tomorrow night. The offering is marvelous and I—we—have special plans for it."

Reverend Kassley wondered at the "we."

"Yes, I said 'we'. . . the one greater than I, greater than all like me, will be with us. I have sensed it for many hours now. He has honored me with his presence two times before on very special occasions. The first occasion was two hundred years ago, on a slave ship sailing from Africa. I had done wondrous things with crew and cargo alike—the tangle of human filth . . . ahhh! . . . wondrous things . . . and he came, my master came. And again, only twenty-four years ago, at a place called My Lai, half a world from here. I am sure you have heard of it. Women, children, old men . . . all ripped up by bullets . . . strewn about the village . . . yes . . . yes, a very fruitful day. My master told me of his approval as we smelled the blood together."

The demon fell silent and caused the smell of blood to

come to Reverend Kassley, and he watched as the man's nostrils flared slightly.

"I tell you this so that you will recognize the great nature of this ceremony. My master only comes to very special ceremonies, and this one will be most special, will it not? You know, do you not, what you and your friends must do?"

Reverend Kassley's body trembled and the heavy cloth of the robe prickled his flesh.

"I am waitiiiing!" the demon hissed.

"Yes . . . we know."

CHAPTER FOURTEEN

Darren Starmann awoke with the sound of the key in the latch of the heavy door that sealed him in his room. He rubbed his eyes and rose on one elbow as the door opened. The tall man was dressed in a white shirt and tie, the knife-like creases in his black trouser legs pointing to shining leather dress boots. His eyes bore into Rooster, and although his lips hinted at a smile, it was an unclean thing to the boy. The sight of it repulsed him.

"I trust you slept well on your comfortable little bed." It was a statement rather than a question.

Silence, as the boy stared at him for an instant before dropping his gaze.

"I have some business to attend to this morning, so I will be gone for a time. After you go to the bathroom and get some food, I expect you to continue your good behavior. Perhaps this afternoon, when I return, you may have the little television set I mentioned earlier. I doubt that there would be anything enjoyable for you to watch this morning. Do you know what today is?"

Another shake of the head, eyes fixed on the man's chin.

"Today is Sunday . . . the television programs would be . . . preachers, you know . . . ranting and wailing on the screen."

Reverend Kassley laughed easily, as if he could see the

television preachers in his mind's eye. "Ah . . . no, I doubt you would like that much, would you, my little friend."

"I'm not your . . . friend."

"Oh, so you do have your voice. Marvelous. We can have a conversation."

The voice had changed, like last night, and Rooster could feel the chill crawl up his spine.

"Do you go to . . . chuuuurch?"

Silence.

"Answer my question, boy, or I will open your mouth and determine for myself if your tongue functions."

"Y—yes."

"Ahhh! So you are a good Chrisssstian boy?"

Rooster nodded his head but could not open his mouth to speak.

"What do you suppose they are doing now, your church people? Perhaps groveling in prayer for you, hmmmm?" He, or *it,* said. The boy could not identify the being whence the voice came, and he knew that if he did not swallow carefully and slowly, he would vomit. Eyes clamped shut now, he could not look at the face. He could smell the being now, closer to him, though he had not heard it move. Then the smell was gone, and the raspy breathing gone with it.

Rooster cracked his eyelids a fuzzy fraction and allowed the features of the tall man's face to form. It was the man again, a strange look on his face, one of bewilderment, as if he too had only witnessed the horrifying spectacle just past. His long hands trembled slightly, and he pressed them against his trousers to steady them.

"I—I must go soon . . . now. Come . . . upstairs and go about your business before I leave."

Joanie Starmann sat between her parents on the front pew and looked through cloudy eyes at the candle flame ten feet from her face. She had managed three or four hours of sleep and Norma had gotten enough food in her stomach to make a real difference in her strength. But the gnawing emptiness within her, the incredible void of her child's absence, these things would not leave her. Joanie Starmann did not feel guilt; she was a mother, a mother to whom God had given a beautiful child, and now the child was in harm's way. No, God would understand; it was not a lack of faith that allowed the emptiness and void to fill her. It was simply the fact that she was a mother. How else would God expect her to feel?

Pastor Rosecrans rose from his chair on the podium and stepped to the lectern.

"Oh, beloved brothers and sisters, does not the Spirit fill this place up? *Hallelujah!*"

"*Yes! Yes, Preacher,*" came a dozen voices.

"We cannot yet touch our young brother Darren, but *you* can touch him with fingers of angels, *sweet Lord Jesus!*"

"*Yeeesss.*" The voice of the congregation was one now and three hundred arms jutted to the ceiling.

"Praise God, brothers and sisters, praise God Almighty." His voice was soft now, almost a whisper. "There is no sermon in me today, people. My heart is filled as yours are. My eyes are on the candle down here—Darren's candle. We will fight his fight today, the fight in the air. We will call upon God's angels, in all their might, to be where we cannot be, where the police cannot be, where Joanie cannot be—but where they *can be!*

"I'm going to come down there with you, beloved, no lofty pulpit this Sunday morning. I need your touch; you need mine. Joanie and Floyd and Norma—they need all of us close enough to touch. Everyone in this place is going to come and lay hands on Joanie's head and kneel at her feet and pray whatever prayer you're led to pray . . . I don't care if it takes all morning. If you have something really important that needs tending to, then go take care of it and come back. I think—I *know,* most of us are going to be here till this thing's over with."

The pastor backed away from the podium and quickly

made his way to Joanie. His wife met him, and as one they knelt at Joanie's feet; six hands clasped together in prayer, and the words were hushed and urgent, and they came from souls beseeching God. They prayed for long minutes as the tears from six eyes plopped onto the knot of hands, and when they had finished, Kathy Rosecrans looked up into Joanie's face and held her eyes before she spoke.

"Your son will walk down this aisle here and blow out the candle. You must see that in your own mind—clearly. I have."

The women smiled crooked, wet smiles at one another before they parted. The pastor helped Kathy to her feet, and as they moved away, another couple took their place. It was when Kathy walked by the center aisle and glanced at the line of people that she saw the old woman, standing at the end of the line. Kathy Rosecrans had never before seen the woman. Although the woman stood very close to many people, she seemed somehow separate from the throng—dignified, yet not aloof, and her eyes held a radiance that seemed out of place in an old woman's face.

"Honey," Kathy said, touching her husband's shoulder, "do you know that lady back there at the end of the line?"

He looked discreetly at the woman for a moment, and she returned his look with a smile and a nod of the head. "Why . . . no, Kathy, I don't believe I've ever seen her before. Must be a friend of Floyd and Norma's, I suppose. How thoughtful of her to come. Let's say a word to her."

The woman smiled again as they neared her and extended her hand when it became clear that she was to be greeted.

"How do you do, pastor . . . Mrs. Rosecrans," came the soft voice.

"Why, just fine, ma'am . . . uh, thank you so much for coming. I—I don't believe we've met, have we?"

"No, pastor, we have not."

"Are you a friend of Floyd and Norma?"

"Yes—yes I am that, although . . . I have not known them long."

"Yes . . . well, again, thank you so much for coming. Are you from around here?"

"Yes . . . I am from . . . around here, as you say." The deep blue eyes bore into the pastor's, and he could not hold them, but he did not know why.

"I'm sorry you are at the end of the line," Kathy said. "I'm sure the others wouldn't mind if . . ."

"No. Thank you for the thought. I am much stronger than I appear. I do not tire easily." The beautiful smile touched her face again. "You two go about your business here. Mingle and strengthen your flock with your presence. I will wait to touch the mother's head. There is time . . . there is time."

The couple drifted away from her, down the aisle, touching hands and embracing the others as they shuffled slowly forward. When they reached the front of the line they stepped to one side and looked back over it.

"Can you believe it?" Kathy asked. "We didn't even ask the lady her name, but she knew ours."

"Why—yes, she did, and—you're right. We didn't. I don't think I've forgotten to do that in fifteen years."

"I can't quite put my finger on it, but there's something about her—haunting, but beautiful. Does that make sense?"

"If I hadn't met her myself, I'd say you're reading too much into it. But, I have met her—and—yes, it makes perfect sense, although I can't explain it either."

They stood silently for a moment, hand-in-hand, wanting to say something, but neither could articulate their feelings. In spite of the silence, it was not an awkward moment, and in truth, both took great comfort in it and each knew of the other's comfort.

"Listen, I need to get on over to the nursing home and two hospitals for visits. I should be back in a couple of hours, maybe closer to three. We're set up to feed supper in the assembly hall, aren't we?"

"Yes. Edna Mae and Ruth have it all organized. People can just slip over five and six at a time and grab a bite or some coffee or whatever. They have shifts set up all night to serve. It's all taken care of. Go on, honey. Tell the old folks what's going on. Their prayers will go to the same place ours go."

He leaned over and tenderly kissed her head before he walked away.

It was an hour and a half before the old woman finally reached Joanie Starmann and her parents. There was no one else behind her; all who had come before to pray for Joanie had filtered to various locations on the varnished wood rows of pews. Except for Kathy Rosecrans, every head in the sanctuary was bowed; her eyes were locked on the old woman who now approached the candle on the communion table. The woman's movements were slow, yet graceful, and her body was held erect as she stood before the candle. It was as if Kathy watched a dream come to life, and she could feel her heartbeat quicken.

The long fingers of the woman's hands opened like flower petals to the sun and then she cupped them on both sides of the flame for a moment as the light bathed her face. Her head bowed and as it did, her hands left the flame and rotated upward, palms facing the heavens, as if she had freed a bird to return to the skies. Her arms extended from her sides and she held them there effortlessly for long moments, and then her head pointed heavenward. Kathy could see her lips move and her eyes were open, blue and radiant, and it was as if she were speaking with someone rather than praying. Kathy glanced from the spectacle to the three people on the pew just behind the woman. Only Norma Hunt was looking up, and she caught Kathy's eyes for a moment before she returned her gaze to the woman at the candle.

The arms slowly descended now, the hands folding in prayer under her chin as she turned to Joanie Starmann and knelt at her feet. The hands unfolded and sought Joanie's head and as they touched her, Joanie sensed a power she had never known before, like a tiny electrical current that flowed gently through her body.

It was when the great blue eyes left Joanie for a moment and came to Norma that she knew beyond all doubt. Part of Norma had wanted to believe the night she could not find the old woman in the parking lot, but she passed it off as wishful thinking, the product of a weary, struggling mind in turmoil. But not now, not when the presence was two feet from her, not when she could look into eyes that held power beyond measure. Norma Hunt trembled in stunned silence as she witnessed an angel of God speaking to her daughter.

"Beloved daughter in Christ, I come to tell you that your son is not alone. Rest now, and fear not the evil one."

Despite the growing urge to reach out to the angel—to touch the great face, to speak words ready to tumble out— Norma could only watch as the woman who was not a woman arose and walked past Kathy toward the side door to the sanctuary.

It was three full minutes before Norma Hunt could think clearly, much less speak. Kathy was on the pew beside her, holding her hand and speaking insistently. Norma became aware of the touch of her hand before she heard her voice.

"Norma—Norma. Who *was* that woman? I've had the strangest feeling since I met her . . . we didn't even ask her name, for heaven's sake . . ." the words tumbled one over the other before Norma held up her hand for silence.

Norma shook her head slowly as if attempting to awake, but it had not been a dream. She looked at Joanie, her head resting in Floyd's lap, hands folded under her head. She was not asleep, but the look on her face was faraway and peaceful. Norma was not certain that Floyd shared her knowledge of the unearthly visitor. She had been aware of no one other than the angel since her glance at Kathy several minutes before. Floyd seemed to be a part of the peace that had come to Joanie. His thick fingers stroked her hair, and the lines in his face were soft as he watched the flame of the candle.

"Kathy—I don't know exactly what to say right now . . . I'll try to explain later . . ."

"Explain what, Norma? Who was she? That's all I want to know. I've never seen an old woman with such presence."

"Yes—yes, I know, Kathy, I—I don't know a name to give you. Look, I know I'm not making any sense about this. Just bear with me, all right? We'll talk in a few minutes, okay?"

"Whatever, Norma. Whatever you say. But I'm going out there and meet her again, and this time I'm going to keep my wits about me and ask some questions."

"You can go out there if you want, Kathy, but—it won't do any good. I promise you—you won't find her."

CHAPTER FIFTEEN

Reverend Kassley steered his Suburban up the gravel driveway beside his house and slowly braked to a stop. He could remember very little of the sermon just delivered; he only knew that it must have been substandard, possibly disjointed, judging from some of the remarks he heard as he shook hands at the door. Two of the deacons had made discreet comments regarding his workload. Perhaps, they wondered, he should make better use of the church secretary, or take more time off during the week, for it surely appeared as if some strain was present.

Razzom had whispered filthy curses inside Reverend Kassley's head as he spoke with his congregation, and it had taken all of the man's energy to keep them from spilling over his lips. He looked at the dark mass of clouds that painted an ominous, swirling mural on the windshield of the vehicle. The first drops of wind-driven rain splatted on the thick glass. Reverend Kassley thought of the boy locked in his basement. Razzom spoke the command to him urgently in a raspy whisper.

"Go to the altar. He waits for us."

Reverend Kassley shouldered open the door and leaned against the wind as he began the walk through the woods. The rain pelted him like tiny stones as he climbed the last few yards to the clearing, and he shielded his eyes as he squinted toward the altar. He could see it now, dark and slick with the rain, but Razzom was leading him away from it. Their destination was the ruin of the old house.

When Reverend Kassley was ten steps from the gray boards that had once formed the corner of his room, he sensed a change in Razzom. His presence had diminished somehow and his voice was reduced to a pitiful, fawning sound, like the mewing of a frightened cat. Reverend Kassley took five more steps before he looked into the yellow eyes peering from the dark corner, and then he knew why the powerful demon had withered. The form was taller than his own height, nearly reaching to the top of the broken door frame, and the head from which the eyes beamed was too large even for a body so great. Reverend Kassley was amazed that he felt no fear despite his nearness to the one he knew was Satan.

"Come closer." The voice was deep and measured, but without the coarseness of Razzom's.

The man shuffled two steps closer to the yellow eyes.

"You know who I am, do you not?"

A silent nod.

"Remember the night long ago when I sent Razzom to your aid? We stand in the very place where you were delivered from the man who lusted after your flesh. I have served you well, have I not?"

"Ye—yes."

"Yes, indeed." A long arm rose from his side and then a finger, hooked like a great claw, pointed down the hill in the direction of Reverend Kassley's house. "I ask now that a worthy offering be made in return for all I have done for you. I desire the child greatly. You have done well thus far, and I trust that you will complete your service very soon."

"Yes . . . that is my intention."

"Very well, but I must warn you, there are—others, who would interfere with our plans. Pay them no heed. Do you understand me? *No heed.*"

"I understand."

The intensity of the storm had decreased and Reverend Kassley could see the face before him more clearly. The smile was thin and crooked and the head tilted to one side.

"Remember. I took the hairy man from you, and now all I ask for in return is one sniveling child. A fair bargain, that?"

"Yes . . . a fair bargain."

A laugh came from the dark corner, and Reverend Kassley could barely see the tall form now, but the words were distinct in the cool wind.

"In the wonderful hour to come, Razzom will be with you and fill you up." He paused and spoke once more before he was gone. "And so will I."

Rooster could hear the cadence of the heavy footfalls on the stairs, and then the click of the latch. The boy stood in the corner of the room, beyond the foot of the bed, his hands clenched into fists at his sides. He had begun to feel vulnerable lying on the bed, somehow less than himself, more of a target for the tall man's eyes. He did not delude himself with the belief that he was really safer on his feet; no one could be safe alone in a small room with the likes of the hard-eyed tall man who spoke with two voices. But it made him feel a tiny bit better, and even a tiny bit was worth snatching at this point.

The door opened, and the man filled the space. His clothing was dripping wet, and the water trickled from his hair and beard, catching the harsh light from the overhead bulb in the ceiling fixture. He seemed unaware of his condition, his eyes downcast, staring blankly at a point on the floor. Rooster's first impulse was one of curiosity, but it quickly turned to fear. There could be no good reason for the man to behave so strangely. Something was clearly and terribly wrong.

Rooster stole another glance at his face and sensed that he could study it for a moment; there seemed to be no desire on the part of the man to lift his eyes from the floor. After a moment, Rooster was certain that tears mingled with the rainwater on the man's cheeks. When he finally looked up and found Rooster's eyes, the boy was certain that he had never before seen sorrow so clearly etched in another human being's face. It was a sorrow so great that the boy lost touch for a moment with his own plight. He thought of the sadness in his mother's eyes, and in his grandparents' eyes, as they sat in the metal folding chairs beside the open grave that would swallow his father's body. What he saw in the bedraggled man was undeniably the equal of that great sorrow.

As the tall form began to move toward him, Rooster retreated a half step before bumping into the corner of the room, and the fear returned to him. He watched, spellbound, as the man grasped the bed with one hand and slid it to the center of the room, directly under the bare light bulb, and then lay down on it. Unblinking, he stared directly at the bulb, and his chin trembled for an instant before he spoke.

"In my room, long ago, there was a light like that one. When it would go out . . . terrible things would happen." He paused and his wide chest rose and fell quickly. "My . . . mother . . . let them happen. She should not have let them happen. If the hairy man had not come—if only he had not come . . . then . . ."

Great sobs racked the man's frame, and the little bed shook with the heavy movements. His hands covered his face now and his fingertips dug at his flesh as he wept like a child.

Rooster looked beyond the strange sight; the door stood open and the stairs just beyond beckoned to him. The boy weighed his chances. The man had been reduced to a pitiful wretch of a human and seemed no more capable of causing him harm than the weeping child which he resembled. Rooster was certain that he could creep to the open doorway and make a dash up the stairs. It could not be that difficult to locate an outside door. But then what? The man had told him that they were out in the country, far from other houses. Where could he run to? His brain whirled and he fought for control of his thoughts. It was clear now; he had to seize the golden opportunity. He would run until he found a road. There had to be a road nearby—and cars—and people. It would work out somehow . . . if he could just get free of the house.

Three slow sideways steps now, smooth and silent, close to the wall, his eyes never leaving the man's hand-covered face. Two more steps, and the hands still covered the man's eyes; the sobs still shook his body. Three more steps and he would be in the clear. Yes! Yes! The boy's heart pounded so loudly in his ears that he feared the man would hear it, but he did not.

Razzom did.

Rooster's fingers neared the door frame, and he gathered his weight on one foot for the final spring through the opening, but before he could make the lunge to freedom, the door crashed shut with such force that the walls of the room vibrated. He froze, slamming his back to the wall as his outstretched hand pressed against the door frame. The boy recoiled in disbelief as he felt the intense heat from the metal doorknob radiating toward his hand. Quickly, and as quietly as he could manage, Rooster slid along the wall away from the door until he wedged into a corner. The tall man was no longer weeping. The pitiful sadness of a moment ago was replaced with a look full of controlled menace.

The long body coiled snake-like for an instant and then sprang open as the man jumped to his feet. The other thing was in him now, and Rooster swallowed against the lump of fear lodged in his throat.

"Soooo. . . you would leave me, would you?" he snarled.

The boy did not answer, but strangely, the fear that had risen in him lost its momentum, and he looked the man-thing in the eyes.

"I see you are feeling brave today. You will soon need all of your bravery." The demon laughed softly. "Since you are so brave with me today, I will tell you some things about tomorrow . . . night."

Tomorrow . . . night. The words hung in Rooster's ears. Would he leave the house then? Would he be exchanged for money? Had his mother and grandparents arranged to get him back? The hope was fleeting; the hatred in its voice told him tomorrow night was something to dread.

"Others will come to our worship service—to help me with you. You are the guest of honor." He laughed again, louder this time. "Ah, yes . . . we have great plans for you. What plans do you think we have for you, brave Christian boy?"

"I—I don't know—but . . ."

"No! You do not know! You cannot imagine what plans we have for you. Spend some of your quiet time in here wondering about our plans and . . ."

"Jesus loves me." The words popped out of Rooster's mouth confidently, and they were as great a surprise to the boy as to the demon.

"How dare you interrupt me, you filthy little—"

"Jesus loves me!" The words shot from his mouth, aimed like arrows at the ugly face. Rooster was firmly on his feet, and he stepped from the corner of the room. He felt his arms rise, as if guided by unseen hands, and he felt his two stubby forefingers jut out and lap over one another in the form of a tiny cross. The cross slowly extended upward toward the face now contorted in rage, and as Rooster looked beyond his fingers, his eyes met those of the demon.

"Be silent, you miserable little piece of filth," the demon commanded, but some of the power had left him and the boy knew it. "If *Jeeesus* loves you, where is *He?* Where is your *mother?* Yes, I know your father is *dead.* He surely cannot help you! If . . ."

"You be silent yourself. I'm not—afraid of you anymore. If you're so strong, see if you can take this cross apart." Rooster stepped closer to the demon, the finger cross raised in front of him like a weapon. The man-thing retreated a step, saliva dripping from the corners of its quivering mouth. "You go away and leave me alone!" the boy commanded.

The room filled with strange animal-like sounds—snarls and grunts—and the air reeked with the sharp odor of burned things. It was moving now, circling away from the boy and toward the door, and as the demon neared it, the knob turned and the door swung open though he did not touch it. Then the tall figure filled the doorway and the eyes of hatred locked on Rooster's eyes a final time.

"I will return tomorrow . . . and there will be one present who will pay no heed to your little signs and words."

The demon's eyes darted toward the light bulb in the ceiling fixture and it popped into a hundred fragments which tinkled softly to the vinyl-covered floor. "Think about *his* plans in your dark little chamber." The door slammed shut and darkness took the room.

Rooster stepped backward cautiously until he felt the wall at his back, and then he relaxed and allowed his body to slide down to the floor. His legs were weak from the tension of the moments just past, and the finger cross began to tremble but he clutched it to his chest. *Tomorrow* . . . what had the man-thing meant about tomorrow? And the *one* who would come . . . and the plans for him? The unlit room seemed to close about him now, and for a moment he thought the wonderful presence that had sustained him might have passed from the room with the demon. But, even as the darkness began to trouble him, he knew the presence was still with him.

The light came to the room in degrees—like when he toyed with the dimmer switch in the dining room of his home. Only this light was whiter, cleaner somehow, and it washed the room in a way that soothed him and made him drowsy. He wondered if the woman's voice would come to him; he thought that it surely would. But it did not come; the light was enough, and the child lay down on his side and slept.

Wesley Livingston had grown very fond of his newfound power over his wife. Since the day he began to hate her—in that thrilling, transcendent moment when he was made aware that the darker powers within him were the most promising—Wesley had expanded his power greatly.

Now, with merely a glance, or perhaps a word or two, he could allow her to touch the edge of his power, and yet hide the totality of it. It was a most wonderful game of cat and mouse, and the fact that the woman was ignorant of the viciousness of the cat added a delightful dimension indeed.

Twila Livingston knew that her husband was not the same person of a few weeks before. Before the change, words had been her weapons, and now, alarmingly, they had become his weapons. Twila was perplexed by the turning of the tables. How had the simple man acquired the knack for cutting her with words—words that were somehow ominous when he spoke them despite the fact that, taken at face value, they should have been harmless? There was one fact that Twila knew beyond all doubt: The change was linked directly to Reverend Arvil Kassley, the great man of the cloth.

Twila could hear the scraping sounds coming from the back porch, sounds of metal being drawn over a whetstone. The knife sharpening had been going on for fifteen minutes and, scrape by scrape, the sounds had become so irritating that she could barely contain her displeasure. Even in the bedroom with the door closed, she thought she could hear the wet, ugly sounds. She watched him now from the kitchen as his right arm swung in perfect, grating cadence.

"How sharp does it have to be, Wesley?"

"When I stop, you'll know, won't you?" The voice was even, calm, with only a hint of insolence, but it was there.

He stopped and held the long fillet knife up to the light bulb for a close inspection, and then, after a measured glance at Twila, resumed the sharpening.

"You can leave if you don't like it."

"It ain't a real pretty day for a walk or a drive, mister, in case you ain't looked outside lately."

The brunt of the storm had passed, but the rain continued steadily, and the wind shoved the dirty, low clouds about mercilessly.

"Blade has got to be just right," he said.

"It ain't deer season. What you got to skin out?"

"Oh, you never know when you might need one. Me and Jessie and the reverend might go catfishin' tomorrow evening. Got to skin a catfish, you know. We got our eye on a real big one down at the creek. I think we can get him."

"How have you seen a big catfish in the likes of that cloudy water?"

"We just know. You ain't no fisherman." He paused and inspected the blade again before drawing it carefully for a half inch along the back of his bare arm. The hairs fell cleanly to the blade. "There," he said, "that'll do it. Why, I reckon this thing would skin just about anything now."

He turned and smiled, extending the knife, handle first, toward Twila. "Want to try it on your arm hairs?"

"No, Wesley, I don't want to try it on *anything,* okay?"

"I didn't figure you'd appreciate a keen edge, woman."

Twila whirled and stalked from the kitchen and even after she was out of sight, Wesley held out the knife and smiled. If only she knew of his latest little secret—the thing that had taken place just last night—she would die of fright. Wesley had tested the blade on her as she slept.

Wesley closed his eyes and savored the moment when the moonlight shone white on the tender skin of her neck as the blade touched her ever so gently. His smile was gone now.

She would die if she only knew.

CHAPTER SIXTEEN

Jessie thought it very strange that his mother had not attended Sunday morning services. He could not remember the last time she had missed a service. Just as strange was the fact that breakfast had amounted to nothing more than cereal boxes placed on the kitchen table. Allene's Sunday breakfasts were normally hearty affairs, complete with bubbling conversation that always expressed her joy at being a part of another Lord's day. But talk of such things had dwindled for several days; Allene Pacely was not herself by any stretch of the imagination.

The lack of a hot breakfast, or even the noon meal now past, was a trivial concern for Jessie; his stomach was tied in such knots that most of the time the mere thought of food was unpleasant. He had subsisted for days mainly on black coffee, sodas, and occasional packaged snacks.

It was mid-afternoon, and Allene had scarcely moved from her favorite living room chair near the window. Her closed Bible lay in her lap, both hands resting on the worn leather cover as if it was some sort of heat source on a cold day. She watched the gray weather patterns unfold through the window and they only added to her burden. Maybe if the yellow sun would sear a hole in the rain clouds she could collect herself and find the energy to fight against the unspoken thing that had descended like a pall over her life and that of her son. She had prayed until she was weary of prayer; she had laid it all out as best she could. God *had* to help her deal with it in whatever manner He deemed appropriate. She sensed that it was too great a thing to bear and she had pleaded for guidance through the night and into the gray day, but God seemed as hidden from the woman as was the sun.

As she blinked away the tears that had begun to collect in her eyes, the little photograph of Jessie popped into her mind's eye and with it the urgent feeling that had led her to give it to him in the first place. The beautiful little-boy face filled her vision and replaced the pane of window glass. It was Jessie's face—it had to be—and yet somehow it was different. The lips a bit thicker than his had been? The color of his hair a shade lighter? The eyes more penetrating? Something. It was Jessie, and yet it was not.

Jessie peered through the kitchen window over the sink, but he saw nothing. His mind was filled with the image of the boy lying on the small bed in Reverend Kassley's basement. He took the photograph from his pocket and felt the edges, now curled and tattered. He did not want to look at it, but he could not resist the urge within him to lower his vision to the palm of his hand, and as he did, he knew his mother was watching him.

He closed his fingers tightly over the photograph and turned around to face her. She found his eyes, holding them for a moment, before her gaze dropped to his clenched right hand.

"It's your picture, isn't it, Jessie?"

He shuffled his feet nervously and started to turn away from her.

"No. Don't shut me out anymore, son. Something real bad is happening around here, and I won't just sit around any longer and let it happen."

"Oh, Mom, just let me . . ."

"No! I will not just let you alone any longer, Jessie. When have I ever not tried to do the best I could for you? When have I not loved you? God only knows, it ain't been an easy life for either of us—but we do have each other—we *do* have that, son. I *know* what's in your hand, I just don't know why."

She paused and sought Jessie's eyes again, closing the distance between them, and she took his hands in hers.

"I do know this much, son. Arvil Kassley is somehow in the middle of all this. He has to be! I'm not blind or dumb, son. He's not a man of God! And something's happening that you and him both are caught up in, and I'm afraid for you, Jessie. Please—I'm afraid for you! Please let me help."

Allene's words stung him and his eyes burned but he would not speak. His mind reeled with it all, but above all else, Reverend Kassley's presence was a living thing in his brain and he could not make it go away. He ripped his hands from Allene's and bolted from the kitchen. He took the stairs three at a time and then his bedroom door slammed shut. Allene's head dropped toward her breast, and she grabbed the edge of the sink for balance. Her suspicions were true; evil was loose, and her only son was caught in its snare. She stood still for a moment, breathing deeply as she cleared her head and ordered her thoughts. The battle was joined, that much was clear, and Allene Pacely resolved to fight for her son with the courage of any soldier who had ever fought in battle.

She stooped to the floor and picked up the photograph, pressing it flat against the countertop. Strong fingers lovingly smoothed the worn edges of the heavy paper and then slipped it into her dress pocket. Allene climbed the stairs quietly, and walked to Jessie's door and opened it. He lay on the bed facing the wall, and he did not turn toward the sound of her entry into the room. She spoke in calm, reassuring tones as she silently made her way to the dresser top and the metal ring with the car keys on it.

"We're in this together, son. I'll be right here all the way. You'll want me to help you soon—trust me . . ."

Allene's fingers closed carefully around the keys and before she lifted them from the dresser, she made certain that they would not clink together. When the door closed behind her Jessie was still facing the wall.

When Clarence Rosecrans drove into the church parking lot at four o'clock that afternoon, he smiled and shook his head as he scanned the lot; there were over thirty vehicles. He parked and sidestepped puddles as he jogged through the light rain toward the side door to the sanctuary.

Kathy was looking at him when he stepped into the sanctuary, urgently patting the place on the pew beside her. She began to speak in a loud whisper even before he sat down.

"Honey, Norma thinks—and I do too—that we've had . . . a . . . *visitor.*"

"What do you mean by 'visitor'?"

"Clarence, it gives me goosebumps just to think about her—him—what are angels, honey?" Kathy smiled, but it was not a mischievous smile that he saw on his wife's face.

"Kathy, will you kindly tell me what's going on here?"

"You can talk to Norma herself later, because you need to hear her tell it. It's so beautiful to hear her tell what happened. But—you remember that elderly lady we spoke with—forgot to even ask her name . . ."

"Yes, of course I remember, Kathy, but what—"

"Just listen, okay? I know this sounds a little far-fetched maybe, even for us, but—but Norma says she's positive that the old lady—isn't an old lady."

"You mean she thinks the old lady is—?"

"Yes, honey. That's exactly what she says. She's sure. If anybody's down-to-earth, it's Norma Hunt. You know that as well as I do. You listen to what she tells you happened over there a while ago, and see if you doubt it."

"Who says I doubt it, Kathy?"

He looked over to the front pew where Norma and Floyd flanked Joanie. Norma looked up at him, then raised her forefinger toward the ceiling for a moment and simply nodded her head a few times. Then she made a tight fist with her right hand and shook it defiantly as a smile crossed her face.

"Praise God," Clarence said quietly, and the two words were a prayer. "An angel of God Almighty in our little church." He shook his head slowly. "We're in the middle of something here, Kathy, something far beyond what we can imagine."

"I know, honey . . . I know." Kathy rested her head against his shoulder.

"Well, well," he said, "it appears that this little army has been assigned a real general."

Arvil Kassley lay in a disheveled heap on the floor of his living room. Parts of his clothing were still damp, but the physical discomfort was a small thing, a faraway thing. Arvil had never been so weary of mind and body in his life. The demon had left him, for how long he could not be sure. He could not be sure of anything about Razzom except that he was never far away. Strange scenes flashed in movie-like fashion within his mind—Razzom's snarling voice, strong and full of malice; a pair of small hands and short, crossed fingers; Razzom's voice, now subdued by the other tiny voice—it was all too much to comprehend, too much to sort out.

Arvil tested his mind with a quick touch of pity as he thought of the boy. Razzom did not respond. Arvil allowed his thoughts to wander to the boy's parents, surely beside themselves with grief and fear. Still, the demon did not fill him. Perhaps it was a game with him; Razzom enjoyed his little mind games immensely, but it did not feel like one of his games to Arvil.

Could it be? Could it really be? So many times, the man had fleeting glimpses of life apart from his demon, only to be reminded in disgusting ways that it could never be so. The possibility of freedom from the demon had never been a concern in his life for as long as he could remember. Life before Razzom was nothing more than ugly fragments of memory, a time full of sorrow and longings never fulfilled. Life after Razzom had been controlled, driven, full of energy; there was no right or wrong, only cruel power over others.

And now . . . these confusing bits of sympathy for his victims, things that Razzom had never before allowed. Arvil was surprised at how quickly the tiny seeds of decency had sprouted in a soil so infertile as his brain. And yet, he could not deny it—things were changing with the demon. He tested more thoughts, daring to attempt remembrance of the thing called love—a thing so lost that the very idea that he, Arvil Kassley, could grasp a fraction of it—it was simply beyond belief.

A shudder passed through his body. He quickly shrank from this thought, for as soon as he began to dwell on it, the foreboding passed over him as darkly as a shadow, and with the shadow came the memory of his meeting with the one greater than Razzom—the one with the yellow eyes.

He was not far away.

The burning desire to speak with Reverend Kassley grew within Jessie as the twilight claimed his bedroom. He had lain on his bed for over three hours, scarcely moving his body, but his mind had not been quiet. He rolled over and sat on the edge of the bed for a moment, adjusting to the upright position. His immediate concern was getting past his mother without any commotion. Once in his car, he could concentrate his thoughts on Reverend Kassley, the one man with the power to help him deal with his newfound doubts.

In the poor light, his fingers groped over the dresser top, feeling for the key ring. Irritated, he reached for the light switch, but when he squinted through the harsh glare he could not locate the keys. He squatted to the floor and looked over it and then under the dresser. There was no other place to look; he always put the keys in that very spot. Always.

It was her; it had to be. Yes—the short visit after their confrontation—the soothing words. If she intended to make him a prisoner in his own house, she was in for a rude awakening.

Allene sat in the living room, listening for the angry stomp of footsteps that she knew would come sooner or later. Jessie clambered down the stairs and whirled around the newel post.

"I'm only gonna ask this once. Where are my car keys?" His tone was controlled, but barely so.

"Jessie, your car keys are in a safe place. We're going to have to talk this thing out sometime soon, and your running off in your car won't help a thing."

"If I want to leave, there ain't a thing you can do about it, and you know it." The voice bordered on the edge of menace now, and Allene braced herself for trouble.

"Son, I'm your mother, and I'm due some respect. I won't just sit here and—"

"This is crazy! I'm grown and I want to go for a ride and you hid my car keys! This is nuts!"

"If it wasn't for Arvil Kassley, it would be crazy, me doing such a thing. But, he *is* tied to this, and there's no use you trying to squirm away from it."

"Why are you so sure he's so bad? What's he ever done to you, or anybody you know? Huh?"

"Jessie, why are you trying to protect him? And what is it about the picture? Do you realize that I gave it to you because I felt led by the Lord to do it? Think about that for a minute and maybe . . ."

"I ain't gonna think about it for a minute, or even another second." The rage in his face was no longer masked. "I got a good mind to turn this place upside down, just to teach you a lesson, but I don't want to waste the time."

"Teach me a lesson! Listen, mister, just you remember who it is you're talking like that to."

They were both standing now, Allene in front of the door and Jessie two steps from her. Allene knew that very soon she would have to attempt to stop him physically unless he could be softened somehow. The words were loud inside her head.

Dear God! Dear God! Help me . . . please!

Jessie's hands were clenched into fists, and his lips trembled. The back door was not an option. He would leave through the front door if he pleased, even if it meant hurling his mother away from it first.

As he began to take the first step, the knock on the door froze him for a moment, but it did not matter now; whoever had blundered into the situation would get bowled over just like his stupid mother.

"Jessie! Don't—"

Allene clutched at his shirt but the cloth tore through her fingers as he brushed her aside. He threw the door open and did not even bother to glance at the figure standing in the open doorway. He raised an arm with which to wedge his body into the space between the person and the door frame, but the hand that touched his chest could not be moved. It was not a large hand, nor did the arm to which it was attached appear to amount to anything. Within the span of a second, puzzlement replaced rage as Jessie jerked his head sideways into the face of an old woman, her features serene despite the intensity of the situation. Jessie could not hold her eyes; they were oddly bright in the gloom of the unlit porch, and they frightened him. The unyielding hand gently guided him back through the doorway, and then the old woman followed.

Allene was dumbfounded at the strange scene. She recognized the woman from church services, although nothing more than pleasantries had ever been exchanged with her. She was the old woman called Gladys—the one who always waited at the end of the line to talk with Reverend Kassley.

"My apologies to you, Mrs. Pacely, and to you, young man, for coming at a time of trouble, but I believe I may be able to help. May I come in and sit with you for a while?"

Allene had been shoved into the wall with such force that

her left shoulder throbbed from the impact, and her legs were weak as she attempted to gather herself and salvage a fraction of dignity—it was, after all, a stranger who had entered her home; maybe the terrible situation could be hidden until she left. Allene could think of no reason whatever that would cause this old woman to presume to be in a position to help.

"Well—I—" Allene could think of no rational reply.

"I know this is a trying time, Mrs. Pacely, and I know that it must be very difficult to have someone you barely know come unannounced. But I ask you to trust me, please. I come in love, and I am a—servant—of the same Christ you honor."

It was the manner in which the word "servant" came from her that caused Allene to begin to feel at ease with her presence, although she did not understand why. The word hung beautifully in Allene's ears, like two soft musical notes.

"Please . . . come in." Allene said. "I don't—"

"Mrs. Pacely, there is no need to explain. I attend your church also—you may have seen me there—and I know of the trouble there."

The old woman walked confidently into the living room with Jessie at her side. Her arm was at his back, gently guiding him forward. More than anything else, Jessie wanted to run from the house and this strange old woman, but he could not make his legs do what he desired. She led him to the sofa, and he slumped into a corner, quickly diverting his eyes to the floor. She turned and motioned for Allene to take a place on the sofa, two feet from Jessie, and then the old woman effortlessly lifted a high-backed armchair and placed it in front of the sofa for herself. The room was quiet for a moment, Allene searching for words that would not come and Jessie frozen in stunned silence. The old woman carefully locked her fingers together and rested her hands in her lap; the silver-covered head bowed forward.

"Lord and Master, we gather to do your business here and ask that you hear our humble prayers."

She raised her head slowly until her eyes looked nearly

straight up for a moment, and then she spoke in tranquil tones.

"I know that Reverend Kassley is at the heart of the problem."

Both Allene and Jessie jerked their heads at the woman, but Jessie's quickly dropped to its original position.

"You see . . . I am a good observer of people, especially preachers. I have had many years of experience. Many years. Mrs. Pacely, I suspect that you have grave doubts about him now. And you, Jessie, you know what he is about, do you not?"

Jessie struggled mightily against the feeling that the old woman was somehow listening to his thoughts, picking through his brain like a gardener searching for weeds. He squirmed on the sofa, attempting to shut out her words, but he could not.

"You must no longer be a part of what he is about, Jessie. I know of the hold he has on you, and I know of the one who has a hold on him. There is a being of great power and evil who drives Arvil Kassley, Jessie. There is no defense against this evil save for Christ the Lord. Your mother and I will show you the way to Christ, and you will be set free.

"Mrs. Pacely, strange as it must seem, I am a part of the answer to your prayers. Do not trouble yourself with exactly how for now, just know that I speak the truth. I have helped others through terrible times, and I will help you and Jessie."

"Mrs. . . . Miss . . ."

"Fairchild, Mrs. Pacely, Gladys Fairchild, and I am unmarried."

"Miss Fairchild, I don't know how you know all you do, but—yes, I'm not surprised about Arvil Kassley. And yes, my son is caught up with him in a terrible way, I'm afraid. Help us. In the precious name of Jesus, help us."

The angel's hands uncoupled, palms upward, and extended toward the sofa, the right to Jessie and the left to Allene. Allene grasped the hand with both of hers and her trembling ceased at once. Jessie's hands were knotted in his lap, and he made no effort to take the hand offered, but it closed over his. The sensation was similar to touching a low voltage electrical current—tingly, yet linked with great power—and it coursed through his body, releasing the tension.

"The power you both feel inside yourselves is not mine; the power is our Lord's, through the Holy Spirit. Open yourself to it, Jessie, allow it to cleanse you. Do not fight against it. Part of what you feel is your mother's love; I feel it also, flowing through our circle of love."

Jessie's will to fight ebbed with the passing of each second, and the burden of the evils committed pressed on him like a great weight. It was more than he could bear, these memories of prayers to Satan and blood and eyes filled with horror and dread. A groan escaped his lips and his body was racked with great sobs.

"Hold your son, beloved woman. Hold him as if he were your little child of days long past. He has fallen to powers of darkness, but only for a time; he will become whole again, for many have prayed."

The angel released the hands of mother and son, but they were joined now and Allene wrapped her free hand and arm around Jessie's shoulders and drew him to her.

"Let him weep and cleanse himself; it will require much of the night. Simply hold him and love him. After a time, he will need to tell you of hurtful things which he cannot bear alone, and they will be difficult for you to hear. But neither will you bear them alone."

The angel paused, reaching out and touching Allene's hand a final time. "The Spirit will never leave you, good woman. Be assured of that. Love our Lord, and the Spirit will dwell in you forever."

Allene buried her head in Jessie's shoulder and rocked him tenderly. She was unaware of footsteps, but when the front door squeaked open, she raised her head to the sound.

"Miss Fairchild, I—I will thank you properly—soon, I promise . . ."

"Mrs. Pacely, the sight before me now represents a measure of gratitude that will sustain me for longer than you might imagine."

"How will you get—"

"Do not concern yourself with me." The smile that came to Allene was warm and radiant, even from the shadows near the door. "I have a way home."

The door squeaked and then closed firmly.

CHAPTER SEVENTEEN

Allene awoke as the thin light of dawn began to claim the room. She did not know how long she had slept—perhaps two or three hours at most—but she felt surprisingly alert. Jessie's head rested in her lap, his body curled up on the sofa. Allene had pulled an afghan from the top of the sofa and draped it over him after sleep had finally come. Before that, Allene was only able to hold him and whisper soothing words in his ears. The pitiful sobs had shaken his body long into the night; he had said nothing intelligible, although several times, Allene thought that he attempted to form phrases. She was certain of one thing, beyond the shadow of a doubt: Jessie had suffered mental agony, the like of which she could not imagine.

She carefully lifted his head from her lap and eased her legs from under it. She stretched against the stiffness in her limbs before she reached down and arranged the afghan over his body. The room was cool following the afternoon and night of rain, the breeze still strong in the leaves of the big silver maple near the front porch. After a few minutes in the kitchen, the sumptuous aroma of coffee filled her nostrils. She popped open a can of biscuits and spread them on a cookie sheet; they would both need something to eat, although she had little appetite and doubted if Jessie would either. When he awoke, reality would take hold of him with a vengeance, and the thoughts which caused him to moan in the night would be nightmares come to life.

But they would deal with them, however terrible. Allene Pacely did not stand alone; the Spirit infused her, just as Gladys Fairchild had promised. The mere thought of the old woman brought strength to Allene. She wondered where the woman lived and how she had found them last night. And then something came back to her that made no sense at all. The woman had arrived in a steady rain, and yet Allene could not remember her clothing being wet. She had worn no raincoat, nor did she carry an umbrella. Strange indeed . . .

Her thoughts were broken with the sound of Jessie stirring in the living room. She went quickly to him and sat down near his head.

"Morning, son." She smiled down at him and his hand found hers and squeezed it. "I'm going to put some biscuits in the oven. We need to get something in our stomachs before we start to sort this . . ."

The look on his face stopped Allene in mid-sentence as he pushed himself up to a sitting position; it was a mixture of fear and sorrow, and she was certain that these feelings were about to become a part of her.

An hour later, Allene still knew that fear and sorrow would be hers to share with her son, but she did not know when. Jessie had simply slumped back into her lap and no amount of coaxing could draw him into a conversation. Allene again laid his head on the sofa and replaced the afghan over his body. She returned to the kitchen and cooked the biscuits, forcing herself to eat two with a bit of jelly before drinking another cup of coffee.

When she sat down in the living room and looked at the expressionless face, drawn and colorless, the urge to seek help welled up within her. Clearly, this was a situation far beyond her, and yet Gladys Fairchild had left little doubt that mother and son could . . . no, *should* work it out together with the Spirit. Still, what harm could there be in seeking reliable help of some sort? She huffed bitterly at the thought that, as a member of a Christian congregation, her first step should be her pastor. Another trusted friend from the church possibly; there were several who could surely be trusted. But what sort of situation would she be dragging them into? The police maybe, but that might be unnecessary, although she admitted that this was probably wishful thinking. Her mind turned the possibilities over and over, but she remained unresolved.

Another hour passed as Allene thought and prayed, but still no firm conviction came to her regarding an immediate course of action. The need to watch over Jessie seemed to be her only task for the time being, and she accepted the tiny bit of satisfaction that came with the responsibility. It was like watching over him when he was small and feverish. The minutes seemed to race by, quickly becoming hours, just as they had so long ago when she willed her thoughts to center around happier times—times when he ran yelping through the yard, imitating Brownie, the little beagle, times when no fever raged within the small body. Allene watched over the little boy, now become a man, lost in their past—comforting, soothing, humming childhood songs. When the strained voice broke her reverie, it was nearly one o'clock on Monday afternoon.

"Mom! Mom! I've got to figure a way to get him out of there before tonight!"

"Who, Jessie? Out of where?" Allene struggled to shift her thoughts back to the present.

"The little boy—the kid . . ."

Jessie had pushed himself up against the back of the sofa and his arms trembled with the effort. He was lightheaded and Allene came into focus slowly, as if his eyes were a camera lens and each blink a click of the ring. Allene sprang to the sofa beside him and steadied his body.

"Jessie, calm down now, and talk sense to me. What is going on?"

"Oh, Mom—Oh, God, please forgive me . . ."

Allene swallowed against the nausea pushing up her throat. *A boy—a child in danger—where? Had there been others before this child? Had Jessie somehow harmed a child? Kassley! That evil, lying . . .*

"Mom, help me figure out what to do. I'm afraid! I'm afraid for the little boy and me both."

Allene took him by both shoulders and shook him firmly. "Jessie, listen to me, son. I *can* help if you just stop and make sense. Now, what boy? Where? At Kassley's?"

Jessie nodded silently.

"Why does Arvil Kassley have a child, and what have you got to do with it?"

"Mom, if we don't get him out of there—they're gonna—"

"Gonna what? In the Lord's name, son, why would he want to hurt—"

"Not hurt him, Mom. Sacrifice him."

Sacrifice.

The word stuck in the woman's ears like the point of an ice pick. *Oh, sweet Jesus,* she thought. *Sacrifice.* Arvil Kassley and her only son were involved with the darkest force of evil on the face of the earth—Satan.

Calm now, stay calm. To panic now might be to lose all, for both her son and the child. Maybe the boy was not yet harmed; Jessie indicated the . . . she could not form the word, even in her mind . . . the thing was to take place later. But how much later?

"Jessie! When? When is this thing to take place?"

"Tonight. He—he's supposed to call."

"Jessie Pacely! In the name of God Almighty! Were *you* going to—were you . . ." The pitiful moans were the mother's now, and she collapsed into Jessie's arms.

"No, Mom—I swear to you—I couldn't have. The picture you gave me the other day—it's been different since then. But the things in my mind are—were—so strong! Mom, you can't imagine the powers in that man. It's like he ain't even a real human sometimes. But after last night—the old woman. I can't explain, Mom. *Things* went from me last night. I don't know how to tell you."

Allene's crying subsided, and she raised her face in front of his, nearly touching it.

"Jessie, just answer me one thing. Did you ever . . ." the word stuck in her throat, but she knew she had to utter it, "kill . . . anyone?"

"No, Mom. I swear. I was there once when him and another guy—did. They killed a hitchhiker and they made me . . . touch him with the knife . . . but he was dead, I swear. He was dead before I touched him."

Allene pushed away from him and lurched to her feet, staggering out of the room toward the half bath twenty feet away. Jessie could hear the sounds of her wretching and then the flush of the toilet. He wanted to go to her, to hold her and comfort her, but he did not trust his legs. He could hear the sound of water splashing in the lavatory, and then it became very still in the little room which sheltered his mother. Jessie Pacely loathed what he had become a part of; he was certain that, if possible, he would trade his life if only he could turn back the clock a few months.

But it was done, all done—the helpless animals, the lonely hitchhiker, a child stolen from his parents and in mortal danger, his own mother physically ill with the horrible knowledge of it all—dear God, it was all done.

"Mom! I'm so sorry . . . please forgive me! I never meant for it to go this far . . ."

Allene stepped from the half bath and placed both hands on the back of a living room chair for support. Her face was pale and she stood silently until she felt clear-headed enough to speak.

"Son, please stop torturing yourself. It won't help anything, or anybody—including the little boy. I forgive you. God forgives you. You have been a part of something so evil that the flesh is as nothing to resist it. You fell away from your Christian roots and became a target for evil . . . but that's all done now. All we can do now is help the child—stop the madness—now."

The few sentences sapped her strength, and she slowly made her way back to the sofa and sat down.

"We've got to think this out clearly, Jessie. There doesn't seem to me to be much of a choice. What else can we do besides call the police?"

"No, Mom, I—I don't think he would just give up without a fight. I know he's got at least one revolver and a shotgun—not even counting knives. If they think they can just storm in there and take the boy . . ."

"Jessie, they're experts with situations like this. It would just become like a hostage situation—they would try to talk sense to him on the phone, or with a loudspeaker or something. They would know better than to storm in there after you told them what you know about Kassley."

"Mom, they couldn't talk sense to him—not if he's—beyond himself. I can't do a good job of explaining, but it's not like dealing with a normal man."

"Son, I believe you, but there isn't any other reasonable choice. There's nothing else we can do."

"Yes there is. It's the only chance the boy has, Mom."

Jessie averted his eyes for only a moment, but in that instant, Allene realized what he meant.

"No! No! Jessie, don't even think about doing that. You'll never be near him again in your life if I can help . . ."

"Mom, listen to me." He held up a hand. "Think about it. As far as he knows, everything is still on. He doesn't know what happened here last night. I'm the only person in the world that can walk in that house without him knowing he's been had."

"So what, son? What if you did go back in there? What then? He's a giant of a man—and the other one—you said there was another man—what chance would you have in there? They've already killed once that you know of. There's nothing to stop them from killing you once they figure you out. No!"

"I admit, it don't seem too good, but they trust me. There's bound to be a few seconds somewhere in there when I could just grab him and make a run for it—I'm telling you, it's the only chance the kid's got."

"But even if you could do that, where would you run to? You'd never make it to your car. The child's bound to be hysterical. He'll fight you—he won't know what you're trying to do. You just can't do this alone, Jessie."

"Okay, you're probably right about getting off his place once I got the boy. Okay, so the police . . . maybe they could sneak close to the house. He don't have any dogs. Sure, they could do that. Then, all I got to do is just get past the back door."

Allene's mind sprang at the mention of police. If she could just manage to get them involved, they could talk sense to Jessie. They would simply take over and do their jobs and rescue the child without endangering her son. He had been through enough already with the evil Kassley.

"Good, son. Good. You can see that we have to have their help for the child's sake. We can't get him back by ourselves. Let's talk it out with them."

Jessie nodded solemnly. The thought of facing the police, of telling them everything he had been a part of, fell on him like a heavy weight. Yet he had no choice. The things of the night had left him; he would be a part of the light now and forever. Even if it meant spending time in prison.

"Mom, you know that—there's a good chance—I'll go to . . ."

"Stop, Jessie. One thing at a time. It will all get sorted out in God's good time. We'll deal with all that later. All that matters now is the little boy."

She stood in front of him and bent forward to kiss his head before she walked into the kitchen and dialed 911.

Allene and Jessie watched through the living room window as the black and white Wrightville police cruiser pulled to a stop in front of the house. An officer emerged from each of the front doors, and they walked unhurriedly, side by side, to the front porch. Allene saw one of the officers smile slightly and shake his head at the other man as they neared the front door. Allene opened the door before they could knock.

"Allene Pacely?" the older of the two asked.

"Yes, sir. Please come in," Allene said.

The two men stepped into the living room and took the chairs that Allene indicated for them. The younger man held a clipboard, but his pen was still clipped to his shirt pocket. The older man spoke first.

"Ma'am, let's go over the phone call again—uh, it was a little hard to follow according to . . ."

"Yes sir," she interrupted, "I know it must have been. This is something that—well, it's hard for me to deal with, if you can imagine."

"Yes, ma'am, we understand. Now, you say that your son here . . . what is your name, sir?"

"It's Jessie—Jessie Pacely." It was hard for him to look the policeman in the eye at first.

"Right, so Jessie here has knowledge of a kidnapping victim, is that correct?"

Jessie nodded.

"And this—boy, you say, is being held by a reverend?" The officer was barely able to suppress the incredulity in his voice.

"Yes, sir," Jessie replied, "Reverend Arvil Kassley. At his house."

The two officers exchanged expressionless glances before the older man continued. "What church would Reverend Kassley be pastor of?"

"Oak Tree Missionary," Allene answered. "I'm a member there."

The older man placed a finger under his right eyebrow and thoughtfully pushed it upward before smoothing it back down. "Has Reverend Kassley ever shown signs of being . . . unusual, folks?" His eyes swept over both Jessie and Allene.

"Well, yes—and no, officer," Allene stammered. "I've known for some time that my son was not acting normal, and here lately . . . well . . ."

"Mrs. Pacely, I'm sure you're aware of the seriousness of what you both are saying."

"Mom," Jessie cut him off as he addressed Allene, "where are my car keys?"

"Jessie, you can't—"

"No, Mom, I ain't planning to leave. I want in the trunk."

Allene got up and walked into the kitchen; the three men sat in strained silence. The sound of a cabinet door opening and then banging shut came to them. She walked back into the room and handed the key ring to Jessie. Without a word, he stood and walked toward the back door. The officers stared a question at Allene.

"I—I don't know what he's after," she said.

When Jessie came back into the room, Allene could see that he held a small plastic bag in one hand. As he passed her, he reached down with his other hand and touched her on the shoulder.

"I'm sorry, Mom, but we're wasting time."

He stopped directly in front of the older policeman and tossed the bag in his lap. The man's body tensed as if jolted with electricity as his eyes focused on the decaying human ear in the bag.

"I watched Reverend Kassley cut that off of a hitchhiker a few weeks ago just before him and another man killed him. He gave it to me as a souvenir. He's always wanted to do a kid."

"Oh, dear God!" the words were moans from Allene's mouth.

The two men jumped to their feet at once, nearly bumping shoulders, the older man holding the bag between his thumb and forefinger. "Billy," he ordered, "go radio in what we got

here and tell them to get the captain back if he's out somewhere."

The young man darted from the room, leaving the front
door standing open after he swept through it.

"Folks, we're going downtown. Please get your purse if you
care to, ma'am."

CHAPTER EIGHTEEN

The desk sergeant thoughtfully tapped his ballpoint pen on the pad of paper in front of him; there were several matters which required his attention, but he was unable to concentrate on them. His gaze bored through the half-glassed walls of the captain's office and onto the occupants. It had been almost ten minutes since the moving commotion had swirled through the Wrightville city police station and into the small office, which was now crowded with people, some seated, others standing.

Two civilians, a woman and a younger man, were seated in front of the desk, directly across from the captain. He was flanked by Sergeant Charlie Stanhouse on his right and Lieutenant Gilbert Fields on his left; both men stood and each held a notepad and a pen at the ready. The imposing bulk of Banes County Sheriff Ted Arens displaced the area between one corner of the desk and the two walls nearest it. Near the other front corner of the desk stood the two officers who had brought the man and woman in. Three times already, Captain Pruitt had been on the telephone, but only one conversation had lasted for more than a few seconds. The talk bounced rapidly now, from one person to the next, heads bobbing in earnest along with gesticulations of every sort.

An officer carrying an armful of file folders approached

the desk sergeant and plopped the stack on the scarred wood two feet from the tapping ink pen.

"What's going down in there, sarge?"

"Not for sure, but it's heavy-duty. Haven't seen the captain's face turn that shade of red in a good while."

"What's Arens doing in there?"

"I just caught pieces of it when the lab tech ran out . . . had an evidence envelope with him. Said there's a guy holding a kid out in the county somewhere . . . the civilians are in the middle of it I'll bet. At least, that's what their faces look like to me. Whatever . . . look's like it's Arens' party . . . it's going down out in the county."

"Reckon he'll need help with it?"

"Who can say. He could get a S.W.A.T. team from the Highway Patrol if it comes to that. Probably won't though, likely the usual—liquor poured over a domestic situation. Wait until the guy sobers up enough to realize what he's doing . . . have a relative talk sense to him . . . you know the routine."

"Hey, sarge!" the voice boomed into the room from the half-opened door. "You hear what the lab jockey came out of there with?"

"No, what was it?"

"Hacked-off ear—human variety." The door banged shut.

The desk sergeant looked up at the officer whose hand rested on the stack of file folders. "I take it all back. He needs help."

The captain popped up from his chair and motioned for the man and woman to be escorted out by the two officers who had brought them in. The office quickly emptied behind them. Two sheriff's deputies walked into the station and spoke briefly with the sheriff before leaving with the man and woman. The sheriff and Captain Pruitt exchanged a few more words before Pruitt reached out and patted Arens' shoulder in a parting gesture, and then the big man pushed open the door and was gone.

Pruitt and the lieutenant who had been in the office with him stood ten feet from the desk sergeant, and he could hear their conversation.

"Think he'll get the Feds in on it?" the lieutenant asked.

"I think he should. . . . I would. He's got interstate transportation of a kidnap victim, and what must be a real loony tune with this preacher. They'd be down here from Kansas City in a big hurry. All he's gotta do is ask."

"I'm a little surprised the Charlotte cop wants in on it so bad. That's a pretty good-sized city. . . . I'm sure he's up to his ears with a lot of things."

The captain shook his head. "I'm not surprised. Sounds like he let this one get a little too close to him." He paused and huffed at his own words. "Listen to me, will you? I'd probably be up here on the first plane out, too, if it was me." He paused again for a moment before looking into the eyes of the lieutenant. "You don't have kids do you, Gilbert?"

The man shook his head in answer to the question.

"My son is twenty-four now, but I can still close my eyes and feel him sitting on my lap as a little boy . . . all soapy-smelling, in his pajamas, just before bedtime. I have a feeling Captain Stoner has a son. No, I'm not surprised at all, Gilbert."

The ringing of the telephone startled the woman sitting in the pastor's office despite the fact that she had just volunteered for the latest duty shift. It was two o'clock in the afternoon and she had spent most of last night in the sanctuary praying with the others; the cushioned chair had lulled her to drowsiness.

"Cedar Valley Baptist Church."

"Yes ma'am, this is Captain Marlon Stoner of the Charlotte Police Department. To whom am I speaking, please?"

"Uh—this is Lucy—Lucy Beltman." Her heart began to pound.

"Lucy, I have some precise instructions I want you to follow please." The voice was somehow friendly, reassuring, even though there could be no doubt that something of great import had happened. If there had been time before his flight, Stoner would have driven out personally, but there was not. And although he had several capable subordinates who could be trusted with the situation, he felt compelled to handle it himself.

"Yes, sir."

"Where are you located in the building?"

"In the pastor's office, we're taking turns . . ."

"Good. Do you know where Mr. Hunt is right now?"

"Well, yes, well, he was in the sanctuary just a little while ago. He was with Joanie and Norma, down on the front pew. I'm sure that's where he still is."

"Okay. I want you to go very calmly to him and get his attention, from as far away as possible. Maybe just point at him when he sees you and make a gesture like a phone to your ear . . . very calmly, all right? I just want to speak with him, nobody else."

"Yes, sir—I'll try. Hang on."

In less than a minute, Floyd Hunt's strained baritone came over the line. "What's happened, Captain?"

"Mr. Hunt, I've just spoken with the police in Wrightville, Missouri. They're dealing with a situation involving a kidnapped boy. He's being held in a house several miles out of town. Evidently, one of the perpetrators has had a change of heart. It's fairly complicated, but I don't have time to explain in detail. I fly out of here in twenty minutes. This guy knows the child came from Charlotte and he gave a very detailed description. It's him, Mr. Hunt, I have no doubt."

"Dear God . . . dear God . . ."

"I'm going to give it to you straight. There's a down side to this. The person holding him is . . . very unstable, according to our source. It will take some real pros to talk him out . . . or go after him, if that's what it comes to."

Stoner could hear the sound of Floyd's breathing as he

paused for a moment before continuing. "Your daughter will want to come out here, but it's not the thing to do, believe me. Just keep somebody on this phone and don't take any calls except from me or other officials. Just leave this line open. I'll be at the scene in less than three hours." He paused. "I don't intend to speak with anyone but you back here."

In the short silence that followed, Floyd Hunt felt the last sentence stab at him. Stoner meant that if the news was bad, it would fall on Floyd to handle breaking it to Joanie.

"Mr. Hunt, I hate to unload this on you, but the news might not—"

"I understand what you're saying."

"Yes, well—I'm sorry to be blunt."

"It's all right. The world is blunt sometimes."

"I'll call back as soon as I get a read on the situation."

The phone line was dead in Floyd's ear but he did not replace the receiver until the insistent screeching of a phone off the hook jolted him back to his senses. His brain churned with the incredible rush of what he had just heard. Part of him wanted to shout for joy; the boy was found. But the sinister fact remained—he was still far from safe. "Unstable," Stoner had labeled the faceless person who held his grandson. "Unstable." A professional-sounding word, no hard edges, a perfect word for a police captain to use under the circumstances, but . . . The images Floyd Hunt conjured up had very hard edges.

He cradled the receiver, moistened his lips, and drew his lungs full of air. He had news for the little army. He walked briskly out of the office.

Floyd returned to the sanctuary as discreetly as he had left it a few minutes before; neither Joanie nor Norma realized the reason for his brief absence. He leaned forward and placed a hand on the shoulders of the two women and whispered as he helped them to their feet. Several heads rose from the pews behind them, and Floyd turned to face them.

"We need to talk for a few minutes, folks. We'll be right back and let you know what's going on."

He led Joanie and Norma through the door and down the short corridor to the pastor's office.

"Excuse us for a few minutes please, Lucy. We'll regroup in the sanctuary and let you all know what's going on."

He waited for the woman to leave the office; the door closed softly behind her.

"Daddy, what's happened? What!?"

"I'm sorry, honey, but I wanted us to have some privacy." He paused, looking first at Joanie and then at Norma. "Stoner called. He's ninety-nine percent sure they've located Rooster."

"Where? Is he all right? Oh, God . . . please tell me he's all right!" The words tumbled one over another from Joanie's mouth.

"As far as they can tell—yes, but . . ."

"Where, Floyd? Where is he?" Norma asked, but there was no desperation in her voice; the words merely formed the question.

"A town in Missouri . . . Wrightville, he said. Must not be too big, I haven't heard of it. He's being held by somebody in a house a few miles out of town. Evidently, one of the people in on it has given up and come to the police."

"In on *what*, Daddy?"

"Honey, they don't know a lot of details yet. Stoner doesn't even know." Floyd wondered just what Stoner *did* know; he felt as if he had told Joanie a white lie. "He's flying out there right now."

Joanie bolted to her feet. "I'm going out there too! Daddy, help me find out when—"

Floyd took her in his arms and held her gently but firmly as he spoke. "Listen a minute, baby, let's think this out."

"Daddy! I can't stand to—"

"Shhhh . . . just listen for a second. We don't even know when the next flight might be going to St. Louis or Kansas

City. Beyond that, I doubt if there is a direct flight to this place. Stoner has law enforcement connections, and it will take him three or four hours, even with all that, to get there. Think of all the time you would be out of touch. That phone in there is ten seconds away, Joanie. He promised he would keep us on top of it."

He could feel the tension in her body ease slightly. Norma's arms encircled them both, and she spoke calmly and confidently.

"Daddy's right, baby. We can do more here together than we can chasing across the country in a plane. Look at what we've done already without even knowing where Rooster is. His whereabouts have been made known to us, and now we can direct our prayers like arrows, straight at the target—a man in a house, near a place called Wrightville, in the state of Missouri."

Floyd felt Joanie's head nod against his shoulder. "Come on, ladies, we have some good news to pass along to our little army. Then we're going to crank it up a notch in there."

Reverend Kassley sat on the basement floor outside the child's room; he had no memory of how he had come to this strange resting place. He was alone with himself now, his brain untainted by the monster who lived in the air, and he wondered how long this condition would last. More than anything else he had ever hoped for in his life—more even than the love from his mother which he had never known, back in what seemed to be another lifetime—Arvil Kassley hoped the demon would leave him alone for just a few minutes longer. Long enough for him to wrap his right hand around the revolver, send a bullet into his brain, and be free of the hideous thing. For if he could not accomplish this act, Arvil knew with a terrible certainty that the boy on the other side of the door would soon die horribly.

He gathered himself and stood on unsteady legs.

He looked down at the wrinkled clothing on his body, the

tail of his once-starched white shirt hanging out, trouser legs with only the remnants of a crease remaining. Except for the defiant face of the child and the tiny cross of fingers, he could remember little of the previous hours. It had been as if he were a spectator observing the confrontation between the child and the demon from a faraway place inside his head—watching, not even really caring about the outcome, just watching . . . watching a battle in the spirit world.

Arvil grabbed the handrail with his left hand and began to pull himself forward, up the twelve steps that led to the main level. The soft thumps of his feet on the treads were the only sounds in the house. Quietly now, past the kitchen table and into the carpeted living room, crept the tall figure. The door to the half bath passed his right shoulder, and then his bedroom was directly before him. Eight feet now—two long strides to the nightstand drawer and the cold, blue steel of the snub-nosed .38 caliber revolver. His heart hammered, piston-like, against his ribcage.

It was when he began to slide the drawer open that Arvil became aware of the demon's presence. Before he could grasp the gun, the drawer closed firmly on his hand, trapping it at the wrist. He could feel the gun brushing his fingertips, but he was powerless against the unseen force that held the drawer. The pressure increased gradually; Arvil's fingertips could no longer move over the revolver, and within seconds the sense of feel was gone from his fingers.

"Noooo . . . nooo, surely you do not believe that I would allow you to escape your highest duty." The familiar hiss of a voice filled the room.

The drawer opened slightly, allowing Arvil to pull his hand from the vise-like grip of the wood. The deep creases on the top and bottom of his wrist were bloodless, and the feeling in his fingers began to return. He slumped to the floor beside his bed.

"No, I have not harmed your hand. It will be strong and functional a bit later when we attend to the child. I am looking very forward to that." An ugly scratch of a laugh filled Arvil's ears and then his head as the demon became one with his being. There was no weakness in the man-thing as it arose from the floor. The long hand reached down into the drawer, bringing out the revolver. The cylinder swung open with a soft click. With one hand grasping the frame and the other securing the cylinder, cruel fingers twisted the parts against one another until a sharp, metallic pop filled the air, and then came the two thuds in the bottom of the drawer before the silence.

The man-thing's attention turned to more important matters now. It would soon be time to call his two helpers.

CHAPTER NINETEEN

The decision to seek the assistance of the Kansas City office of the F.B.I. had been made very quickly after ten more minutes of enlightening conversation with Jessie Pacely. Sheriff Ted Arens had never been one to allow petty jealousies to become a hindrance to sound law enforcement. There was no doubt in his mind that the life of a child teetered precariously on the brink of a grisly death.

Arens was proud of his department; there were many good men and women under his command, deputies worthy of trust, willing and able to wade into situations fraught with all manner of thorny problems. Arens and his deputies had successfully dealt with many volatile domestic situations, often involving guns, knives, liquor, drugs, hatred—the whole ugly bag full of horrors that haunted every county in the state. But the things he had heard in the last half hour . . . no, he had never dealt with anything like that. Or, more precisely, any*one* like the preacher who was not a preacher.

Along with the Pacelys, Arens waited with two deputies in his office for the telephone call from the Kansas City office of the Federal Bureau of Investigation. He had spoken with several people during his initial conversation, but the special investigator whose call he now awaited was in transit back to the office. A man named McCain would return his call, they said, the man with whom he really needed to speak. The tension in the small office was palpable; no one even bothered to attempt small talk. It was already far beyond that. The telephone on Arens' desk rang only once before he snatched it to his ear.

"Yeah, Donna, put him on." Arens fidgeted with the receiver, waiting. "Yes, this is Sheriff Ted Arens."

"Sheriff, I'm Agent Troy McCain. I've been briefed on your situation, and I believe I can help."

The bass voice was steady and professional, yet, strangely, Arens thought to himself, he was sure he could detect a hint of sadness around the edges of it.

"I'm very hopeful of that," Arens said.

"Can we get Mr. Pacely on the line with us, please?"

"Sure. Can I just put the phone on open intercom? Besides Pacely and his mother, there's only two of my deputies in the office."

"Yes, but close the door if it's not already."

"Okay," Arens said, "the floor is yours."

"Mr. Pacely, first allow me to say that I very much admire what you have done here. If we manage to avoid another tragedy, you will have had a great deal to do with it. I will do all I can to help you once this is over."

McCain did not wait for a reply. "Have you ever been a part of a sacrificial service in daylight hours?"

"No, sir."

"Good, that's what I expected. It means that we have at least five hours to get set up at the altar as well as the Kassley house and for you to brief me regarding the floor plan, outbuildings, trees and shrubbery, the sacrificial site itself, things like that—not to mention Kassley himself. What we do *not* have a great deal of time with is the possibility that he might call you soon to set up the exact time of the sacrifice. Am I correct?"

It seemed strange to Jessie that McCain used the word "sacrifice" so routinely, as if he were familiar with it.

"Yes—yes, sir. He doesn't call to set it up at any certain time."

"I want you there when he calls; if you're not, he might suspect something is wrong. Sheriff, I want your best female deputy in civilian clothes and a personal vehicle—not an unmarked—but a *personal* vehicle, to take Mr. Pacely and his mother home. I want a lot of waves and loud, friendly chatter when they part company, got it?"

"Yes. We can handle it," Arens said.

"Good. Now, I want you to wait at least ten minutes after he calls before you phone the sheriff. If he forgets to mention something, or if he's actually checking up on you—either way—it wouldn't look good if the phone was busy immediately after your conversation. Then phone Sheriff Arens' office and he'll have you picked back up. Hopefully, by then my team and I will be waiting in his office, and we'll decide on a plan. Another thing: if you can, get a good read on his mindset. Does he sound like usual? Does he say anything that doesn't fit—you understand?"

"Yes, sir."

"Don't say anything more than absolutely necessary to him. The less you say, the less likely he can get inside your head and snoop around. I imagine he's very good at that?"

"Very."

"Yes . . . okay then. Questions, Sheriff?"

"What's your ETA?"

"Between sixty-five and seventy minutes. You have a pen handy?"

"Yes."

McCain gave Arens a mobile telephone number.

"Let me know if Kassley calls before we arrive."

"You got it. We'll be waiting."

A click and then an electronic tone hummed for a second before Arens broke the connection.

Jessie and Allene Pacely had been home for almost an hour before the jangling of the telephone touched raw nerves. With the first ring, Allene locked her eyes on Jessie and made a quick folded-hand signal below her chin.

"Remember what the man said, son. Be calm as you can. I'll be praying for all I'm worth."

"I'm okay, Mom." He lifted the reciever from its plastic cradle after the third ring. "Hello."

"Jessie, all is in readiness here." Reverend Kassley's most powerful voice registered in Jessie's ear; it was the voice Kassley used when he was in total control.

"Yes, sir." It sounded normal enough to Jessie.

"I am very eager to proceed with this work, Jessie. I see no need to wait long past dusk. I will expect you here by seven-thirty. Is that a problem?"

"N—No, sir, that's fine." Jessie bit down on his lip and clenched his fist. Where had the rotten, lousy stutter come from? He could not believe his ears. The line was silent for five of the longest seconds Jessie had ever experienced. Allene's eyes were closed in prayer.

"I trust all is well with you, Jessie. This is hardly the time to waver."

Jessie's brain whirred in the instant before he replied. Would it be a simple "yes sir" and hope for the best as McCain had suggested, or was it necessary to risk a sentence or two?

"I'm okay, Reverend Kassley. It's just that—well, this is a big step for us tonight, and I can't help but be a little excited."

Sweet relief flooded through Jessie as the deep laugh told him he had made the correct decision.

"That is certainly understandable . . . yes, I'm more than a bit excited myself, Jessie. It should be a marvelous evening. Until then."

"Yes, sir—until then."

Jessie lowered the telephone and steadied himself with two long breaths as he took Allene's hand.

"You did fine, son, just fine." She looked up at the wall clock. "Ten minutes, he said. Then we'll call the sheriff."

The unmarked Ford van cruised east down Interstate 70 at a steady seventy-five miles per hour. Troy McCain sat in the front passenger seat, staring out the window at the lush Missouri landscape. With a thumb and forefinger, he stroked his square jawline and then passed a hand over close-cropped black hair. He wore a black moustache, neatly trimmed and extending only to the corners of his mouth. A strong nose swept upward to dark eyes—the only feature with a hint of softness. They were his mother's eyes, and though the years had hardened the rest of him, the softness of his mother's eyes refused to succumb. At six-feet-three-inches, the two hundred and ten lean pounds were twenty more than anyone would have guessed. Special Agent Troy McCain did not look to be fifty-two years old, but for several years, this knowledge had ceased to be even a point of minor pride. His body had become merely one more necessary tool of his trade, and it had served him well during more than one potentially deadly situation.

He was free to think his own thoughts now, at least for the next few minutes. The time of the intended sacrifice had just been relayed to him by Arens. There was no great hurry. The quiet business of his team members checking out their equipment in the compartment behind drifted forward in muffled clinks and rustles. He had heard the sounds of men preparing to fight other men many times—sounds at once simple, and yet profound, for it could never be just a simple thing when one human being contemplated the death of another. On this elegant late summer afternoon, with the rain clouds swept away into the east and the sun warm on the side of his face, McCain knew that it was very possible that human beings would die when darkness came to the house north of Wrightville, Missouri.

It was on such a summer night eight years before that a girl named Cynthia was lured away from a party at a friend's house by two teenage boys who held hands with Satan. They had taken her across the state line into Kansas where she was delivered to a satanic coven which gathered from time to time at the edge of a heavily wooded state park. When this particular coven assembled, McCain learned later, something—human or animal—always died horribly. On that night, it was a beautiful fifteen-year-old girl named Cynthia who perished. Positive identification of the body was made from dental records.

The last McCain had heard, the girl's mother was drifting through life in a quiet room in Hastings State Mental Institution. The father had committed suicide two days after the funeral. McCain had thrown himself into the case for the eighteen exhausting months it had taken to piece it all together. There were two meaningful convictions of a man and his wife, a couple who, for many years, had appeared to all their acquaintances as any ordinary couple—minding their own business, paying their bills, living their lives in an orderly fashion. How wrong the acquaintances had been, McCain thought to himself. How incredibly wrong.

In the years that followed McCain's involvement in the case, two great changes had taken place in his life: he had come to accept the reality of both Jesus Christ and Satan, and he pledged himself against the work of the latter. There were only two fellow Christians in the local office with him, although neither of the men worked directly with him. There had been sidelong glances and turned shoulders in the beginning, but McCain understood this and accepted it as a part of the Christian walk. Quietly and steadfastly, he performed his duties, and the issue of his "getting God," as he had overheard another agent refer to his conversion back then, had become an accepted part of him, unmistakable and unhidden, yet no longer a problem for either superior or subordinate. The simple fact was that Troy McCain was an extremely capable F.B.I. agent, Christian or not.

The six men who readied themselves behind him would follow him anywhere. McCain knew that they followed him now into a piece of hell on earth. He glanced at his watch. The piece of hell was ten minutes away.

Within thirty minutes of his arrival at the sheriff's office, Agent Troy McCain concluded that the situation was extremely grave. The basis for this conclusion was drawn mainly from his private conversation with Jessie Pacely. There was no doubt in McCain's mind that Kassley had presided over at least one human sacrifice. Pacely's detailed description of the horror, as well as his newfound conviction to prevent another, were proof positive for McCain. The revelations about Kassley were not shocking, not even the fact that the Satan worshiper was a pastor. McCain had long ago concluded that he was no longer shockable; there was simply no set of circumstances imaginable that would cause him surprise. Such was the depth of darkness to which Satan could lure a dedicated follower.

The bits of knowledge that stuck in McCain's throat like sharp bones were Pacely's descriptions of Kassley's drastic and frequent changes in facial expression, voice tone, and mannerisms—changes which caused Pacely to say that it seemed as if there were really two people inside the man. On two prior occasions, McCain had been exposed to demon-possessed persons. The most recent involved a young woman who had been a satanic high priestess. During the course of a ninety minute prayer struggle, McCain and a minister watched as her fingers curled like claws and swiped at them. The curses which spewed from her foaming mouth were vile beyond description. A shudder passed down his spine with the memory of it all.

Yes, it could very well be that Reverend Kassley's soul actually belonged to something from the dark world. And if this was indeed the case, McCain knew that a company of Marines would make no difference in the outcome if the boy was not brought out of the windowless, isolated basement room that Pacely had described. Of course, at this point, there was no reason to doubt that the child would be taken to the usual sacrificial site. They *had* to take him there. McCain shuddered at the thought of a scenario involving the use of the basement room as the killing place.

Within minutes, McCain would learn of details at the Kassley place. A two-man spotting team had been dispatched immediately. Aerial photographs provided by the local Department of Agriculture had revealed good spotting sites from one hundred to two hundred yards away from the house. With twenty power spotting scopes aimed at the house, it would be very easy for his men to assess the situation.

McCain watched with Ted Arens and Jessie Pacely as the tall camo-clad agent half trotted toward the office. McCain waved the man in before he had a chance to knock on the glass.

"Let's have it, Mark."

"Sir, I've just been in radio contact with Starkes and Jiminez. They've covered the house—a full three-sixty—and nothing's moving. The window shades are up. They have the main floor plan down solid, but there's no windows at basement level . . . just no way to know what's going on down there. Our sound pick-ups are negative. The place is—" he started to say "dead" but swallowed the word, "real quiet, sir."

"Okay, Mark. Tell them to stay put and keep you posted. What about the sacrificial site by the house ruins?"

"Looks good there, sir. Dunleavy and Cox report that the woods line is within forty-five to sixty yards from the stone. Two partial walls of the old house within twenty yards. That's where we need to spring him, sir; there are several options open to us."

"Good, Mark. Stay on the horn."

"Yes, sir." The door banged shut.

McCain rubbed two fingers across the short stubble on his chin for a moment before he looked up at the other two men. He looked down to the desk top again as he made a final review of the situation. He could set it up according to the book—perimeter coverage, telephone communication if possible, speaker system if not, try to talk him out before they even brought the child out. Some chance with that, possibly, but it was a long shot at best and no shot at all if Reverend Kassley had a helper from hell inside his head.

The thought of a silent assault only flickered through McCain's mind. Even with the main floor plan down pat and a perfect approach, they might not get down the basement stairs to the holding room quickly enough. Their chances of overpowering both Kassley and Livingston before the child was harmed were infinitesimal. The decision to allow Livingston to enter the house unalarmed was relatively easy. If Pacely was right about him, Livingston had grown very fond of his participation in Reverend Kassley's bloody rituals. Without a doubt, Kassley would know he had been found out if Livingston did not show up for this most special of occasions. Kassley would possibly tolerate Pacely's absence—he had shown signs of cold feet last time. Still, it would be very risky, especially after what Pacely had said during his last phone conversation with Kassley.

McCain shook his head silently. It was really a simple thing to weigh out—Pacely had it right, he had to go back into the basement with the madman to ensure that the child would be brought out. McCain could not take a chance on spooking Kassley into holing up in the basement. When he looked up, Pacely was staring directly at his face.

"I told you it's the only way," Jessie said softly.

McCain nodded. "I know, son . . . I know." He glanced at Arens. "Sheriff, would you get Mrs. Pacely in here, please?" Allene was escorted into the office and seated beside Jessie, who reached over and took her hand in his. Arens closed the door behind him and stood near it.

"Mrs. Pacely, I am sure you are aware of the situation by now. It is a most difficult situation, to be sure, but I have dealt with worse. Now, I know that you want Jessie to be forever separated from Kassley—rightly so, ma'am, so would any parent in your shoes."

He paused to allow Allene a chance to speak, but she sat stone-faced and silent, and McCain knew that she was aware of his intentions for her son.

"Mrs. Pacely, it all really boils down to one hard fact: the child *must* be brought out of that house. If for any reason things go sour and Kassley keeps him in the basement . . . well, we just cannot have it turn out that way."

Before McCain could continue, Allene raised a hand to silence him. "Mr. McCain . . . I know where you're leading with all this, and I don't mind telling you that I don't like it one bit."

"Mom—"

"No, Jessie, it's all right," McCain said. He turned his head to Allene. "Mrs. Pacely, I won't be dishonest with you; I hope very much that Jessie does try to see this thing through, but I will not—cannot—force him to do it. Technically, he is actually within custody as a possible accessory to homicide, and as such, is in my care. I'm out on a bit of a limb here, too, but it's my call and my responsibility. I think it's reasonable to believe that Jessie can go back in there and play along with their plan long enough to clear the house. And once he's out of the house and at the altar site, I can tell you that I'm ninety-nine percent sure he will be in the clear."

"How can you be so sure, Mr. McCain? This Kassley is very bad—worse than you can imagine . . ."

"Yes, ma'am, I have no doubt he is very bad, but I have had considerable experience with his kind. I'm no stranger to Satan's followers."

It was the way he said it that gave Allene a touch of confidence; there was no fear, no awe, just the strong assurance that he knew of what he spoke.

"Kassley has never used firearms during these rituals, and the knife, or knives, that he and Livingston carry will not be in a ready position when we spring the trap. When we start the action, all Jessie has to do is run toward us; it will be over within a matter of seconds. My people are extremely good at this, Mrs. Pacely."

"I—I can accept that—what you say about it once it gets out in the open, but what really worries me is the part *inside* the house—the part where your men can't help anybody. What if Kassley . . . somehow . . . sees through Jessie? What then?"

"I can't deny that as a possibility, but—"

"Mom, I can handle it—now. After last night—I can pull it off. She changed everything."

"She?" The word shot from McCain's mouth. "Is there someone else who knows about all this?"

"Well, yes, I suppose you could say she does," Allene answered. "We had a—very timely—visit from a lady in our congregation last night. She seemed to know that Kassley wasn't what he pretended to be, and—"

"What is her name, ma'am?"

"Fairchild—we really didn't know her well at all. Gladys Fairchild is her name. I don't see . . ."

"If anyone knows about Kassley's actions, there is a chance that they, or someone they have told, might do something that would jeopardize our plans. We can't take any chances at this point. Sheriff, would you run this down for me? Get hold of the church secretary . . . some member of the congregation . . . someone who can get an address on this woman and go seal her off. Make sure she hasn't told anyone else. If she has, you'll have to find them, too, and quickly."

"We'll take care of it right now," Arens said as he reached for the doorknob.

McCain turned back to Jessie and Allene. "I'm going to give you a few minutes alone. Think it all through once more, and then decide for sure, one way or the other. You both have to be one hundred percent behind this, or we'll just take our chances that Jessie's absence won't spook him. Simple as that."

Five minutes later, as McCain sipped coffee from a paper cup, his eye caught movement from inside the glass office. Jessie took his mother in his arms as they stood, and when he locked on McCain's eyes, he gave a thumbs-up sign with his right hand.

CHAPTER TWENTY

The two sheriff's deputies popped out of the tan-colored patrol car and walked toward the front door of the white house at the end of the quiet street. The older deputy, a tall, ruddy-faced man in his early fifties, waved his left arm, pointing to the neighboring houses located on the same side of the street.

"Guy named Fulton owns all these rental houses here. Four or five of them I think. You know the guy . . . has a couple of shoddy apartment complexes out in the country . . . bad reputation."

"Yeah, I know him," the other man said, "about half a jerk, best I recall."

"More than half," the older man chuckled. He wrapped his knuckles sharply on the front door, while his partner walked to the corner of the house and then back to the small front porch. There were no sounds from inside the house.

"Check around back, Charlie," the older deputy instructed. The man disappeared around one corner of the house and returned around the opposite corner.

"They gave us the wrong address, Jed. This place is empty. I could see through the curtains . . . no furniture in there . . . light meter's at a dead stop too."

"Aw, for cryin' out loud," Jed huffed, "why can't people get the simple things right? We're in the middle of a big time kidnap, the F.B.I. is in town, and nobody can even jot down a lousy street address. Let's go radio back in and see if they can get it right."

When the deputies turned toward the car, they noticed a girl across the street standing astraddle her bicycle. Her gaze shifted between the men and the white house as she thoughtfully tongued a paper-stemmed candy from cheek to cheek. Jed nodded to her as he approached the car door.

"Hi there, honey."

"Is she okay?" the girl called out softly. Jed stopped beside the car and glanced at Charlie. Together, they crossed the street to the girl.

"Is who okay, honey?" Jed asked.

"Her," the girl pointed to the white house.

"You think somebody lives there, huh?"

The girl nodded in reply as the ball of candy smacked from her lips. "I wave to her. We're friends, sort of."

"You're sure you've seen her go in *that* house?"

"Yep. She always waves back and smiles at me."

"Do you know her name?"

"Huh-uh. We didn't talk. Is she okay?"

"Well . . . yeah, I'm sure she is, honey. We just wanted to talk to her for a minute. No big deal. Wait here for a minute, okay?"

The two men walked back across the asphalt street and onto the front porch. Jed tested the doorknob.

"It's unlocked. Help me remember to call old Fulton. Place is probably trashed." He pushed the door open and stuck his head inside. "Anyone home?" he shouted. "Sheriff's deputy here."

Both men stepped inside the house and walked through the small rooms.

"No doubt about it, Charlie, there hasn't been a soul in this place since the last tenant. The girl must have seen some old bag lady wander in and out of here a couple of times. That's all I can figure." He shook his head.

"That's got to be it, Jed. I'm just surprised she hasn't trashed it up some. Neat as a pin everywhere."

"Well, we know we got at least one tidy bag lady in town. Let's go call in now."

When they stepped out on the porch, the girl with the bicycle was nowhere in sight.

"Doesn't mind very well, does she?" Jed laughed.

"Didn't matter anyway, partner. That ain't the lady we're looking for."

Charlie leaned against the patrol car and studied the old, tree-lined street while Jed radioed in. Three minutes later, Jed unfolded himself from the car seat and stood, his left arm draped over the top of the door.

"Dispatcher called the woman from the church back . . . we're at the right house. She must have moved out within the last day or so, but the kid sure didn't talk like she knew about it."

"What's it matter, Jed? Seems pretty clear she's out of the picture around here. That's all that matters to us . . . no problem."

"I'll go along with that. If she's gone, she's gone." He shrugged his shoulders and turned his hands palms up. "Surely Mr. F.B.I. can find something more productive for us to do than chase after old women. Let's ride."

The young deputy sheriff who drove Marlon Stoner from the Wrightville airport filled in very few of the blanks regarding the situation at Kassley's house. At first, Stoner was mildly irritated with the deputy's lack of detailed knowledge, but he soon realized that the young man could hardly be expected to know such things. Stoner's irritation was now self-directed; there was no reason to bark at a stranger, even if he was a law enforcement officer of lesser experience and rank. The deputy sat stone-faced behind the wheel of the patrol car; he had no intention of speaking again unless spoken to.

"What's your name, son?"

"Perry, Mike Perry."

"Mike, I apologize. I'm not usually a jerk. This one's got to me more than I'd like to admit—the kid and his family . . ."

"Forget it. Everybody's a little edgy around here. You'll fit right in."

They both laughed quietly at the cold humor.

"This F.B.I. agent in charge, does he seem like he's got his act together?"

"That much I do know. He just took over like some kind of general. Sheriff's perfectly happy to let him too. We don't get many deals like this around here. He brought a team that looks like something left over from Nam. Van full of guns and gadgets, one of the guys told me. I haven't had a close look in it yet."

"About what I'd expect," Stoner said. "I've been around the Feds before."

"You think they'll just load up and charge in there after the kid?"

"Doubt it. Not with the kind of guy this Kassley sounds like."

"Some deal, huh? A *preacher,* of all people." The incredulity in his voice made him sound even younger.

"To tell you the truth, Mike, I'm not shockable anymore. You stay in this line of work for many years, you won't be either."

They rode in silence for a couple of minutes.

"How much longer?"

"Three more blocks." The deputy tossed a quick smile at Stoner. "Then you can talk to the general himself."

Troy McCain was standing beside the desk in Sheriff Arens' office when he looked up to see who was walking through the main door into the station. Stoner's eyes darted about for only a moment before they found McCain's, and although the two men had never before seen one another, each knew instantly who the other was. McCain motioned with his hand for Stoner to enter the office. During the six seconds that passed before Stoner reached the door, McCain's brain processed initial bits of information: excellent physical bearing—neat, compact, hard-looking, eyes that beamed with a controlled intensity; the tiny bulge of the handgun and shoulder holster invisible to the untrained eye; no wedding ring, probably divorced.

Stoner opened the door and stepped inside the office as McCain extended his hand. "Troy McCain, Captain Stoner. Just Troy suits me fine."

"Marlon for me."

"Sit, please." McCain waited for him to sit down before taking the sheriff's desk chair. They were alone in the small office. Before McCain could speak again, Stoner raised his right hand slightly.

"Shoot," McCain said.

"Just this. I haven't the slightest desire to notch my gun handle here. The last thing I want is to be a hindrance. I'm a good cop—have been for a very long time, and I'll do anything I can to help. I'm smart enough to know that there probably isn't much I can do, and I'm honest enough to tell you I came because I got too close to this one."

He paused and held McCain's eyes with little lasers. "All I want is to take this kid back to Charlotte with every drop of blood still in his body."

McCain nodded. "I could have guessed all that, but it's good to hear you say it. Let me lay it out. I suppose you already know about the intended satanic sacrifice?"

Stoner nodded. "I've not had much experience with . . . cults."

It was the way he spoke the last word, as if they were discussing pesky juveniles who spray painted tombstones on Halloween night. McCain slowly shook his head. "There are cults . . . and there are *cults*, Marlon. A true satanic worshiper is as close to a human boogeyman as you can get in this life. I have had considerable experience. Believe me, I know what I'm talking about."

Stoner did not reply.

"Best case scenario goes like this—all thanks to our insider, the Pacely boy. I don't know what turned him around, but without him, me and you aren't even sitting here and the Starmann boy is sacrificed before midnight. Maybe nobody ever even finds the pieces."

McCain paused for a moment and glanced up at the ceiling tiles. "Whatever. He did turn around, and we know everything he knows, which is a lot. He's going to the Kassley house as planned. Just has to. I don't like it, but he just has to. He doesn't show . . . Kassley smells a rat . . . maybe just stays in the house and does the boy there. There's another accomplice named Livingston who we have to let alone for the same reason. Everything has to appear normal so that they bring the boy *out* of the house. That's the key to everything—*out* of the house. He's got him in a corner basement room, no windows, one door . . . might as well be in a bank vault down there. But once they bring him out and head for the sacrificial site, it's a whole new game.

"The house area isn't good . . . no close cover to amount to anything, but it doesn't really matter. The sacrificial site is perfect—ringed by woods, forty yards max, plus partial walls of an old house ruin. We'll be set up along the route—it's very short—and track them by radio. I've got a sniper with ice water in his veins and a night-scoped AR-15. He can drill a fifty-cent piece tossed in the air at that distance. We jump 'em first time there's good separation between Kassley and the boy. Pacely covers the boy with his body. If Kassley's hands don't go straight up in the air, my guy head shoots him. Same with Livingston—one little move toward the boy, he goes down too. Party's over."

Stoner nodded. "Worst case scenario is if they hole up in the basement then, huh?"

"Yeah."

"Seems to me if this guy Pacely can hold it together, it's a lock. Is he solid?"

Chambers **185**

"Feels solid to me. I have been wrong, but not many times. He's not really the one I'm worried about though."

Stoner furrowed his brow at McCain.

"You don't quite have the whole worst case deal yet. Do you believe in demonic possession?"

Stoner's eyes narrowed. "I believe in schizophrenia."

"No, Marlon, I'm not talking clinical definitions here. I know all about that too. I'm talking about *demons*—living things—inside someone's head."

"Well—I, uh—I saw that movie several years ago. What was it . . ."

"The Exorcist."

"Yeah, I saw that, but . . ."

"But it was just a good scary movie, right?"

Stoner shifted his weight in the chair. "Look, I've dealt with some very bad people before—crazy people, some of them—but, they were just—people. Very bad people."

"We'll talk sometime about all that, when we have more time. I won't argue with you now. But Pacely has given me a detailed portrait of this guy, and I can't totally suppress this ugly little thought about him having a bloody helper whispering in his head. And *that,* my fellow cop, is the worst case scenario."

"Even if this demon thing is real, wouldn't Kassley still want to go to the place and do the boy?"

"Most likely, yes. As long as the demon didn't sense anything amiss . . . see through Pacely's act maybe. You have to understand that a demon is a totally distinct being—with an incredibly powerful mind of its own. A mind tied to the greatest evil mind in the world."

"And whose would that be?"

"That would be Satan's, Marlon. That would be Satan's."

The orderly bustle of activity leaked into the office from the outer area but neither man heard the sound; each pair of unblinking eyes held the other. In the few seconds that passed, Marlon Stoner learned beyond all doubt that Troy McCain had fought enemies of children, the likes of which Stoner had never imagined. The knowledge at once frightened and encouraged him. Only a man who had fought and survived in the darkest pits of earth could be trusted to enter there again. Stoner hoped fervently that it would not come to that.

"Troy, knowing how you feel about that kind of thing now, let me tell you where the boy's mother and grandparents are right now. I think you'd probably want to know."

"Please, tell me."

"They and a bunch of other church members are sitting in a small church house just outside of Charlotte . . . praying for the boy. I can tell you that they feel very strongly about their—efforts."

"Thank you—very much for that, Marlon. The power of what they do is infinitely stronger than anything my men or I can do. I don't claim to know many things about this life with absolute certainty, but I do claim to know that."

Stoner lowered his gaze to the desk top. McCain could see the big wall clock beyond the glass boundaries of the office. The red hand swept casually, yet relentlessly over the black tick marks as the seconds evaporated from the late afternoon.

"I'm sure you've got a line open down there?"

"Yeah, supposed to be," Stoner said.

"Do something for me, will you, Marlon?"

"Name it."

"We've got about an hour before we leave to get set up. Sometime before we leave here, will you call down there and mention me and Pacely—Jessie Pacely, by name. It's important to me that they know us by name."

Stoner nodded silently.

"And I know this won't sound quite right to you, but I want you to tell them Kassley's name. It's Arvil—Arvil Kassley. Tell them that he may be possessed by a demon."

"What—uh, whatever you say, sure—but it seems to me that—uh, it might . . ."

"Scare them, Marlon?"

"Yes."

"No, it won't do that. It will just make them pray with more power. They'll understand, don't worry." He paused for a moment. "You didn't mention the father. Divorced?"

Stoner shook his head. "Dead. Just last spring—heart attack. One more reason this is all so deep under my skin."

"I understand . . . believe me, I do."

CHAPTER TWENTY-ONE

When Rooster awoke, he had no idea how long he had slept. The soothing white light still washed the room. The boy marveled at its presence; he had only a vague memory of the light that had come almost simultaneously with the deep sleep. His recollection of the encounter with the man-thing was equally fuzzy. His lips parted, tongue dryly probing the corners of his mouth as his thirst raged. He peered at the floor in the adjacent corner of the room, knowing that the water cup that sat there would be empty. But it was not. To his amazement, he could see water brimming near the rim, and he scurried across the floor on hands and knees. He took the cup in both hands and raised it to his lips; the water was cool and sweet as he gulped it down.

Tomorrow night. He did remember that. The words, the promise, of the man-thing came back to him and Rooster wondered how long he had been asleep. How near was tomorrow night? Could it already *be* tomorrow night? Suddenly the silence began to close around him and despite the strange light, the dread of things to come filled his mind. There would be others who would also come, the man-thing had promised. Others—one of whom would be even stronger than the monster with the snarling face that took over the man.

Just before the chill in Rooster's heart caused him to tremble, the voice of the woman came gently to him. "You are not alone, child. I will be with you in the hour to come." Just as before, the voice was comforting, soothing, and Rooster was again unfazed by the fact that it was not attached to any visible body. But something was different this time. There was an element of strength infused in the words, as if the voice knew that "the hour to come" would be one of struggle. After a few moments' reflection on the two simple sentences, the boy was certain that his ordeal would soon be over—one way or the other. He drew his knees up to his chest and wrapped his arms around his legs. He would pray them again, the beautiful words of the Lord's Prayer, slowly and with conviction—just as his father had taught him, two years before death took him. Only now, the boy decided, when he came to the place where Jesus had said "deliver *us* from evil," he would substitute the word *me*.

So it was that nine-year-old Rooster Starmann, on the night of his intended murder, sat calmly on the hard basement floor and prayed the Lord's Prayer with as much fervor as any mortal who ever lived.

And above him, on the wooden floor just beyond the thin Sheetrock ceiling, steady footsteps fell in heavy cadence as the man-thing enjoyed thoughts of the coming darkness.

Reverend Kassley and Razzom listened intently for the crunch of vehicle tires on the county road at the end of the driveway. It was twenty minutes past seven; Wesley and Jessie were never late on a sacrificial night. Their black robes were neatly folded and placed on the kitchen table. Reverend Kassley had already donned his robe, and now his hands fondled the familiar objects in the deep left pocket. The leather sheath of the dagger, the silver chalice, and the pentagram sent welcome sensations to his fingertips, but the tingling that came from the new instrument in his right pocket surpassed anything he had ever dreamed possible.

He withdrew it and studied it in the fading light. It was a perfectly marvelous straight razor; the yellowed ivory of the old handle had great character, and the blade surface was generous—over four inches of steel edge, honed to perfection by his own strong hands. The man-thing smiled with the knowledge that it had never been put to the use for which it was now intended.

The sound of an approaching vehicle filled his ears now, and as he listened to the tires turn into the driveway, the sound of a second car could be heard, its big engine rumbling in the still air. Reverend Kassley was most pleased that his helpers had arrived precisely on time; it was a good sign, he surmised—the promise of an eventful evening. The two vehicles slid quietly to the usual hiding place behind the barn. As they approached the house, Wesley walked a few paces in front of Jessie as Reverend Kassley studied their faces. He swung the back door open and bowed slightly with a sweep of his arm as they stepped inside.

"Welcome, brethren. A fine evening to serve him, is it not?"

"That it is, Arvil," Wesley answered.

Jessie nodded in affirmation, but his glimpse at Kassley's face was too perfunctory, and he regretted the imperfect beginning. Jessie's stomach knotted even tighter and he strained for control; already, there was an obstacle to overcome. Hopefully, Kassley would pass it off as nerves.

"Calm yourself, Jessie. Breathe deeply and focus your mind on the duties to come. It will be the purest pleasure of your life. I promise." Kassley smiled thinly as Jessie forced himself to meet the hard eyes.

"Yes, sir. I'll be fine when the time comes."

"I certainly hope you will, Jessie. I have a great deal of trust invested in you. Do not allow thoughts of failure to even enter your mind."

He pointed to the robes on the table. "Prepare yourselves. We will meditate and pray as night falls."

Marlon Stoner punched in the digits of the telephone number from memory. Before the end of the first ring, the woman's voice came over the line.

"Cedar Valley Baptist."

"Yes, this is Captain Stoner. Please get Floyd Hunt on the line for me."

Stoner waited through twenty seconds of silence. "Captain Stoner, what's happened there?"

"Mr. Hunt, the situation is basically unchanged concerning Darren, but there is other information I need to pass on to you all."

"Let's have it."

"This is going to sound crazy, I know—but—uh, the man holding Darren is the pastor of a local church."

"Dear God Almighty!"

"I know, it's hard to believe, but we're absolutely positive. One of his accomplices had a change of heart, without which we still wouldn't know a single thing. It's believed that this pastor's into satanism, or that he might even be—demon possessed." The words did not come easily from Stoner.

Several moments were passed in silence. "What else?"

"Actually, the F.B.I. agent in charge here asked me to call you. He's a—religious man, Mr. Hunt, a deeply religious man. He wants you all down there to—pray for him by name. His name is Troy McCain. He wants you to remember the young man who has switched sides. His name is Jessie Pacely, and he will play an extremely important role tonight. He's going to go back into the house tonight as originally planned."

"What do you mean 'originally planned'? *What* was originally planned?" Floyd felt his skin begin to crawl as his mind fought against the answer he knew he would hear.

"Mr. Hunt, I don't really think it matters exactly what they plan to do, we're not . . ."

"They plan to sacrifice him, don't they?" The words were like a scream in Stoner's ear even though they were calmly spoken, and he gathered himself for a moment before answering.

"That's, uh, what the insider claims, Mr. Hunt. You'll have to decide whether or not to tell everything to the others."

"That's not a difficult decision to make, Captain. Knowledge, however terrible, is power to those who pray. Prayers are most effective when aimed directly."

"Well, as I said, it's your call."

"Are you going out there to the house with them tonight?"

"Yes, I am."

"Then we'll pray for you, too, Captain Stoner. The foes aligned against you are powerful beyond your worst nightmares."

For an instant, Stoner felt the urge to reply, but it passed quickly and he said nothing.

"You've forgotten to give me one name, Captain."

"So I have. His name is Kassley, Arvil Kassley."

McCain and Stoner crouched in the gathering gloom at the edge of the woods line, one hundred yards from Reverend Kassley's handsome white house. The camouflage fatigues provided for Stoner were nearly a size too large, but the ill-fitting clothing was of no concern to him. His eyes were riveted on the benign-looking house.

Behind them on the quiet county road, a half mile to the west, Sheriff Ted Arens sat in civilian clothes behind the wheel of his personal car at one of the roadblocks. Two of his deputies, also in civilian clothes, waited in line behind him in their personal vehicles. A half mile east of the house, three more deputies were stationed in the same fashion at the other roadblock. Any driver who approached the house from either direction would be quietly turned around, with one of the county officers completing the trip past the Kassley house. In this manner, the normal traffic pattern would be simulated while insuring against any inadvertant intrusions into Reverend Kassley's plans for the evening.

McCain's gaze swept over the house and yard, left to right, right to left, his head barely moving. The decision to set up at the house was easily made. If there was trouble anywhere, it would almost certainly be here. And then there was the trim, dark-eyed agent named Dunleavy who was in charge of the remainder of the team at the sacrificial site. It was a great comfort to McCain, though haunting and sad, to know that Roger Dunleavy would trade his own life for the safety of Darren Starmann without a moment's hesitation. The same could be said of any of the other team members; the same could be said of McCain. He no longer felt any pride in this knowledge, and he doubted if the other men did either. In the end, if it should ever come down to that, it would simply be a matter of making a proper trade. It would be the right thing to do.

It was an unspoken thing—the death-trade pact—that they all lived with. Sometime, possibly this very night, the dark side which had the power to devour a man's soul could force a trade. It was a hard fact of their lives.

McCain turned his head to the left and waited for the agent peering through the night scope atop his AR-15 rifle to lower the weapon. As the rifle slowly made its way down, McCain looked a silent question at the man. The bill of his cap knifed through the air in three short, precise sideways movements which told McCain nothing moved inside the house. Stoner watched the exchange between the two men and then shifted his weight to his other knee in an attempt to find some semblance of comfort. It could be another hour, perhaps two, before they came out of the house. Stoner forced himself to breathe steadily and deeply; the heavy, green smells of the Missouri night were lovely things, and he was sorry that he could not appreciate them. On another night, he promised himself, he would separate each fragrance and enjoy its offerings.

But not this night. As the darkness thickened around Reverend Kassley's house, Stoner could only watch and wait and worry.

Rooster had prayed the Lord's Prayer over a hundred times before he heard footsteps falling on the wooden staircase, and his heart began to pound with the knowledge that more than one man was descending to the basement. He wondered if he would look into the eyes of the normal man or if he would see the man-thing. When he heard the sound of the doorknob turning, the soft, white light faded away and for an instant, the room was dark. Quickly, the light was replaced with the eerie glow from the two tall candles held in the right hands of two of the men. They wore robes with hoods over their heads; the boy could not distinguish any facial features, but when the tall one in the middle spoke, Rooster knew that it was the man-thing.

"So, how has our brave little Christian boy endured the darkness?"

Before Rooster's hands could come together and form the finger cross, a dark blur of motion shot at him and two vise-like hands closed about his wrists.

"Speak but a word, and I will tear your tongue from your mouth."

Rooster's hands were jerked behind him and bound with coarse twine. The man-thing reached into the left pocket of the robe and pulled out a roll of white adhesive tape, ripping loose a three inch piece and covering the child's mouth.

"Now, that is much better. I do not suspect that you desired conversation anyway." A scratchy laugh filled the room as Rooster felt his body being dragged across the floor toward the small bed, but it was a faraway thing, and the sensations were not hurtful or worrisome. He could hear the sweet voice of the woman now, singing softly, "Jesus loves me, this I know . . . ," and his mind sought other places to be—places where his mother and grandparents smiled and tended to his needs, places where his father's wide smile and bright eyes shined at him like a beacon.

He could see another great candle now, much taller and whiter than the ones held by the men who had come for him, and the light from it was a wondrous thing to behold. The warmth from its flame filled him and soothed him and it was all he could see now. And though his eyes remained open, he could not see the man-thing, nor could he feel its hands, as they tore his clothing from his body.

"Come closer now," it said to Wesley and Jessie.

The two candle flames moved toward the bed, but one moved steadily and the other did not.

"Kneel."

Closer now, the light from Jessie's candle found the edge of the bed and then the flesh of Darren Starmann and when it did, Jessie could no longer control the pace of his breathing. The candle flame trembled visibly, and he could feel Reverend Kassley's eyes seek his.

"Jessie?"

Jessie's brain whirred and his teeth were clenched as he struggled to find words that would defuse the situation, but he could not.

"Jessieeee?" Louder this time, and menacing. "Look at me."

In that incredibly clear, transcendent moment when the demon knew Jessie's heart, the horror of a thousand nightmares hung in the close air of the room. The red eyes that bore into Jessie's were not those of a man, and he knew that he had only moments to live. Regret flooded through him, and he would have traded fifty more years of life if only he could talk with his mother for an hour. He waited, frozen in place, as the interminable moments passed in a haze of fear. The man-thing lowered his head and looked at the claw-like right hand with fingernails that had not been cut in two weeks.

The first blow was open-handed, the force of it hurling Jessie backwards into the wall, but he did not lose consciousness. With a swiftness beyond anything Wesley Livingston had ever witnessed, the man-thing sprang on top of Jessie and covered his face with the open hand. The claw-like hand moved slowly, downward from Jessie's forehead, as guttural sounds mingled with Jessie's weeping pleas.

Unconsciousness came, deep and merciful, as the whirling kaleidoscopes of bright reds and oranges slowed and faded into muted grays and whites. The hand continued downwardly to the point of his chin, and when the man-thing stood, it held Jessie's body by one arm like a limp cloth doll. The great head turned toward Wesley and in the faint light he could barely discern the tight smile.

"How is your resolve, Wesley?"

Wesley attempted to reply, but he could not. He nodded his head vigorously.

"The traitor no doubt has friends outside. We will hold the service here, Wesley—after I return him to his friends."

It moved easily with the body in its hand, stepping to the place where Jessie's fallen candle still glowed. It quickly stamped out the tiny fire before turning again to Wesley.

"It would be a terrible thing to burn, would it not?" It laughed and walked toward the open door.

At nearly the same instant, Troy McCain and the rifleman with the night scope spotted the movement of the white front door. Before the rifleman could open his mouth to whisper, the fingers of McCain's left hand jutted into the air and silenced him. Stoner saw it now; the door was slowly swinging open, but the blackness inside the house showed no sign of a person.

McCain whispered calmly to the agent beside him; the rifle was now trained on the open doorway. McCain was now looking through a spotting scope of his own. "I don't like this. Pacely said they would use the back door. If we have to shoot here, I'll number the targets: one, two, three, in the order they come out. Got it? My command *only.*"

"Got it."

McCain did not have to make any decisions. When he heard the strange laughter spew from the doorway, he knew with a terrible certainty that there would be no battle with guns. The voice that shrieked into the night made Stoner's hair stand on end as if electrified.

"Before they put him on the slab, let his mother see his face!"

Even without the aid of a night scope, Stoner knew that the dark lump which hurtled through the air from the doorway was a human being. It fell to the ground after reaching a height of at least ten feet, bouncing and skidding to a halt a hundred feet from the house.

"Dear God! Dear God, be with me now," McCain said aloud as he sprang to his feet. He pointed to the rifleman as the commands shot rapid-fire from his mouth. "David, cover the other two while they go get him. Then radio Dunleavy to get down here and bring the EMTs forward. If Pacely's alive and they leave with him, I want another rescue vehicle and team on the way *now!*"

"Yes sir."

"Under no circumstances does anyone follow me in there!" He had trotted three steps toward the house when Stoner shouted at him.

"I'm going in there with you."

"*No!* I don't have time to argue, Marlon. The fight's not in your world any longer. Help with Pacely."

Stoner stood in stunned silence as McCain's form grew ever smaller in the darkness.

CHAPTER TWENTY-TWO

When McCain reached the front porch steps, he sat on the second tread and ripped at his boot laces, snatching them through the eyelets. The door stood open, its hinges creaking softly as the night breeze nudged against it. His sock-covered feet made no sound as they crept into the dark house. His left hand engulfed the little New Testament just retrieved from the wide shirt pocket. He strained to hear any sounds from below, but the silence was heavy and foreboding. The inside of the house was darker than the outdoors and his eyelids snapped impatiently as his pupils dilated.

McCain began moving to his left, the details of his team member's floor plan drawing etched into his brain. Maybe fifteen feet through the living room, dark shapes of furniture guiding his path. On through the doorless opening into the kitchen, the silence broken only by the pounding of his heart. Past the edge of the cabinets, his fingertips brushing the counter. Eight more feet over the vinyl-covered floor and then it was before him—the open door to the basement. McCain felt the cooler air drift toward him as his right foot sought the first step. Beads of perspiration leaked through his eyebrows and he blinked against the sting.

It was the eighth tread that squeaked, but it did not matter.

Razzom had been waiting patiently since McCain had crossed the threshold of the front door.

"Hurry now, brave hero, there are four more steps, and I am growing impatient."

McCain sucked in his breath at the sound of the demon's lilting, gravelly voice. It came from inside a separate room—twelve feet, possibly fifteen, from the bottom of the staircase.

"Here, allow me to direct you into our little chamber." Although McCain did not hear the strike of a match or the wheel of a lighter, the glow of a candle suddenly shed its tiny light. McCain moved slowly forward, holding the New Testament in both hands over his heart. He could barely see the hooded face, but the partial features which were visible did not resemble anything human. Slowly, the man-thing lowered the candle and wedged it between the child's right arm and body. "As you can see, my candle holders have departed . . . one, involuntarily as you know." The laugh was a loud hissing. "I suspect you will find Mr. Livingston cowering somewhere in the woods. Things must have gotten a bit intense for him. I am somewhat surprised . . . but, then again, he is after all just another sniveling piece of human garbage."

McCain's gaze swept over the small face of the child, and his mind filled with dread as the open, unfocused eyes looked at nothing.

"No . . . no, do not fear. He is alive—for now. I desire that you see my plans fulfilled."

McCain thrust the little New Testament forward like a weapon. "In the precious name of Jesus Christ, leave this man! In *Jesus' name* . . ."

The wad of spittle shot from the demon's mouth like a bullet, striking McCain high on the cheekbone. "That is what I think of your *Jesus!*"

McCain took a step forward, the tiny book jabbing in front of him. "By the precious blood of Jesus . . . the holy, precious blood of Jesus the Lord . . ."

"*Blood!* Yes . . . blood from the slaughter, you swine." The words slithered from the demon with the drool of its mouth. "It was marvelous . . . beautiful . . . I was *there,* I heard his pitiful wails of agony . . ."

"Silence! I command you by the authority of God's Word and the power of the Holy Spirit. Leave this man."

McCain had taken three more steps forward; one more, and the demon would be pinned to the wall, and McCain would be between it and the child. The thing spat on him again, but he ignored the clinging wetness. The noises it made now were half animal, half human—deep, throaty sounds that McCain could barely understand. He took the last step and positioned himself at the foot of the bed. When he did, the man-thing jerked the razor blade from the pocket of the robe and held it high over his head. McCain could not see any white in the eyes which were partly crossed.

"Blooood . . . yes, blooood. I will give you your own blood and that of the child to wallow in . . ."

"Stop and be silent, I command you in the name of the risen Lord Jesus."

The razor blade shook in the demon's right hand and its bared teeth clicked loudly before it spoke. "Oh, come master . . . come to me now in my need . . . rid me of this wretch."

"Satan cannot help you . . . the blood of Jesus washes over the child and me. Come, Holy Spirit, in the precious name of Jesus . . . come to this place . . ."

"*Nooooo! Come Masteeeeer!*"

The thing was on the floor now, coiled grotesquely like a snake, the head turned in a sharp angle as its tongue flicked in and out. The razor blade sliced crazily into the vinyl floor covering before it broke in half, but the hand that held it continued to twitch spasmodically.

McCain knelt on the floor in front of the demon. "He *cannot* come to this place . . . the Holy Spirit fills this place.

Leave the man! Now, in the name of Jesus Christ—*leave him, I command you!*

For the longest half hour of McCain's life, the battle raged, the demon hurling vile curses between serpentine hisses and flicks of its tongue. McCain began to tremble from the tension of the struggle, fearing for the first time that the powerful demon would resist long into the night. But it was not to be.

In the same instant that the candle was snuffed out, the warm, white light filled the room, and McCain watched spellbound as the coiled body rose two feet above the floor and straightened to its full length. McCain's eyes were tightly closed in prayer when the long scream of agony began to escape the demon, but he opened them and drew back involuntarily from the spectacle before him. The face was contorted into a mask so horrible that McCain feared for Kassley's life; surely no man could survive such an ordeal. The red eyes rolled wildly. Blood trickled from the corners of its mouth as the clicking teeth found the edges of its tongue. McCain's effort at prayer was reduced to the only four words that would come from his mouth.

"Help him, sweet Jesus . . . help him, sweet Jesus . . ."

At first, Stoner and the men around him could not identify the scream, but within seconds it increased in intensity. The shear savagery of the scream, the inhumanity of it, was far beyond anything Stoner had ever imagined possible. His breathing came in shallow, sucking spurts, and his head pounded with each beat of his heart. McCain was right. The fight was not of the world he knew. Stoner looked at the two agents standing to his left, their faces a mixture of concern and dread. The powerful rifles hung from their hands like toys of war rendered impotent by invisible forces that swirled about in the air.

So they stood, the three men, with others like them surrounding the house, unable to aid the man whose only weapon was a tiny Bible.

Still on his knees, McCain pushed backward against the

metal frame of the child's bed as the ear-splitting wail grew to a crescendo that was physically painful. With a forefinger and thumb, he pinched the smoking wick and flung the candle away from the child. Knee-walking, he shoved the bed to the opposite wall, laid the New Testament on the boy's body, and clamped his own hands over the child's ears. He fought the impulse to gag on the foul odors that wafted about the little room. The thin, Sheetrock walls reverberated from the sound waves, and McCain was certain that the entire house was shaking. The body levitated ever higher, now six feet over the floor, and when it dropped, the silence was for an instant as loud as the scream had been.

Stoner and the others were startled by the sudden cessation of the sound, but before they could even exchange glances, the wind began to swirl around the house as they watched, spellbound. It was as if the wind came from the earth itself, straight up through the yard, and yet Stoner could not feel the slightest breath of air. The branches of the great shade trees looked like the arms of giants, extended upwardly, with leafy fingers straining to touch the sky. Ever higher the fingers rose, many torn from the wooden hands as they were carried away in the maelstrom. And then, as with the wailing of the demon, the wind ceased in the blink of an eye.

After carefully peeling the tape from the child's mouth, McCain cut the rope from his hands with the broken razor blade. He jerked the sheet from the mattress and gently wrapped the naked body of the child. Save for the bruise on his chin, there were no signs of harm. His eyes were still open, though unfocused. A strong, steady pulse reassured McCain. He quickly turned to Kassley. The long body trembled slightly; it was a human thing now, and the pulse at McCain's fingertips was elevated, but not alarmingly.

For the first time, McCain was aware of the strange, white light in the room. He glanced at the ceiling fixture and noted the jagged neck of the broken bulb. When he stood on weak legs to leave the room, he saw an old woman standing in the doorway.

"What . . . how?"

The angel raised a hand and silenced him. "All is well, faithful servant, the light is the Master's, and I come to do His bidding."

The angel smiled at McCain, who understood immediately. Tears welled up in his eyes, and he wanted to speak, but knew that he could not.

"The child is unharmed. So it is also with the man, though travail will follow him for the remainder of his days. Cling to him, even in his final hours. When I come for him, you will know."

McCain felt the soft words sear into his brain. For the rest of his life, he would remember the sound of every syllable. The image of the woman began to fade, but before it did, there was a final promise.

"Know this also. I go now to seek the enemies who took the child."

McCain stared into the emptiness beyond the doorway, his heart pounding in his ears. He knelt on the hard floor a final time, praying and calming himself, before he returned to the duties awaiting in his temporary life.

It was nine o'clock when Floyd Hunt heard the insistent ringing of the telephone from the church office. He had just stepped outside for a moment of fresh air and was passing close to the office. Without a word, the lady sitting at the desk arose from the chair and extended the receiver to him.

"It's him," she said as Floyd took the phone.

"What's happened?"

"We have him back, Mr. Hunt—safe and sound." Stoner could not choke back the emotion in his voice.

"*Yes . . . yes,* sweet Lord Jesus . . ." The sound of Floyd's sobs filled Stoner's ears for several seconds. "Is he with you now?"

"I'm at the hospital. They've checked him over throughly, Mr. Hunt, and the doctors assure me that no physical harm has occurred. The F.B.I. agent who got him out—Troy McCain—he and I have been with him for the last thirty minutes, and he seems fine. He's said nothing about the ordeal, really—just wants his mother and you two. Just wants to go home. Asked for a Whopper from Burger King and ate every bite, must have drunk a gallon of water. He's just—just—fine."

"When will you bring him home?"

"In the morning, the doctor says. He'd like to monitor him through the night, just to be doubly safe, but you can look for us around mid-morning. I'll call in the morning with details. Do you have a pen and paper handy?"

"Yes." Stoner gave him the telephone number of the hospital room.

"Call him after you've shared the good news. The sooner, the better."

Stoner could hear the loud sigh clearly over the line, and then the sound of Floyd blowing his nose. "The others, Captain? I assume McCain is all right, but . . ."

"The Pacely boy is in the Intensive Care Unit, Mr. Hunt. Kassley—or what was in him—must have sensed something wrong in the house. It was—very violent. We won't know for a while yet."

"We won't stop praying for him. Kassley?"

"He's in police custody here at the hospital too. It's a long story. McCain would be the one to tell you the details. He wants to talk to you later. But, the things that happened to him have caused some damage, though nothing major. He's talking. It seems absolutely incredible to hear and see him— like a normal man—lying there in the bed. Mr. Hunt, if you can believe it, he's actually asked about Darren. He had no idea what happened in the room."

"I have no trouble believing that, Captain."

"Well, I know you can't stand it much longer. Go tell them. I wish I could be there."

"Just go outside and listen—you'll probably hear the shouting clear up there." Stoner smiled as he heard the loud click.

Floyd's hands were raised high over his head as he burst into the sanctuary. Even as he shouted the joyous words, he was running to Joanie and Norma.

"Hallelujaaaaaaaah! He's safe! Hallelujaaaaaaah!"

Allene Pacely looked up from the edge of the padded chair in the Operating Room waiting area. A hospital volunteer in a candy-striped uniform was walking directly toward her.

"Mrs. Pacely?"

Allene nodded in reply.

"The doctor will be out of surgery in a few minutes. Please follow me and I'll take you to his consultation room."

When Allene and the girl turned the corner near the small room, Allene looked directly into the eyes of Troy McCain. They held each other's gaze for a moment before McCain broke the silence.

"Thank you, miss. I'll direct her from here."

The girl nodded and walked down the corridor.

McCain took two steps forward. "Mrs. Pacely, I'll leave in a minute . . . I know I'm the last person in the world you want to see right now, but please listen . . . please." He paused and swallowed slowly. "I assume full responsibility for what happened to your son out there. I didn't think it would come to anything like that, but, it did. It was my call, and I made it, and I have to live with it—whatever this doctor is about to tell you. I'm so very sorry for what—"

"Mr. McCain, you hear me, now. Not you, or anyone on this earth should—or can—assume responsibility for what happened. You are not the author of this evil. God's shoulders are wider than yours—let Him assume responsibility for Jessie's care now. Even though the mother in me didn't want him to go out there, I knew it was the right thing to do. A child's life was at stake." Her chin began to quiver and she batted the tears away with quick snaps of her eyelids. "Since— uh—I seem to be a member of a pastorless church now, I'd appreciate it if you'd go in there with me and give me a hand to hold."

"It would be my honor, Mrs. Pacely."

McCain could see the doctor approaching down the corridor, and he took Allene's hand and, together, they turned to meet him. The doctor's rumpled green operating room uniform disguised the speed of his approach.

"Please come on in and sit down." He gestured with a hand. "My name is Cannelly." He paused and looked at Allene. "Mrs. Pacely, overall, I'm encouraged right now, and you should be too."

The sobs came quickly and Allene made no attempt to control them, rocking against McCain's shoulder. "Praise God."

"Amen." The word came from McCain softly, as a prayer.

The doctor gave them a moment before continuing. "Your son's condition is still technically critical, and I don't want to paint too bright a picture. Very serious conditions could present which we would have to deal with later. The important facts are these: there is no paralysis. I'm confident of that— and I was almost certain when we began that there would be. There is no significant damage to any internal organs. He does have a serious concussion, but I expect that to clear up in timely fashion. One arm and one leg are broken and he has several cracked ribs on his right side, multiple body contusions and lacerations and the like . . ."

He stopped for a moment and handed Allene a tissue from the box on the coffee table. "On the down side, his face will require extensive reconstructive surgery, and he did lose his right eye. But, please hear me now, plastic surgery is a modern marvel, and they have already begun to work on him in there. It will be a long process, but don't be discouraged in the beginning, all right? Trust me on that."

Allene nodded. The doctor rose to leave and McCain stood and extended his hand. "Thank you, doctor. Thank you so much."

"I haven't heard yet, was it a one-car accident?"

"It wasn't a—car accident, doctor."

"We assumed he was thrown from a moving vehicle."

"No . . . it wasn't that."

"Hum . . . well, whatever, I'm going back in there now. We'll talk again later."

CHAPTER TWENTY-THREE

McCain and Stoner stood in the edge of the yellow haze cast by the parking lot light. The giant box of the hospital loomed behind them, outlined by three rows of windows, some well-lighted, others faintly so, and some dark. Twenty feet away, a deputy sheriff waited patiently for McCain behind the wheel of a patrol car. The two had stood nearly motionless and totally silent for five minutes. Stoner spoke first.

"Suppose you'll go back to Kansas City tonight?"

"Yeah, I'd like to get these guys a few hours with their families. They're all married, every last one."

"Hope they can manage to stay that way." There was only a hint of sadness in Stoner's tone, but McCain heard it.

"How long?"

"Seems like a lifetime—three years—she was—is—a good woman."

"I'm sorry."

Stoner was sorry he had opened the old wound; he had not intended to. He turned away from it. "How will it shake out with Kassley?"

Wesley Livingston had been found within a mile of the Kassley house. His statement had been taken, regarding both the kidnapping and the murder of the hitchhiker. Wesley had held nothing back, not even the location of the bag of salt in Arvil Kassley's basement which held certain mementos.

"Interesting question," McCain answered softly. "If it's murder one, who did it, the man or his demon? I assure you, Kassley is as normal right now as you or me. Psychiatric evaluations won't turn up a thing abnormal. The truth is—the simple, terrible truth is that a demon from the spirit world possessed him, body and soul, and that ninety-nine percent of the world, and probably all twelve people in a jury box, won't quite be able to swallow it."

"I imagine that you're a better than average witness."

"Before it's all over, what I will be, above all else, is a *Christian* witness. My beliefs will be dragged all over the courtroom floor, as will those of any defense witnesses who testify about demon-possession."

"No, I can't believe they'll make murder one stick."

"Don't be too sure."

Neither man spoke for several moments.

"Tell the boy's family I look forward to speaking with them soon."

"Believe me, Troy, you won't have to wait long; they'll be in touch."

"You stay in touch, too, okay?"

"Count on it."

"We'll talk more someday about it all, Marlon, you've just seen the dark side. There's a side to Christianity that blots all this madness out, believe me. Don't say anything now, just think about it . . . read about it. You have a Bible?"

"We had one when we were all together, a coffee table ornament, really. I don't think I could find one in my apartment."

"There will be one for you in the mail within a week. Don't worry," he smiled, "I'll wrap it in plain brown paper and you can unwrap it at home. Read Matthew, Mark, Luke, and John—the beginning of the New Testament. Some of the words will be printed in red. Pay very close attention to those words, Marlon. The One who conquered this demon speaks them."

Stoner nodded but did not speak.

"End of sermon, Marlon, relax. I've got to hit I-70."

McCain extended his hand and Stoner shook it as they clapped each other on the upper arm before parting. Stoner watched as the tall man folded his body into the front seat of the patrol car. The engine roared to life and within seconds, the red taillights disappeared into the night.

Emergency Medical Technician Eric Stevenson turned his head away from the churning air as the medical helicopter bearing the man with no arms clambered skyward from the wide shoulder of Highway 74, twelve miles east of Charlotte, North Carolina. The red and blue flashes from the emergency vehicles and Highway Patrol cruisers whirled crazily into the night. For a moment, Stevenson let his guard down, taking in the eerie sights through non-professional eyes—the same eyes which he saw through as a twelve-year-old viewing the riveting horror of his first accident scene. It had been nearly twenty years ago, but the collage of images which he knew would never leave him was keenly focused now, as it always was when he allowed himself to remember. But the single image that haunted him above all others was the stillness—the stillness of the bodies. Eric Stevenson had fought against the stillness of death for nine years, fighting in some victorious battles, and struggling for naught in other, losing conflicts. Tonight he was not certain if the most recent battle would be won or lost. At least it had been carried to the emergency room at Charlotte Memorial.

The victim had lost a great deal of blood, but the Good Samaritan who had been the first to arrive on the grisly scene had done all the right things. He had ripped off his own shirt, and then his undershirt, using the garments like giant compression bandages as he clamped his hands over the two stubs. When Stevenson and his partner shouldered against him, it was only with considerable force that they were able to pry his hands free. The rescuer was in a state of near-shock himself. Stevenson looked into the front seat of the Highway Patrol cruiser sitting ten feet away and sought the man's eyes. He sat hunched forward with the trooper's jacket draped over his bare shoulders. When he looked up through the windshield, Stevenson smiled grimly and gave a thumbs-up sign to the stranger—now and forever, another soldier in the fight against the stillness. Stevenson fervently hoped that the man would be able to cope in the days to come when the bloody collage revisited his mind. The man acknowledged the bond and managed a small nod before he returned his gaze to his trembling hands.

The voice of his partner, level and calm, was in Stevenson's ears now. "You ready to clean up and get out of here, Eric?"

"Yeah. Yeah, Pat."

"Pretty cool head, huh?" Pat gestured toward the man in the patrol car.

"You got that right, pard. He doesn't clamp the stubs. They got a D.O.A. at Memorial." He paused. "Think he'll make it?"

"Yeah, I think he'll pull through. You?"

"Me, too, I guess. He ought to make it," Stevenson said quietly.

"He's strong enough to, no doubt about that. Geez! You ever see such a body? He must be a bodybuilder."

"A better than average one at that," Stevenson added.

"Well, that's history now, huh?"

Stevenson nodded silently, pondering the finality of the half second which altered the man's life forever—the horrible instant when the tree limb gouged through the front window of the van. The limb had been sheared at an angle, transformed into a six-inch-diameter wooden blade which had not only severed the man's arms, but also ripped most of the sinew from the bones. There was no possibility of re-plantation. He had seen incidents stranger than the dreadful misfortune of the man, but—he shook his head—the woman on the passenger side—no, he had never seen such a thing. She was being transported by ground ambulance, and Stevenson turned in unison with his partner as the blocky vehicle lumbered into the westbound lane of the highway.

His partner had seen Stevenson's head shake in bewilderment. "I know what you're thinking, Eric. I've never been close to one like that either. The only thing I can figure is that a small branch off the main limb just—somehow . . ."

Stevenson finished the sentence for him. "Somehow put out both of her eyes while barely scratching the bridge of her nose. No other marks on her face!" The last sentence was spoken with unmasked disbelief.

"Yeah, man, I don't know. . . . It had to be a sharp branch—somehow . . ."

"Somehow," Stevenson echoed.

A highway patrolman walked up to them, clipboard in hand. "Ugly one, huh, fellows?"

"Aren't they all?" Stevenson said.

"You got a point there," the trooper nodded.

"How'd he manage to run it off the road?"

"The Samaritan was just five or six car lengths behind him. Says he saw something flash in the van's headlights just before the guy starts to swerve, and, well, you know the rest. He just lost it. Did a great job really, though. I can't believe he didn't roll it. Hadn't been for that low limb . . ."

"A deer I suppose—some animal?"

"Well, that's what I figured, too, but this guy . . ." he shook his head and pointed the clipboard toward the patrol car, "he swears it was a person. Me and three other guys stomped all around back there, and there's no sign of a human anywhere. Ground's still muddy after yesterday's rain. Should be a footprint—something—back there, if it was a person. 'Not likely,' I tell him, but I can't shake him off it. He just keeps repeating that it was 'upright—like a person.' Whatever, or whoever, it was, was in the wrong place at the wrong time for those two."

"They married?" Stevenson asked.

"Don't know. Strange deal. Neither one of them had any I.D. that we could find. The woman wouldn't say a word. Shock, I guess, huh? Anyway, I ran the vehicle and it's registered to a Carol Ashford—Charlotte address."

"Carol?" Stevenson asked, "you sure it was Carol?"

"Yeah, why?"

"He was moaning something when we strapped him down. I put my ear close to his mouth and I thought at first he was saying, 'leave us . . . leave us', but the more he said it, the more I knew he was saying a name."

"What do you think it was?" the trooper asked.

"I don't *think*—I *know*. It was Leva. He was crying for Leva."

St. Louis City Fire Inspector Aubry Jameson looked through the windshield of his parked car at the door to Building No. 4 of Cascades Apartments. The coordinating call from the police department had come last night at eleven-thirty. Jameson had spent over two hours at the scene in Apartment 2-B, not to mention half a sleepless night with the strange sights plastered against the back of his eyelids. Now, at ten o'clock on the morning after, he was no closer to writing a report than when he had first set foot in the apartment. He would look one more time; there *had* to be something he missed, some clue that would lead to a plausible explanation.

He passed a hand over tired eyes and massaged his temples with his thumb and middle finger. He pushed open the car door and stepped onto the asphalt parking lot. As he walked slowly toward the four-unit building, he hoped that the other three tenants were absent; more questions and distractions would only make the puzzle more difficult. Jameson slid the manager's key into the lock; the door opened quietly. As he moved silently over the carpeted living room floor, the faint odor of burned things caused his nostrils to flare. Aubry Jameson had smelled the sharp blackness that wafted from hundreds of extinguished fires, but each fire resulted in distinct lingering odors, and this fire left the most terrible of all reminders—the unmistakable scent of burned flesh.

Jameson had picked through scenes of destruction so vast that they boggled the mind. And yet, the blackened two-foot circle of plywood now before his eyes troubled him more than anything that the monster blazes had left behind. There were always explanations for the great fires—faulty electrical wiring, gas leaks, improper storage techniques, arsonists, the careless flip of a cigarette butt—any one of dozens of possibilities. But this—this crazy little black hole in a man's bedroom carpet . . . . He shook his head as he knelt to the floor.

Both the carpet and the pad had burned completely through to the plywood flooring, but the wood, highly combustible, was only blackened and not burned. There was not the slightest trace of carpet fiber or pad material in the circle. They had simply been consumed by a fire that was incredibly hot and fast. Jameson shook his head at the undamaged bedspread that hung less than eighteen inches from the hole. The electrical circuitry in the entire apartment was in perfect order, as it was in the apartment below.

The lady below, certain that she heard a human scream, had punched 911 within moments of the terrible sound. But the sergeant and the apartment manager on the scene when Jameson arrived had found no one inside the locked unit. They had found a very tidy and well-appointed apartment for a single man. The sergeant also found a half dozen high quality photographs of children strewn on the bed. Jameson shook his head again and shrugged his shoulders. He hoped that the guy wasn't kinky, with a thing for kids, but—it didn't look too good. Still, you had to give him the benefit of the doubt, at least for now. The cops would likely ask a few questions about the photos when the man returned. They figured that he was messing around with something flammable and had an accident, then probably ran helter skelter out the door for help. But if that had been the case, why the locked door? The other two tenants in the building were gone, but the lady below had not reported footsteps or a slamming door after the scream. In fact, she had sworn that there was no other sound except for the scream in the few minutes before the police had come. She was also quick to point out that the man's car was still in the parking lot. The police had also confirmed that no hospital emergency room or medical clinic had treated the man, or even one fitting his general description.

Whatever. All that was a police problem; let them sort it out. The fire was Jameson's problem, and it galled him to the bone that he could not figure it out. The mere thought of "cause undetermined at time of report" popping up on his computer screen was enough to make his stomach roll. He stood now and pulled in a deep breath and pushed the air through loose lips. He would talk more with other experts in the field, but he knew it would be a waste of time. He slowly flicked the green pile of the carpet with the toe of his shoe. The thought nagged at him and he could not shake it—it was possible that nobody would ever know exactly what had taken place in the man's bedroom last night. And from this thought, another was born, much stronger than the first. It was possible—very possible—he thought, that the screaming man would never return to his apartment.

Jameson stood in the room for another five minutes trying to shake the chilling thought, but he could not, and when he locked the front door behind him, he felt as if he had sealed a tomb.

Joanie Starmann paced anxiously over the carpeted floor of the Cedar Valley Baptist Church office; within only minutes now, she would hold Rooster in her arms. Stoner had phoned Floyd from the Charlotte airport with the arrival time. Joanie's eyes were puffy from the near-sleepless night and the joyful tears shed since she had heard her son's small voice over the telephone line the night before. It seemed like a voice from Paradise, and it was the most beautiful sound she had ever heard. Though the conversation lasted for several minutes, the few words spoken were reassuring endearments. They had listened to each other's sobs, mostly; the weeping was a cleansing thing, and already, much of the evil had been washed away. But now, only the touch of him would suffice—the fine, sandy hair in her fingertips, the delicate flesh of his lips, the smoothness of skin unravaged by the callous hand of the world. Yes, only this would satisfy now, only holding him like a baby. A baby who was lost and now was found.

"Joanie, darling, you're gonna wear a trough in this carpet," Norma teased.

"I can't stand still, Mom. Just can't." Joanie glanced at Floyd. "How much longer, Daddy?"

"Soon, baby, soon . . . just a few minutes. They'll bring him straight in here."

Floyd had given Stoner specific instructions regarding the meeting place in the rear parking lot of the church grounds. This would afford the family some privacy at the beginning of the reunion celebration. The congregation was singing in the sanctuary, the strong melodies of the hymns pushing through the walls of the office. Norma tapped a foot and hand in unison with the music.

"I swear, I can hear Chester McCollester's voice from in there," Norma said, shaking her head. "Loudest voice in the history of the church, and he hasn't hit a note in his life."

"Never will either," Floyd said, "but it sounds mighty pretty to me now."

"Amen to that," Norma said.

Joanie stopped in mid-stride and held up a hand. "I hear car doors!" She darted through the office door with Floyd and Norma close behind.

For a magical instant when she first saw him, Joanie stood

motionless as her brain registered every detail of the portrait. He wore a new red short-sleeved shirt with a white collar and navy blue jeans with a belt buckle that glinted in the late morning sunlight. The toes of white tennis shoes peeked from the cuff of the jeans. The bill of his baseball cap was pulled low and he tugged at it with his right hand. His left hand was lost inside a full-sized baseball glove. Joanie waited for him to find her eyes and when he did, they both began to run at the same time.

Stoner stood with one hand resting on the open door of the unmarked patrol car, drinking it all in through blurred eyes. The uniformed officer sitting behind the wheel smiled at the sight of mother and child locked in the wondrous, clumsy embrace.

"Shame they don't all end up like this one, huh Captain?"

"Yeah, Terry. That it is."

Joanie swept Rooster off his feet and turned toward Floyd and Norma. The boy extended his gloved hand toward his grandparents and the circle of joy quickly widened. Heads bobbed left and right and up and down as kisses passed from one tear-stained face to another. Floyd pulled a white handkerchief from his hip pocket as he broke away from the circle and walked toward Stoner. The men shook hands and embraced for a moment in the mannish fashion of grown men.

"Come inside, please, Captain . . . the other officer, too, if he wants. We're going to have a little ceremony before the main service. There's a candle that needs to be snuffed out in there."

"No, thank you kindly, Mr. Hunt, but I don't think I . . ."

"Captain, do me a favor and just stop being a cop for a few minutes. We want you to be a part of this. You *are* a part of this. Just for a few minutes, please."

"Thank you. It would be my honor, but the man who should be here is McCain."

"Well then, you stand in for him. You can tell him about it later, okay? Come on."

Stoner leaned into the patrol car and spoke briefly with the driver. When he approached Joanie and Rooster, Joanie kneeled and gently slid Rooster down to the pavement. "Oh, Captain Stoner . . . I . . . thank you so much. It sounds so silly to say just that." She took his right hand in both of hers.

"Mrs. Starmann, like I just told your father, the man you should thank isn't here."

"I'm sure we'll meet someday—soon I hope. But I know how much you cared. You will always be a part of this family, like it or not."

"I like it."

"I see you're trying to make a ball player out of Rooster." The boy smiled and looked up at Stoner.

"We did talk some baseball, didn't we, partner?"

Rooster nodded.

"Did you play—or coach?" Joanie asked.

"Played a very long time ago . . . coached Little League . . . when my boy was young." The sadness passed over him like a thin cloud and he tried to ignore it, but could not. Joanie saw the sadness touch him and despite her own joy, she touched it with him for a moment. He knew and thanked her with his eyes.

"It's time, big boy," she looked down at Rooster.

"For the candle?" he asked.

"Yep, for the candle. There's a church full of people in there waiting for you. Some of them have been there as long as you have been—away."

"Let's go then." He tugged at the cap again and looked up at Stoner. "You gonna come, too, Mr. Stoner?"

"Yes, son, I'd like to watch this."

"Good." The boy smiled and handed the glove to Stoner. "Can you hold it for me?"

"You bet."

Clarence Rosecrans saw Rooster and Joanie first as they

stepped through the double front doors at the rear of the sanctuary. His uplifted hand swept to and fro, keeping time with the last line of *Amazing Grace* as the words of the great hymn thundered to the ceiling. From the front pew, Kathy Rosecrans watched her husband's gaze fix on the doors of the sanctuary and she turned her head to the rear. Soon other heads turned and hands began to jut high into the air, but the last words of the hymn did not fade.

". . . to sing God's praise . . . than when we first begun."

When the last word faded away, a great hush descended over the room before loud whispers of praise began to spill from the worshipers.

"Oh, sweet Jesus . . ."

"Yes, Lord . . ."

"Praise God . . ."

"Hallelujah . . ."

The pastor's strong voice rose over the quiet praises. "Darren Starmann, a candle burns down here, son, and only you can blow it out." He held out both arms in invitation.

The boy looked up at Joanie. "Prob'ly should take my cap off, huh, Mom?"

She could only nod in reply as she struggled to control her quivering chin.

"You come, too," he said, squeezing her hand. She nodded again and they began to walk, but Rooster stopped after only a couple of steps. "Remember when I told you I was through with crying, down at the ocean?"

"I remember."

"You be through, too, okay? I don't want anybody cryin' around me any more—for a long time."

"Okay, Rooster—it's a deal." She dabbed at her eyes with a tissue.

"Let's go," he said.

Stoner watched from behind Floyd and Norma as mother and son walked down the carpeted aisle. The praises were no longer whispers, now rising to shouts of joy as Rooster and

Joanie neared the tall candle. Rooster placed both hands on the edge of the table and tiptoed, leaning over the table. His chest puffed out as he drew in all the air he could, and then he shot it at the flame which bent sideways for an instant before dying. The pews emptied quickly and soon the two of them were lost in the glad throng.

Stoner turned to leave before he realized he still held the baseball glove. When he turned back around, Floyd was looking at him. Stoner held the glove out toward him.

"About forgot this," he said. Floyd took it from him.

"Don't be a stranger, Captain. Come back and see us soon."

Stoner smiled. "Maybe someday—thanks."

"How about *Sun*day instead of *some*day? It's only five days away. Someday may never come."

Stoner nodded as he turned to leave, but he did not reply.

EPILOGUE

It was the last week of May in southeastern Missouri and the front windows of the car were down so that the two men sitting inside could scent the delicate aromas that floated on the early evening breeze. To the older man, who had known many Missouri springs, the smells were like colors—pastels mostly, whites and lavenders and quiet shades of green and yellow—all swirled together like a beautiful collage in his mind. But these things, however tranquil and soothing to the senses, were of little comfort to the young man. He smoothed his tie with clammy fingers and adjusted his neck inside the stiff, white collar of his dress shirt. His black suit coat hung on the small peg over the backseat window. It was a formal occasion; the two men had come to share the last hours of a man's life.

Potosi Correctional Center sprawled in the distance, but save for the guard tower and the concertina wire that looped like a giant slinky toy around the perimeter, it was unthreatening. Even the death chamber itself, tucked deep in the hospital block, was without menace. All of the inmates knew what the chamber looked like, with its spotless vinyl floor and painted concrete block walls and fluorescent lights. It looked like a hospital examination room, complete with a shiny porcelain lavatory and a silver goose-necked faucet arching over it. But the large metal box mounted on one wall would forever preclude any degree of ordinariness for the room. It was the thing that made the room a chamber of death. The box held the lethal injection machine, and all the inmates knew that when the lights on the delivery module came on, liquid death would flow through the veins of the condemned man.

They all thought about it, the men under death sentences, for it was something that could not be shelved conveniently in the mind like an appointment for dental work. The quiet, antiseptic place, this chamber that masqueraded as a room, waited for them all, and tonight it waited for Arvil Kassley.

The men in the car studied the prison building through the windshield in silence for several minutes, each lost in his own thoughts, each preparing himself in his own way. The older man spoke first.

"Hard to believe that it's finally come down to this. Twelve years—almost a generation."

The young man filled his lungs and exhaled slowly, but did not reply. The older man continued. "I've come here at least twice a year all that time, talked with him for hours on end . . . and still . . . still, I cannot get close to him. I love him, I know he loves me. He's been a Christian for nearly ten years now . . ."

The young man broke his own silence. "He said in his last letter—he said, 'I sometimes feel as if I have never really been a part of this world.' He called his mind 'an inner landscape'. It's not something he is able, or even wants to explain to anyone."

"Yes, I think I can understand that. The only life he's ever known, or had mental control of, has been in that place—and it's not a part of any normal world."

"I don't believe he ever thought he would live this long, I mean, he never really participated in the appeals process. It was like a runaway train that he was caught on. I think he wanted to just jump off sometimes—just get it over with."

The long struggle through the appeals process had been carried out mainly through anti-death-penalty organizations whose leaders had realized early on that Arvil Kassley himself would be of little assistance in the fight against his own execution.

"Ready?" The older man glanced at his watch.

"Ready as I'll ever be."

The prison officer in the guardhouse watched as the two well-dressed men approached.

"Witnesses for tonight, gentlemen?"

"Yes, sir. Well, actually visitors. It's all been arranged. My name is Troy McCain and this is Darren Starmann."

The man ran his finger down the edge of a computer print-out sheet. "May I see some identification?"

Both men pulled a driver's license from his wallet and slid the card under the opening at the bottom of the plexiglass window. The officer carefully matched the photographs on the licenses to the faces in front of him. Satisfied, he slid the cards back through the opening.

"Go ahead to the main gate area." He motioned with one hand. "It's clearly marked. You'll hear it again, but remember that from this point on you're a part of our world, and you've got to play by our rules."

"We'll remember," McCain said.

Once inside and past the security checks, McCain and Darren followed a brown-shirted guard through the labyrinth of corridors, the solid echoes of things steel and concrete chasing after them, reminding them of the netherworld which had closed in around them. The guard turned his head and spoke as he walked.

"The holding cell is just around the corner."

When they turned the corner, he was standing to meet them. The holding cell was unwalled to the front with only a steel mesh curtain separating the occupants from the corridor. The deathwatch officer sat behind a small table in the front corner of the cell, near the mesh. It was his duty to monitor and log every event taking place during the deathwatch period. Arvil Kassley, being a very low-risk prisoner, would spend only the minimum time in the cell—forty-eight hours. There were five hours remaining in his life.

The escort guard locked the steel curtains behind the four men and retreated down the corridor. There was an awkward moment of silence as McCain and Darren met Arvil's gaze. Darren had no recollection of him; it was six years beyond the fateful night before his mother had allowed him to satisfy his curiosity regarding the events that had made nationwide headlines. Three more years passed before the young man was allowed to write the first letter to the man whose demon had once sought his blood.

Arvil's head bowed forward slightly from the tension of the moment. The great head reminded Darren of the statue of Lincoln in Washington, D.C., the long, gaunt features weighed down with burdens untold. The pity came to Darren in a rush, the surprise of its enormity nearly overwhelming him. He attempted to erase it from his face, but he could not, and the other two men sensed it. McCain acted quickly against the thing none of them wanted in the cell, moving to Arvil and embracing him.

"Arvil." It was the only word he could pry from his tongue.

"It is all right, my friend—a strange night it is."

McCain regained his composure at the sound of the deep voice. "Arvil, meet Darren Starmann."

Arvil took the first step forward and extended his hand. Darren's hand was swallowed by the long, thick-fingered hand, but the grip was gentle, with only a hint of firmness.

"It is my great honor, Darren. Thank you so very much for coming. I know it is a difficult thing."

"You're welcome, Mr. Kassley, I—I wanted to come, really."

"Sit, please." Arvil swept a hand toward the two folding chairs near his small table. There was a television set with a VCR machine nearby and an unused box of movie tapes beside it. The cell was well lighted and spotlessly clean. A neat stack of paper was laid out on the table and two ballpoint pens lay side by side.

"I have been writing since the death warrant came down ten days ago." He huffed a little laugh. "I am surprised that I have so many goodbyes to say, but . . . twelve years is a very long time and many people have corresponded with me. Many wonderful people . . ." He was looking at Darren when he spoke the last three words.

"I have always wondered, Darren—and we have never touched on it in our letters—why you ever wrote the first time."

"When I was about fifteen, I nagged my mother to help me research all the old newspaper pieces—about that night and the trial and all. And Mr. McCain—we became friends, and he told me of your conversion—and, I don't know exactly when, but somewhere along the way, I knew that I had to learn more about you."

Arvil reached down into a cardboard box on the floor beside his chair and took out a large manila envelope. The flap was carefully sealed down. "Well, they have come full circle, Darren, and I want you to have them back. To attempt to tell you what they have meant to me is probably a foolish thing—something I am certain I cannot verbalize under the circumstances. But, I did try on paper. It is in here. I hope that I have at least come close to saying what I want you to know." He held the envelope out to Darren.

"Mr. Kassley—I—thank you."

Arvil turned to McCain. "Troy, would you see that the rest of these—mighty epistles—find their destinations." The two men smiled. "Most of them are addressed, but a few I was not sure of, since I had never received anything directly from them."

"Consider it done, Arvil."

Arvil looked around the cell for a moment, gathering his thoughts. "You may have wondered why I asked that you come so late. They would have allowed you to be here all day, you know. But, I thought it best this way, less chance of our time together deteriorating into something maudlin."

"We understand, Arvil," McCain said.

"This is a strange occasion indeed, as I said, but certainly not an unhappy one for me, I assure you. God's timing seems perfect. Together, we have accomplished much in this place." He laughed softly, genuinely. "You know, they call me 'Rev' here—in derision at first, of course, but—it is not in derision now."

"How many, Arvil? How many have you led to Christ?"

"Many—at least for this place. Thirty-one have made professions of faith. The prison chaplain thinks that some have conned me—toyed with me—but I do not believe this to be true. I have grown to be something of an expert at reading cons."

"Have any emerged as leaders?" McCain asked.

"Two of them show great leadership. They will carry on very well, I am certain. They are at peace with my death— and, more important, with their own."

He paused for a moment. "So, Darren, graduation soon, then seminary?" Arvil asked. "Have you settled on one?"

"Yes, sir, American Baptist."

Arvil nodded slowly, savoring the knowledge of Darren's decision. "I trust you will soon lead many down the Roman road to salvation when you acquire your first pastorate."

"Yes, sir. I—I surely intend to, with His help."

"Oh, you will have His help, son. He will always be as close as the air you breathe. Know that, and hold to it even in the trials when you may think He hides His face."

"Yes, sir, I will."

"If I may burden you with one request?"

"Anything."

"One day, perhaps in the first spring with your new church, I would like your congregation to sing *Amazing Grace,* dedicated to an old friend of yours, now passed. I will hear it."

Darren swallowed deliberately, determined to control the emotion rising like a fever inside him. "Count it as done, Mr. Kassley."

"Thank you kindly. I have memorized every song in the

Baptist hymnal, but only one speaks to me like that one." He tilted his head back and sighed. "Written by a slave trader, John Newton—a pagan of the worst ilk—gloriously saved. Most do not realize that he wrote only the first four stanzas. No one knows who wrote the fifth—and it is incredibly beautiful—'When we've been there ten-thousand years, Bright shining as the sun, we've no less days to sing God's praise, than when we first begun.'" The deep bass voice rumbled softly from within his chest, the words more like a prayer than a song.

"I myself believe that no human wrote the last stanza . . . perhaps an angel . . . perhaps the Holy Spirit Himself . . . but no mortal."

The cell grew silent except for the faint sound of men breathing and the faraway mutterings of the prison. The deathwatch officer sat statue-like in the corner, his head bowed slightly toward his table. Arvil sought McCain's eyes before he broke the silence.

"I have often wondered, my friend, will I sneak in the back door to heaven? Or will angels attend me like—like untainted Christians?"

"There are no untainted Christians, Arvil, none. Angels attended John Newton—and St. Paul, who helped murder Stephen. Yes, they will attend you as well. There is no back door to heaven, Arvil."

A single tear slid down Arvil's cheek, but he did not acknowledge it. When he spoke, his voice was firm.

"I am very grateful, Troy, for your taking care of the—arrangements and such."

"It was my honor."

Arvil felt relief that the final thank-you had been uttered and the three men moved away from it and began to reminisce about prior visits and letters. Darren and McCain answered Arvil's questions about life on the outside. But mostly, they told of their own families, and it was a delight to the man who had never known such a life. The minutes flew by for all of them, and soon the irritating sweep of the second hand over the white face of the wall clock could not be ignored. Arvil waited for a pause in the conversation.

"They will come for me soon. It has all been explained in detail. They will need three more hours for the final processing. The appointed time is 12:01 A.M. I—hope that you both will stay on the grounds until then—it will be a comfort knowing that."

"We'll be just outside the walls, Arvil—or we stand ready to serve as witnesses if you have changed your mind."

Arvil had the right to choose up to five witnesses to the execution, but he had declined, preferring to be remembered in life. "I have not changed my mind. Wait outside the walls, where the spring breeze touches your faces. Go quickly now. I will be on the breeze just past midnight."

Arvil and McCain came together and embraced, each clapping the other on the back for a moment before they opened their arms in offer to Darren. He joined them, all three foreheads touching now, six arms interlocking in love. Darren, drawing strength from the powerful oneness, started the prayer, "Our Father, who art in heaven . . ." and they finished it in unison before breaking the circle.

Barely able to control the sobbing, Darren was nearly blinded by hot tears, but he did not care. Arvil reached down and picked up the box of letters, then handed it to McCain. The guard unlocked the cell and the two men walked through the opening; the clank of the latch came quickly behind them. After a few steps, they turned back for the last time to see the tall man looking at them through the steel mesh. He raised his hand in farewell.

"Shed no tears for me. For my entire life, either my mind or my body has been locked in a chamber—and tonight—in the final chamber—I will be set free."

At two minutes before midnight, the guardhouse officer watched as the two men stepped from the car and walked, hand in hand, to the edge of the parking lot. They stopped, and for reasons he could not understand, shuffled a half turn to the left, their heads held high and their free arms raised skyward. The officer had no way of knowing that they turned to face into the night wind. He was amazed that they were able to hold their arms in the air for several minutes. As they finally lowered them, the telephone rang in the guardhouse.

"Post one. Duncan."

The voice on the line was crisp and businesslike. "Stand down. The exercise is complete."

Darren and McCain walked slowly toward the car, pausing as they neared it.

"It eats at me—it will always eat at me," Darren said, "that so many considered him liable for the actions of a demon."

McCain thought for a moment before replying. "You will learn to accept it, son. The world embraces what it can see and rejects what it cannot."

Darren shook his head wearily. "I'm tired—drained."

"Yeah, me too. Go ahead and get in. I just need a couple more minutes out here to clear my head."

"Sure, go ahead."

McCain returned to the place where the light melded with the darkness and stood silently, waiting. He knew the angel would come. The image took shape slowly and indistinctly in the shadows but McCain could see that the form before him was much taller than himself, clearly not the image of the old woman he remembered. Neither was the voice the one he remembered; it was resonant and powerful, yet comforting beyond measure.

"Beloved servant, it was a wondrous sight to behold, when my legion rose with him. Oh, great day it will be when eyes like yours may witness such things."

The angel and the man stood in silence for a moment, and as the angel spoke his final words, he faded from the man's sight.

"Go now, and complete thy tasks."